I0561815

Twenty Thousand Years Under the Sea
and Other Tales of
Steel & Sorrows

BY THE SAME AUTHOR

Return t the Center of the Earth

Twenty Thousand Years Under the Sea
and Other Tales of
Steel & Sorrows

by
John Peel

A Black Coat Press Book

Stories Copyright © 2020 by John Peel.
Foreword Copyright © 2020 by Paul Magrs.
Cover illustration Copyright © 2020 by Mariusz Gandzel.

Visit our website at www.blackcoatpress.com

ISBN 978-1-61227-997-8. First Printing. September 2020.
Published by Black Coat Press, an imprint of Hollywood
Comics.com, LLC, P.O. Box 17270, Encino, CA 91416. All
rights reserved. Except for review purposes, no part of this
book may be reproduced or transmitted in any form or by any
means, electronic or mechanical, including photocopying,
recording or by any information storage and retrieval system,
without permission in writing from the publisher. The stories
and characters depicted in this anthology are entirely fictional.
Printed in the United States of America.

TABLE OF CONTENTS

Foreword
The Celestial Sandpit

When I think about John Peel I think about a certain period in my life when everything was quite uncertain. I was twenty-one and all I wanted was to be a writer. I was finishing my degree and about to go straight into an MA in Creative Writing: I was jumping with both feet into living my dream. All was uncertain at the start of the 1990s, including *Doctor Who*. The TV show had ended and Target Books had almost run out of episodes to novelise. The very existence of one of the staples of my life—new *Doctor Who* books—was suddenly in question.

But then—John Peel was one of the names that came to my (and many others' rescue) as he wrote some of those final few novelisations of classic shows and then published the first in what would become a very long series of books of the kind I had endlessly, joyously anticipated: original *Doctor Who* novels.

And with John we were transported into a vaster, wider, even more colourful *Doctor Who* universe. The books got longer than 126 pages! They were actually novel-length for just about the first time, and committed, addicted readers like myself got to steep themselves longer in their immersive reality.

I still remember the feeling of elation at the first of those *Virgin New Adventures* coming out. A whole new complete *Who* story that continued the adventures of the Seventh Doctor and Ace. For many years *Doctor Who* had seemed under threat, and I'd had unhappy times trying to watch each new episode in a student house shared with unsympathetic friends. Now the Doctor's new story was even better because it was both portable and all mine. I felt like the boy at the beginning of *The Neverending Story*, running away, clutching to my chest the only book that mattered in the whole world, a story I didn't have to share with anyone... and I was so ready to be transported back to Mesopotamia and to find out more about the mysterious Timewyrm...

Like his Dalek books, *Genesys* feels rather like an epic movie from a vintage era. What is it about John's writing that conjures up the expansive feel of Cinemascope, the glow of technicolour, and the expectation of Harryhausenesque monsters twitching and lurching their way across our mind's eyes?

I think it's probably because he's such a fan. His adoration of the films, shows, comics, books, toys and ephemera of a golden age of sci-fi , mystery and horror comes leaping off every page he writes. The committed zeal and delight of a fan is evident in his work: there's nothing jaded and stale about his writing even after all these years. He writes this stuff because he loves to do so.

I remember seeing John on a convention panel in Baltimore just a few years ago. It was a panel about the writers of TV and film Tie-In Fiction, and he was on with Keith DeCandido and my lovely friend, George Mann. It was so funny and informed and fascinating a panel and what shone out to all of us in the audience about these three fellas was their huge enthusiasm and enjoyment of what they did. They made the writing of Tie-In Fiction seem like a noble and heroic calling, whether that involved novelising and fleshing out existing tales, or the creation of new *Missing Adventures* taking place within the continuity of a familiar series, or pushing on at the frontier of a timeline of a show that's been cancelled already. They made it seem like a wonderful thing to be entrusted with: the playing with other people's marvellous and abandoned toys in the celestial sandpit.

To me, these stories that take their cues from other people's tales often seem rather like they take place inside a dream. Or, remember when you were a kid, and playing in the schoolyard, inventing your own stories involving favourites from the telly? The stories you and your friends came up with

8

then were always wilder and odder and more brilliant than anything you ever saw on the screen. They were preferable because they were *yours*... You had taken the raw stuff of story from the thing you'd seen on the telly and you'd hammered it and shaped it with your own unfettered imagination to the way you wanted it to go...

To me, all of John's stories read like—in the nicest possible way—strange distorted dreams involving characters we already partially know from a hundred bygone episodes or pulp magazines. His fictive mischief-making transports us to worlds where Cthulhu, Captain Nemo, Carnacki the Ghost Finder, Biggles and Zorro can all combine. His gleeful erudition makes characters from all eras of mystery and adventure fiction step out from the pages and screens of their source texts to team up and collaborate in his own. It's a world of missing scientists, queer cabals and eldritch beings from other realities: a world of wonderful What If and Never Was.

I love the fact that there is a steampunk version of a certain Time Lord who turns out to be French and pre-dates the invention of television itself...! (I won't spoil the fun by listing all the fictional migrations that happen in these stories— I'll just say that I cheered at various points when particular favourites happened into view!)

There's a lovely dream logic to these mirror-universe twists and multiversal mash-ups and giddy-making continuations... At least, that's how it's always seemed to me.

Returning to these books and handling this wonderful gift of his collected short fiction, which is peppered with glimpses of characters teaming up across separate universes, I find myself thinking of Henry Bemis. Remember that character? He was played by Burgess Meredith in the best ever *Twilight Zone* episode, "Time Enough At Last." He was the bank clerk who only wanted enough time to read his beloved books and, when the end of the world suddenly happens, happily finds that he has just that. (Though there's a terrible irony and a twist I won't spoil for anyone here.)

Anyway, thinking about Henry Bemis's bibliomania makes me think that if there was yet another apocalypse any day soon (not so strange to imagine in these very strange days..!) it might be the sort that destroys electronic stuff. What if the end of the world meant the end of video tapes and discs, ebooks and computer records? What then, for our beloved TV shows and films?

Why, then the only part of those narratives remaining might well be the novelisations and Tie-Ins. That grand, shattered library that Burgess Meredith clambers through – that might be filled up with Tie-Ins that are no longer tied to anything. In his longed-for seclusion and joyous self-isolation, the perfect reader and fan Mr Bemis would surely fall delightedly upon the Collected Works of John Peel in order to relive the grand, crazy dreams of an era gone by.

Paul Magrs
Manchester, April 2020.

Paul Magrs is the author of the Doctor Who *novel "Mad Dogs And Englishmen", and the* Lost On Mars *trilogy. He has also created and written the Brenda and Effie mysteries.*

Jules Verne has always been a huge part of my reading life. His incredible tales of improbable journeys have always enthralled me. If A Journey To the Center Of The Earth *is still my favorite, there are so many that run a close second. From* The Earth To The Moon! Off On A Comet! Around The World In Eighty Days! *And the list goes on. And, of course,* 20,000 Leagues Under The Sea. *(It was years before I realized that this didn't mean that they'd dived 20,000 leagues straight down, but traveled them...) Captain Nemo and his heroic, futile attempt to stop war, coupled with his scientific inventions were simply awe-inspiring. Such a great character demanded more. (We got more, of course, in* Mysterious Island...*) Friends of mine were a bit surprised to discover that I'd never read H.P. Lovecraft. I suppose it was a natural progression from my love of A. Merritt, but somehow I'd never made the jump. I'm not a huge reader of horror (despite having written many such stories), and I'd never managed to get around to him. So I bought a collected volume and started reading. The end result is as follows...*

Twenty Thousand Years Under the Sea

The Antipodes, 1865

Amongst the papers of the late Professor Arronax, the following pages were discovered. They had evidently been intended to form part of his memoirs but had, at the final moment, been torn from the manuscript that he delivered to his publisher. Upon examining the pages, it is simple to see the reason. Professor Arronax was a dedicated and thorough man of science, and whilst many of the events he described in his memoirs verge upon the fantastic, never do they unduly stretch the credulity. The excised section, however, is of a very different timbre.

The first reason is that the events that they purport to describe were never witnessed by the Professor himself—they are merely reported to him by the late Captain Nemo. Being a sound man of science, the Professor could not therefore verify their veracity. The second reason is that the events related by Nemo are, in and of themselves, quite fantastic. It is more than likely that Professor Arronax himself did not entirely believe the account that was related to him. The only reason, therefore, that the papers were not simply destroyed is the evident high regard the Professor held for Captain Nemo. He was unwilling to have his name associated with this tale while he was still alive; but now that he has died, he would appear to be less concerned. Attached to the pages was a note stating:

"Publish or destroy this account as you see fit."

As his executor of his papers, I have been torn both ways. Allowing the general public to read this fantastical account seemed to me to perhaps jeopardize the high regard that Professor Arronax has deservedly merited to date. And, yet, such is the public interest still in the exploits of the late Captain Nemo and his astonishing craft the *Nautilus* that it appeared to me to be irresponsible to withhold further details of his remarkable life.

I merely note that Professor Arronax did not vouch for the truth of this tale. Nor can I; I can merely present it.

One evening, after another of the splendid repasts that the skillful chef of the *Nautilus* had dreamed up—against consisting solely of creatures and plants found beneath the surface of the ocean—Ned Land and my incomparable Conseil had retired, leaving me alone in the company of Nemo. At this point, the *Nautilus* was traveling at a depth of some 14 fathoms. The ocean around us was teeming with small fish, but no landscapes could be observed within the range of the electrical lamps. Nemo stood at his portal, staring into the waters, apparently lost in thought. I had made some inconsequential remark about the bravery and loyalty of his crew—the former perhaps not so surprising, given the enterprise upon which they were engaged, but the latter I found unusual in that the members of the *Nautilus* were drawn from many different and sometimes antagonistic nations. Yet they all owed allegiance to this mysterious Captain of theirs. I had begun to believe that Nemo had retreated into his own thoughts and started to make my way from the room when his voice halted me.

"It was not always so, Arronax." There was another pause, which I took for an invitation to return and stand beside him. As he spoke, he did not yet look at me; instead he regarded the waters that he loved. "There was a time when their bravery faltered, and when one of their numbers betrayed me. I hesitate to speak of it not because it faults my crew, but because the events that occurred are so strange that a man of science like yourself would be understandably skeptical of my account."

"It would seem to me, Captain," I assured him, "that your regard for the scientific method is as high as my own. The notes you have allowed me to peruse and the facts you have related to me demonstrate a clear mind—even if it is one with which I cannot always agree."

He gave a slight nod. "Fair enough, Professor, fair enough. Then I shall relate my tale, and you may accept or scoff as seems most suitable to your humor. However, I shall simply preface it by stating that the events I speak of happened, and, while I cannot fully explain them myself, I do not believe that they are entirely beyond the boundaries of science to explain—perhaps one day, when our understanding of the Cosmos has increased.

"It was during the early days, when the *Nautilus* was still being tested and proven. I had, as you know, assembled a crew consisting of mariners from a variety of nations. One among them was a man from the United States named Suydam. He was taciturn, and considered odd by his fellows, though not unliked. He was a good mariner, and I had no complaints with his performance—until his final day in my employ. That he might have ulterior motives for voyaging with me did not at any time until that final day occur to me.

13

"We were voyaging in—no, I shall not tell you the waters, nor give any hint of the location, save to say that it was deep within the Antipodes. I would not have that place discovered again by any human being. The *Nautilus* had descended toward the bed of the sea, and we had on the electrical lamps so that we might study the formations ahead of us. There was nothing extraordinary in any of this, and we were in no hurry, so we meandered somewhat as the fancy took me.

"The area there is rather volcanic, so I was being quite careful. An underwater eruption could well damage my vessel, though I was under no apprehension that we would be unable to flee any lava flows. To the contrary, I was hoping that some vulcanism might be apparent to us in order for me to make a study of how lava flows under the surface of the sea. My only concern was that an underwater eruption might cause some sort of a pressure that might impact the ship. Hence the reason to advance slowly.

"As a result, we came across the artifacts quite slowly, and they were instantly apparent in the gleam of the lights for what they were—artificial constructs, and at considerable depths in the ocean. As you might imagine, I was rather excited by the discovery. At first it was nothing more than a simple wall, but it was of hewn stone, neatly fitted, and progressing in a straight line. It could be nothing but the work of skilled hands, that much was certain from the start. As we progressed, though, the nature of the ruin changed. In the place of a simple wall, pillars began to appear. Some were erect, many were fallen, and none supported anything.

"It was quite obvious that some sort of cataclysm had befallen this place. Plato's description of the casting down of Atlantis immediately sprang to mind, of course, but this was in an ocean far remote from his world. But where one city might have fallen to the fury of the elements, others might also."

"You said that this voyage of yours was in the Antipodes," I objected. "But there have been no city-building nations there until the recent past. And none of those cities, to the best of my recollection, have ever been swallowed by the waves."

"You are quite correct, Professor," Nemo agreed. "There have been none. This was one reason why I was so gripped by excitement—whoever had built this sunken city must have belonged to some civilization that was advanced in mind, and yet unknown to science. As we explored further, it was apparent that we had stumbled upon a major discovery. But it was also a most peculiar one. There was... something... about the architecture.

"Marine organisms had grown all around the stone work—and yet not one had intruded upon the stones themselves. It was almost impossible to judge how old the site was because of this. Why had none of the plants ventured to grow upon the stones? I could not then say, though now I might venture a guess. And then the walls and toppled columns turned into semi-intact structures and then almost perfect buildings as our floodlights swept across the site. Though I was puzzled by the lack of marine growths on the buildings, I was soon deeply disturbed by the buildings themselves.

"Their architecture was—inhuman. I can think of no other word to describe it. The way that the buildings were constructed was not the product of any sane mind. Overall, the sunken city did not appear so strange—there were buildings that must have been dwellings; some small, some larger. There were open spaces where once markets and meets must have been held. And there were temples and larger public structures. This much was clear and understandable. It was only when one's eyes moved from the general to the particular that the peculiar nature of the place became apparent.

"Walls were not quite straight—not in the sense that they were badly built, you must understand, but that they were deliberately constructed in a fashion that seemed out of keeping with a sane mind. The *intentions* of the unknown builders were to construct the structures precisely the way we viewed them. Windows and doorways were not squared, and floor plans were not straightforward. The problem with describing

15

the city is that it was nothing you could quite put a name to—but it was all clearly warped and twisted from the fabric of a normal life. Looking at the city, we all could tell that whatever had built it and whatever had lived there was not entirely human—and possibly not human at all."

I frowned. "You mean to infer, then, that some lesser species than mankind constructed that city?"

"No; such would be absurd, Professor." Nemo considered for a moment. "Certain insects build homes; beavers dam rivers. But they do not quarry stone and use it in their endeavors. No, not a *lesser* species than man—but certainly *another* species."

I confess that I could not follow his reasoning. "But what could you mean by that?" I asked him.

"I am not entirely certain myself," he confessed. "It is simply that all of us who gazed upon that vast field of ruins had a strong conviction—which we later admitted to one another—that human minds could not have imagined that city, and human hands could not have manufactured it. It had the undeniable stamp of something alien to a human mind about it. And, to be perfectly honest, it unnerved us. As you know, Professor, the men I voyage with are some of the proudest, strongest and bravest that our nations have to offer. Yet through all of our hearts and minds at that moment of discovery, a tremor of fear ran. It was as if the place was drenched in evil, and had been so since time immemorial.

"I said *all*, but that is not true. There was one among us who felt only exultation and a sense of purpose achieved—the mariner Suydam. I did not know it at that time, but when he saw the ruins, his face had changed, showing great satisfaction, and, whilst all other eyes were staring at the astonishing and frightening sight, he hurried away. Looking back later, I realized that Suydam had not been surprised to find the sunken city—that, in fact, he had expected to stumble across it some time in our voyaging. One of his fellows told me later that the man had brought with him some ancient book that he studied at night, with a dim lamp, and that he let no other person see. I can only conjecture that it spoke of ancient and forbidden secrets, including the existence of that terrible place. The book vanished with Suydam, which is probably for the best, so I was never able to be certain of this. But it is logical—as much as anything connected with this event conforms to the rules of logic.

"The first that any of us knew of Suydam's vanishing was when the engines gave a strained sound. I was not then as used to the sounds of the *Nautilus* as I now am, and for a few moments I had no clue what might have occurred. I merely understood that our engines were under some sort of strain. Then the noise became a cacophony, and abruptly ceased after a loud banging noise. The lights flickered for a moment, died, and then returned at a lower level of illumination.

"I forgot about the ruins at that moment, hurrying instead to the ship's engine rooms. There we discovered the engineer insensate, and the main generator inoperable. Clearly this was sabotage, and of a potentially lethal type. Without motive force, the *Nautilus* was sinking slowly toward the bed of the ocean. I hurried back to the viewing chamber and saw that we were, indeed, settling on the floor of the sea, amidst the field of ruins. There was a loud scraping sound as the vessel slid down the exterior wall of a temple or some such. Stones broke free, falling with us, as the *Nautilus* came to rest on the bottom.

"Silence then descended, save for the gentle sound of the electric lighting. The air purifiers, powered as they were from the main generator, had closed off. Without them, we had only the air inside the vessel to breathe. We were in a perilous situation—without the generator our air would not circulate, and we could not move from where we lay. I calculated quickly that we had air enough for almost a full day, and that repairs must be effected within that time.

"Clearly, though, the first thing that needed to be done was to identify and isolate the saboteur. If he had struck once, there was the chance that he had further and even deadlier mischief in mind. Accordingly, I had the crew assembled, and it was at that point that Suydam was discovered to be missing.

"The culprit was clear, but his location was not. I had the ship searched while the engineer was tended to, and I examined the generator.

"Suydam had simply and literally thrown a wrench into the machinery—he was not himself an engineer, and clearly did not know the best way to disable my vessel. He had caused damage, but it was repairable. The only question was whether this could be achieved before our air supply became so fetid as to render us unconscious. My engineer, insisting he was recovered sufficiently to aid us, believed that this could be accomplished, and set about organizing his men to begin temporary repairs. We should certainly need to return to our base for a full overhaul, but he expressed publicly his belief that he could manage to repair the *Nautilus* sufficient for us to return home. Privately, however, he admitted that he was not quite as confident as he seemed. However, he did not wish to depress the crew by an open and honest evaluation. I commended him on his wisdom in avoiding the potential for panic, and set him to work.

"Meanwhile, the men I had sent to search for Suydam reported that he was nowhere to be found. There could be only one explanation for this, and I hurried back to the observation room. Thankfully, the searchlights outside the ship were run from a second generator that was still operable. I directed their movement, and in moments we could see a figure that must be the missing saboteur.

"He was walking purposefully through the ruined city in one of my underwater suits. His motivation was unfathomable—he had stranded us here, on the sea bed, and was now taking a walk into the sunken city alone. Surely he understood that he must perish? Even if we were to succeed in repairing the *Nautilus*, he had to be aware that we would not bother to pick him up. And if we died, he would die also. There could be no haven for him in this city that must have been dead for untold millennia.

"And yet—and yet! Suydam had been withdrawn from his fellows, but he had never shown any signs of palpable insanity. So I could only assume that there was purpose in his actions, no matter how inexplicable they seemed. As we watched, he vanished into one of the buildings—one that seemed to be a cross between a temple and a mausoleum.

"One of the sailors had searched Suydam's berth. The book was discovered to be missing, but there had been left behind a slip of paper on which the man had jotted a few notes, Most made no sense at all, but one line did stand out: *In his house at R'lyeh dead Cthulhu waits dreaming.*

"I was not certain there was any sense in this, either—but the building Suydam had entered had the appearance of a mausoleum—and the line spoke of a person who, though dead, yet dreamed. Was it possible that the man thought he was to awaken some sleeper? It made precious little sense—but, then, nothing made any more sense.

"I was seized with a sudden conviction that stranding us here was not all of the malevolence Suydam had planned for us. And if that were to prove to be true, then he had a purpose in his mission in the dead city. I detailed two of my men to accompany me, and left the engineer to make repairs as speedily as possible. The two men and I then suited up carefully for an underwater expedition. We each took along with us harpoon guns and—almost as an afterthought—a small supply of dynamite. I was not sure that any of these weapons would be of any use, but it was better to be prepared for eventualities.

"We then quit the *Nautilus*, and made our slow, determined way to the sunken city. Close up, the ruins were even more ominous, and their strange aura of inhumanity even more pronounced. I was more convinced than ever that nothing human could have built so unholy a place. The lines of the walls, the cut of the stones, their joints and bracing—all of it was done by the plan of something that thought in a very different way from humanity. It was clear that the buildings were ancient, and the thought came to me that they predated human history. Anything this grand, this awful, would have otherwise

19

been noted by scribes of the antediluvian past. Whose hands—
or other appendages—built that ruined city I cannot say—nor
would I wish to venture a guess.

"One thing puzzled me, though: no fish crossed those
ancient walls. Normally, in places such as these there would
be schools of fish, and predatory moray eels or hunting octopi
would lurk. But here there were no signs of life at all. The
ichthyds avoided the place entirely.

"The building the traitor Suydam had entered was now
just ahead of us. It had the vague appearance of a large domed
church or mosque—though larger than any I have seen in the
world above—and constructed in peculiar and inhuman fashion. As we drew close, we could see that there were large
doors that led within. These appeared to be of copper and
yet—despite their millennia of immersion—were as gleaming
fresh as if they had only just been cast. On the surface of the
doors were images—pictures of such grotesque and abomina-
ble form that I try not to recall them, and will not attempt to
describe them to you. Suffice it to say that they were images
that even a madman's nightmares could not surpass. The race
that had raised this city must have gloried in unspeakable acts
of torture and degradation. Not even a fiend steeped in dope
and bred in the gutters of our world's vilest slums could imagine what we saw depicted on those doors. And, as we progressed further, we discovered that the interior doors and walls
were similarly adorned with pictograms of acts that are too
horrific to repeat.

"But there was science behind all of this, too. The beings
who created this city knew their architecture and building, and
they planned for the ages. Some of the buildings had been
wrecked, true, when the city had sunk below the waves, but
many more were still intact, and the temple-mausoleum we
entered was in a perfect state of preservation. Its age was
unguessable, but there was true skill behind it.

"We opened the main doors, and entered the building.
There was a small entranceway, about ten feet deep, and then
a second set of doors similar to the first. One of my men at-

tempted to open them, but they would not budge. Were they bolted from within? Suydam might have expected to be followed, and sealed them behind him, after all.

"Then a thought occurred to me—perhaps they were like the entrance to the underwater chamber on the *Nautilus*. Two sets of doors, as you have seen, Professor, to allow passage in and out of my vessel. Perhaps these doors were serving the same purpose, and the inner doors would not open until the outer ones closed. I gestured to my men to close the doors behind us, and, once they were closed I examined them and saw that, indeed, they appeared to be a very tight fit. With the outer doors closed, opening the inner ones proved to be a simple matter. They did serve, as I had wildly guessed, to conserve air within the building. When they opened, the water with us in the entrance drained swiftly down channels set in the floor, and we stepped into a further small room, which was virtually free of water.

"As I have said, I had no idea how long this city had lain on the sea bed. Yet, there appeared to be air within this building—perhaps completely stale after all the centuries. There was no way to estimate it, so I tried the experiment of removing my helmet whilst gesturing to my men to retain theirs, in case the air should prove stagnant.

"To my surprise, it was breathable. The only problem was that there was a rank odor, one I have never known before or since. It had something of the miasma of decomposition about it, and that proved to be the more pleasant component of the stench. But the smell, no matter how putrid, did not prevent the air from being breathed. I gestured to my men and they both removed their own helmets, and immediately made comments about the foulness of the air. I was convinced, however, that there was something vitally important to our safety that we must discover as swiftly as possible, so I ordered the men to leave their helmets beside this door and to accompany me.

"It was not difficult to see the path Suydam had taken. Wet footprints led deeper into the depraved building. As I have already mentioned, the walls and doors were given over to horrendous depictions, all of which served to make the three of us more and more uneasy as we progressed. There was no sign of life, ourselves excepted, and the feeling that these were halls mankind was never intended to enter grew as we moved onward. I am a man of science, but the only word that I could seize upon to describe that building was *haunted*—and haunted not by some specter that might once have been human, but by one that possibly had no idea even what a human being was.

"As you may imagine, we were a highly nervous trio, and we clutched our harpoon guns for whatever protection and comfort they might afford. We moved through the building in silence, none of us wishing to break the cold, dank silence with speech. But then, ahead of us, we heard someone who was not so constrained. It was a voice raised in arrogance and triumph. I have made the study of many of the languages employed by mankind, but I could make out no words in this chanting that sounded at all familiar. The words, indeed, sounded as if they were designed to be uttered by vocal cords very different from ours. *Cthulhu* was mentioned or invoked more than once, along with various deities and beings from ancient mythology. Other than that, the words were completely meaningless to me.

"We came to a final door, which lay open, explaining how we could heard the voice making invocations to blasphemous beings. As I had expected, it was Suydam. He was standing before what I took to be an ancient altar, arms upraised, and a gloating, evil expression on his twisted face. The altar was large, carved from a single stone, with horns jutting from each corner. Pictographs in some ancient language were carved deeply into the stone, and covered the altar. Suydam appeared to be reading from these writings as he chanted.

"I called a warning to the man, and he turned to look at me, an expression of fierce triumph on his face. 'You are too late, Captain,' he coldly informed me. 'The One I came here to raise already stirs. His dreams are ending, and life returns to his body.'

"I grasped his meaning. 'You speak of Cthulhu?' I asked him.

"He nodded. 'None other,' he agreed. 'The Great One awakens, and he will reclaim his own.'

"The man was clearly demented, or so I thought. He spoke of raising the dead, as if this was an action a mere mortal might accomplish. And not merely the dead, but the dead of some inhuman race. I was tempted to simply walk away and leave him to suffer the fate he deserved—death, alone, within this hollow city—but I was prevented from following this thought with action.

"For there was a stirring in the air. The foul smell somehow managed to intensify, to the point where my men and I were almost sick. There also appeared a feeling in the air almost electrical in nature. The air was moving, stirring as it had not stirred in long, abandoned centuries. I was unable to understand what was happening, and I have no way at all to explain what happened next, or words sufficient to convey the events.

"Somehow, it was as if there were a connection between where we stood and some other, eldritch place. I had the feeling that vast centuries were somehow being spun aside, that space and time as we know them to be abruptly were seized and shaken as a dog shakes a toy. Everything that we knew as logical and scientific and possible was wrenched through 180 degrees, and the impossible, the unthinkable, the unknowable was happening.

"As a man of science, I have no means of explaining what then occurred—I can merely state that it did happen, no matter how impossible it may sound. In the space before us, a shape materialized. One moment, the space was empty, and the next it was occupied by this entity, the likes of which I have never seen before—and which I devoutly hope I shall never see again!

"It was large, though I cannot say exactly its size—taller and broader than a man, at least 12 feet high. Like a man, it stood upright, but that was all the resemblance it had to anything upon this world. I knew, instinctively, that nothing like this beast could have evolved upon our wholesome planet. And the stench from it was so strong and sickening that it almost crippled all of us, Suydam included.

"Its head was like the body of a squid—large, unblinking eyes, and tentacles that fringed a gaping maw, extremities that writhed constantly. Below that terrifying head was a body, but one I scarcely saw. I have the impression of limbs and claws, but I can attest to nothing. For those great eyes bore into us, and I knew the malice that the creature held for us and our kind. I knew that, if loosed upon our world, it would stamp with certainty the demise of humanity. Such creatures as this and we ourselves cannot co-exist. Even Suydam, whose incantations must have called this creature from some abyss, was stunned by the awfulness of this sight.

"One of my men fired his weapon at the monstrosity. I know the harpoon hit and sank into whatever flesh that monster had, for there came a scream of inhuman rage and pain. The creature lashed out, catching my man and crushing the life from him. Then, in a moment of horror that I cannot forget, no matter how I try, it drew him into that great mouth, and began to devour the fresh corpse.

"I knew it intended the same fate for all of us. Like fabled Polyphemus, this creature thrived on the flesh of human beings. But the poor man's efforts had shown that, though a harpoon might cause the monstrosity pain, it could not halt it. My actions were those of instinct and not rational thought. I fired my own harpoon—not at Cthulhu, for this was surely the sleeper awakened—but at Suydam, whose infernal tampering with the laws of Nature had raised this leviathan. The bolt proved far more effective on the man than on the monster. With a gasp of shock, Suydam fell to the floor, dead.

"Cthulhu, having finished its grisly feast, sprang upon this fresh corpse, raising it to that terrible mouth. I had taken out the dynamite I carried, and removed it from the waterproof covering. Striking a lucifer, I ignited the sticks, and then threw them into that all-devouring maw. Hurriedly, I shook my remaining companion, who had been struck silent and still by the horrors we were witnessing. Together, we stumbled toward the exit doors. Behind us, the dynamite exploded, and there was a fresh, titanic scream from Cthulhu. I chanced a backward glance, and saw that the explosion appeared to have taken the head off the creature—but if it had, whence came that chilling scream? The mountainous body didn't fall, however, and its several limbs were writhing, claws opening and closing.

"We fled as swiftly as we could, returning to the entrance chamber where we had stashed our breathing apparatus and helmets. We sealed the inner door behind us, and then worked at opening the outer ones. At that moment, we heard the sound of many limbs beating on the inner doors. They would not open, of course, as long as the outer ones stood ajar, but as we moved as swiftly as we could out of the buildings, I saw that the solid metal was starting to buckle under the rain of so strong and ferocious blows. It was only a matter of time before Cthulhu battered down the doors and came after us.

"As you know from experience, Professor, it is impossible to move swiftly under the water. It seemed to take us forever to bridge the distance between that foul city and the safety of my craft. Somehow, though, we did. It was only later that the reason for our escape occurred to me—when Cthulhu broke down those inner doors, water would have poured into the temple, and even a being as strong as it could not fight against the power of the sea. Cthulhu must have been washed backward by the pressure of the inflowing water, allowing us those moments we needed to effect our escape.

"Back in the comforting walls of the *Nautilus*, I was delighted to discover that my engineers had managed to repair the craft sufficiently for us to power up and begin to move. I had no time for explanations—nor could I find the words to explain my actions. Instead, I merely turned my craft toward the forgotten city and called upon all the power of her turbines.

"We crashed into that great dome with the prow of the *Nautilus*. It was designed to penetrate wood and steel, and those stones could not withstand the blow. The entire vessel rang with the sound of the encounter, and then we were past. I had the searchlights turned to our rear, and, as we watched, the dome collapsed, tearing down most of the superstructure with it. It seemed to fall in slow motion, of course, as the dome fell apart, and then inward. My frantic eyes searched for any sign that Cthulhu might have made its escape before the collapse, but I could see nothing of the monstrosity. I could only pray that it had been buried beneath those monumental inhuman blocks, and that the building I had taken for a mausoleum truly was such now.

"We managed to limp home in the damaged *Nautilus*, which was repaired. But the one man and I had memories that could not be erased. The sight of that creature, Professor, is one I shall never forget, no matter how hard I might wish it to be otherwise. And there is one more thing that still troubles me. That one line in Suydam's writing that had made some sort of sense:

"In his house at R'lyeh dead Cthulhu waits dreaming.

"Perhaps we did somehow kill that creature. Dynamite and the fall of masonry would have killed any entity that this world has ever spawned. But is it enough to slay the being that we saw? Or is Cthulhu still waiting and dreaming again?"

Like many of my contemporaries, I bought most volumes of Ballantine Books' reissues of older fantasy novels in the Seventies, and rather enjoyed the works of William Hope Hodgson. Somehow, though, I'd missed his brilliant tales of Carnacki the Ghost Finder. I remedied this oversight after watching The Rivals Of Sherlock Holmes, *which filmed one of the tales, "The Horse Of The Invisible". Donald Pleasence played Carnacki, and I was hooked. Hodgson wrote only a handful of Carnacki tales, so I decided that it was high time to remedy that oversight. Jean-Marc once again suggested a foil for him – Madame Palmyre, created in 1924 by Renée Dunan for her supernatural novella* Baal *(available from Black Coat Press). She was a delightfully wicked character, and a perfect opponent!*

More Imaginative Sins

London, 1912

My friend Carnacki was a man of unvarying routine. He would invite the four of us over for dinner after one of his cases, and nothing would be spoken of it until after a fine meal was finished and we had settled in comfortable chairs. Carnacki would light his pipe and then commence telling us of his latest adventures. Those adventures were always of an astonishing nature as he is, by profession, a ghost finder. I firmly believe that Carnacki needed the strictly unvarying routine of that social interaction as a counter to the complete unpredictability of his cases. In some instances he would deduce that a human agency was at work and would supply his clients—and by extension the four of us—with an explanation of how something that appeared to be supernatural was achieved by trickery. But in other cases… well, they were the sort that would make the skin crawl.

This evening, I had been strongly tempted to break the routine as Carnacki looked as shaken and pale as I had ever seen him. Before I could remark on his appearance, however, he had caught my eye and shaken his head slightly to dissuade me from such a course of action. The other three all gave a start when they saw Carnacki, but they, too, received that slight shake and held their peace.

After dinner and a fine brandy, Carnacki consented to speak. We settled into familiar chairs and waited until he had lit his pipe and taken a few puffs.

I know you were all surprised by my appearance (he began). To tell the truth, I've had rather a rough time of it in this last case of mine. I've not spoken much about my neighbors here in Cheyne Walk, but there are some interesting types. One in particular—Sâr Dubnotal. He is in a line of business not too unlike mine, though he tends to travel the world and I like to stay in my own little country. He's been able to offer me advice and a little help from time to time, so I wasn't too surprised when he called upon me and asked me to take on a case for him as a favor. It seems the sister of a friend of his had suffered from a curious affliction. He himself would have investigated, save for the fact that it was imperative for him to be in the South of France the following day on crucial business. Naturally I agreed that I would look into the affair, and he supplied me with an address and a letter of introduction.

As I didn't have much to keep me busy, I went around that afternoon to a place in Eaton Place. It was about what you'd expect—reeked of old money and the tweedy inhabitance of several generations. The owner was a Richard Cardinal and he lived there with his wife, two children, one sister and a barrage of servants. The house had been his father's before him, and the grandfather's before that, so he knew the history of the place back to the days when the first brick had been laid. There had never been the hint of a ghost before this, and no signs of anything out of the ordinary. Any self-respecting haunt would have been bored stiff, most likely, in such a staid household. Save when the gentleman of the house was speaking, the only noises to be heard were the ticking of the various clocks. A place less likely to be an outpost of Hell is hard to imagine.

And yet, that is what it appeared to have become. Cardinal's wife and children were in the country with relatives as they simply couldn't stand the house any longer. At precisely eight in the evening, the terror would commence, and it would last until dawn. The events were wholly centered upon the sister, Agnes. She herself could recall nothing of what transpired in her room between those hours, save that she was exhausted and horrified when they were over. And there were no witnesses to what occurred, at least not directly, because the events happened only inside the room and no one else was able to enter the room once eight had struck until the dawn of the following morning. All that anyone else knew was that poor Agnes would scream and scream in horror, and that there was something else in that room, something that cast a putrid light beneath the door and a foul stench that filled the upstairs corridor. The events had commenced a week prior to my arrival and were repeated without change every night.

Naturally, the thought that first occurred to me was that perhaps the sister should leave the house—or, at the very least, occupy some other room in this house in the evening.

"That has been considered," Cardinal informed me. "But it's simply not possible. We cannot remove Agnes from the room at any time."

I confess, this case was certainly an intriguing one, and I was determined to see for myself what was happening. Accordingly, I asked Cardinal to take me to see his sister.

He consulted one of the clocks in the receiving room. "At this hour, she's probably sleeping," he said. "Whatever it is that happens to her, she's left completely exhausted."

"Then you would not advise my seeing her?" I asked. I know I must have scowled, for it would be a great inconvenience if I could not look over the room and examine the young lady in question.

"Oh, no, you may see her," Cardinal explained. "It's merely that you won't be able to question her. She sleeps very deeply, no doubt worn out from the night terrors." He rang for the butler. When that worthy appeared, he sent the man to fetch a Miss Bolton. "She is my sister's ladies maid," he explained to me. "She will accompany you to my sister's room. I..." He paused and then admitted: "I prefer not to enter the room myself." Seeing my expression, he added hastily: "My sister and I have always been close. It distresses me greatly to see the suffering she is subject to."

That I could understand. Miss Bolton arrived—a sharp, nervous woman in her late forties—and she regarded me with some suspicion before leading me up the stairs. The sister's room was down the corridor to the right and I paused outside the door. "You appear suspicious of me," I commented.

Miss Bolton studied me steadily. "I do not approve of meddling with the occult," she stated flatly. "I've told Miss Cardinal this before. It is against my personal beliefs to trespass in realms we are not supposed to traverse."

"I see." This is a common attitude I find in my investigations. "If it is of any comfort to you, I, too, disapprove of trespassing in such realms. Yet, sadly, people constantly do so. It is my task to attempt to save them from their follies, not to encourage further transgressions."

That seemed to change her opinion of me somewhat. "It's a shame that not everyone shares such beliefs," she commented.

"Including Miss Cardinal?" I prompted.

"I will hear nothing spoken against her," Miss Bolton said sharply. "Only...Well, I did warn her not to see that fortune teller."

I hid my smile. "Though many so-called fortune tellers are nothing but fakes, I doubt one could seriously harm her—except in her purse."

"You did not see the one who came here," Miss Bolton snapped. Then she covered her mouth with a thin hand. "I should not have spoken; I gave my word."

Then I could see how little her word was worth. But this seemed a possible line of investigation, but one I shelved for the moment. I wished my inspection of Agnes Cardinal's room to be unprejudiced by suspicions. Instead, I stood outside the bedroom door and studied it.

"Do you not wish to enter?" Miss Bolton asked.

"Only when I am satisfied there is nothing further to discover outside," I informed her, then dismissed her from my mind for the moment as I examined the framework of the door. If, as Mr. Cardinal claimed, the room was impenetrable from this side after eight, there had to be some reason for this.

So-called magic is simply the manipulation of energies as yet little understood or investigated by man. Many rituals have evolved through trial and error, some of which are effective in working those energies, others of which are not. In order to prevent people from either entering or leaving this room, there had to be some force at work, and as a result there must be something close at hand that could affect and focus that force.

At first glance, there was nothing obvious. That led to only two conclusions: either Roger Cardinal's story was a tissue of lies, or else the obvious was incorrect. I seriously considered the former—not from distrust of my client, but simply as a matter of logic. If Cardinal was lying—why? Why employ me if there was nothing wrong? And why tell a lie that could be disproved so simply as to ask other people in the house what was transpiring? Many thoughts came to mind, though I dismissed them rapidly. Perhaps his sister had money he wished to control and he wanted her declared insane? Then would he not have called a doctor and not an occultist? Perhaps he wished to keep her imprisoned in her room for other reasons? Then why call in an outsider at all? No, he had begged my friend Sâr Dubnotal for help, and that must have been a genuine request. Dubnotal was no fool, and could have told if his friend had been lying. So—if Cardinal had been telling the truth, what I sought was too subtle to spot at first glance.

"Now I will see Miss Cardinal," I informed Miss Bolton. She nodded and tapped gently on the door. There was no reply, but she led the way into the room. It was in no obvious way different from a thousand such bedchambers in the City of London. The centerpiece was the canopy bed itself, with laced curtains drawn about it. There was a ladies' dressing table beside the window that overlooked the street below, and a chair drawn up to it. To one side was a couch with an upholstered chair beside a tea table. Though the room had been fitted for electricity, there was a large candelabra standing in the corner. A door led from the end of the room, clearly to a dressing room beyond. It was a pleasant bedchamber, neat and tidy. It looked normal and most charming.

There was a stench of evil thick enough almost to be touched.

Anyone who works in any profession—from banker to rat-catcher—develops a certain sense of their sphere of interest, things that are immediately apparent to them when an outsider detects nothing amiss. I could quite clearly feel the presence of some inhuman force upon the structure of this room. It was nothing definite and in no way could I define what it was I sensed—and yet any lingering doubts as to Cardinal's veracity were gone in that instant. The other-worldly had entered our fragile realm at this point.

"Is anything ever found in this room in the mornings?" I asked Miss Bolton.

"Nothing physical," she replied. "But there is a most unpleasant odor that lingers a short while."

"Yes, I imagined there might be." Other realms have other atmospheres, not often pleasant to our senses. "And are there marks on the body of Miss Cardinal?"

Miss Bolton drew herself up to scowl at me. "It is not polite to enquire about the form of a young lady," she scolded me.

"Quite so," I agreed. "But perhaps you might consider me a doctor of some sort for the duration of this investigation? My interest in her form is professional, and not salacious."

Miss Bolton considered for a moment. "There are... welts," she finally stated. "They do not persist long."

"Would they be visible now?" I asked.

"Not to the likes of you."

I sighed. "Miss Bolton, do you wish your charge to continue to suffer through her nights, or do you wish her freed from her terrors and pains?"

"Of course I want her to be free," the companion said.

"Then please indulge me and allow me to see some evidence of what is left with her after her trauma."

Miss Bolton clearly struggled with her prudish conscience, but finally her affection for her employer overcame her moral scruples, and she reluctantly led the way to the bed. She glared at me in warning, and then pulled aside the curtain.

My first sight of Agnes Cardinal was quite a shock. She was a young woman of perhaps 23 years, but she looked a decade older. She was drawn and her skin pale, though there were indeed raised welts on her exposed cheek and wrists, welts that had clearly been red and livid, but were dying down. Miss Cardinal was sleeping badly, panting slightly, a sweat upon her brow. From time to time she gave off whimpers, much as a beaten dog might, and thrashed about in her bed. When she was well, she would have been a pleasant, if undistinguished, young lady.

I had seen all I needed, and gestured to Miss Bolton that she might close the curtains again—which she did with an audible sigh of relief.

I considered what I had seen. Miss Cardinal clearly suffered physical assaults in these strange nocturnal occurrences, but the effects were not lasting. The fear and horrors, however, seemed to have ingrained themselves in her soul. The events transpiring in this room were very disturbing, but to be sure of what might be causing them I would have to witness one of the attacks. This left me in something of a dilemma, one I would have to discuss with her brother.

"I have two courses of action here," I explained to him a short while later. "The first is to gather information which may aid me in coming to a method of aiding your sister. This means, however, that we should have to allow another attack on her this evening. The second option is that I can attempt to protect her whilst still being uncertain of the exact nature of the problem."

"Which would you recommend?" he asked me. I could hear the pain and evident concern for his sister in his voice. If Mr. Cardinal was somehow behind these attacks for whatever nefarious reason, then he was a better actor than my ability to penetrate. He seemed utterly genuine.

"I am always in favor of gathering as much information as possible," I responded. "I am, in that way, akin to a doctor preparing for surgery. The dilemma here is that your sister would be forced to suffer more agonies."

"And do you think you can help her now, even being uncertain of the forces at work?"

"I do not know," I admitted. "I have methods at my disposal that might—and I stress *might*—alleviate the problem. They are unlikely to be completely effective, but they may ameliorate the pain."

"In which case," he said firmly, "you must try them. Anything that might help relieve the suffering my sister endures must be my primary concern."

Thus in agreement, we began the preparations for that evening's vigil. Miss Cardinal slept through most of the arrangements, waking only at about six in the evening. She was startled to see me and only calmed down when her brother appeared to assure her that I was a friend who would help her.

"I fear nothing can help me, Roger," she replied, her voice tinged with pain and terror. "I am in Hell."

"Not Hell," I assured her, in as kindly a fashion as I could. "Perhaps an outpost of that region, however." As she ate a light meal, I continued my work. Her eyes darted about, following my work, but she refrained from asking questions, which I found most unusual and welcome in a woman.

I set up my electric pentacle on the floor about her bed. I have spoken of this before, as I frequently find it to be very useful in protecting against the forces of evil. I was not certain how effective it would be in this case, as I still had no clear picture of precisely what was attacking the slender woman who ate and drank sparingly and watched my every move. I then quietly invoked the Aalaaron Ritual from the Sigsand Manuscript as further protection about the bed. This combination ought to provide some protection for Agnes Cardinal, whatever the evil might be. Then I sent her brother from the room, remaining only with Miss Cardinal and Miss Bolton as chaperone.

"If you are up to it," I told the victim, "I should appreciate a little information from you. I thought you might speak more freely if your brother was not present. Please think of me as you would a doctor or a priest—whatever secrets you divulge will not be revealed to your family."

[Here Carnacki paused and regarded those of us who were his audience. "I should add," he said, gently, "that I have changed the names of those involved in the household, as well as disguising its true location in order for me to keep my promise. All other details are quite accurate." He then resumed his tale.]

"I can tell you no more than Roger already knows," Miss Cardinal replied. "I know only that at the stroke of eight some monstrous evil invades my room and I recall nothing more until I awaken the following morning with lesions across my body and in terrible fear and agony. During the day I sleep, which enables me to recover slightly, and in the evening the events repeat themselves. They wear me down," she confessed, "and I do not know how much longer I can endure them." She hesitated a moment. "I have been contemplating a grave sin," she added.

"My dear lady," I told her, "in these circumstances I should be most surprised if the thought of suicide had not crossed your mind. But none of this is what I wished to question you on. Rather, I wish to know about your experiences with a certain fortune teller."

A guilty flush brought brief life to her cheeks, and then it faded. "You know of that?" She glanced in some annoyance at her companion. Miss Bolton had the grace to squirm under the accusing gaze.

"I do not judge you," I informed her. "It is merely that there would appear to be some connection between that event and your current predicament. If I am not mistaken, the person involved visited your rooms here at least twice before your misfortunes began? And both times when your brother was not present?"

"Yes," Miss Cardinal admitted. "But I cannot see what possible connection there might be between the visits of Madame Palmyre and my current situation."

"Nevertheless it is there," I assured her. "You seem to be a well-bred woman, and I doubt you are in the habit of receiving strangers here in your room."

"I am not."

"Then my hypothesis would appear sound—the only stranger to visit you was this Madame Palmyre, and subsequent to her visits you suffer nocturnal attacks. Therefore the two events must be linked. Now—a delicate question, I know—I must ask you to tell me the reason for her visits." As she flushed again, I held up a hand. "I understand that it must be of a delicate nature as you kept the visits secret from your brother. That is why I sent him from the room before talking to you. But if I am to help you, I must have a complete grasp of the facts in the case."

"You will think me foolish," Miss Cardinal replied.

"I repeat, I do not judge; I am here only to help, and in order to help, I need information. Whatever your motivations, they have led you to this state and I must know them." I softened my voice a little. "Besides, there is not one human being who does not behave in a foolish manner at some date in their lives. And some live in a perpetual state of folly. If you behaved unwisely, then it proves only that you are as human as the rest of us."

"Thank you for your kind words," she replied, her head bowed. "Very well, I shall tell you—and you will see why it can have no connection to what is befalling me." She looked up, her indecision fled. "There is a friend of my brother's of whom I am extremely fond. I shall not name him, as that cannot be of interest to you—but he is... dear to me. Yet he has given me no signs that he returns my regard. So..." She gestured with her hand. "I had heard of Madame Palmyre, who visits London for a short while, for her skills." She colored again. "She is not a fortune teller as such, but one who promises to help a person achieve their goals."

I began to understand the picture Miss Cardinal was doing her best to avoid painting. "She offers love potions?" I ventured a guess.

"Yes." She looked down at her hands again. "And she promised me that she could deliver one that would be effective in winning his affections."

I nodded. "Hence the two visits," I said. "The first for the consultation and the second to deliver the philter."

The pale woman looked puzzled. "But how could you be so certain that she visited twice?"

"That will become clear shortly," I promised her. "First, did you use the potion?"

Again that feverish flush of the cheeks, which made her words redundant. "Yes," she admitted. "I was instructed to add a little to his wine and a little to my own. Thus we should be linked, and thus would our affections be linked."

"And did it work?" I asked.

"I do not know," she confessed. "That evening was the first when I was attacked. I have not seen the gentleman since. My brother does not invite visitors whilst I am in this state." She started. "You think that the potion may have caused my troubles? I do not see how."

"Nor do I yet," I admitted. "But given the juxtaposition of the two events, cause and effect does seem to be likely."

"But what reason would Madame Palmyre have for offering me such evil?" she asked, bewildered.

"Again, I cannot see a reason—but reason there must be. It is quite clear that she has a hand in these events. Perhaps when I speak with her she will enlighten me."

"You will go to her?"

"Not today," I said, consulting the clock in the room. "It is already past seven, and I cannot leave you alone this night."

"You cannot do anything else," Miss Cardinal said, sadly. "I cannot leave this room and no one can stay with me past eight. There is some... force that prevents either action."

"A force I wish to investigate," I informed her. "Is it painful for you to attempt to exit your room?"

"No—it is merely impossible."

"This I wish to see, then, with my own eyes." I gestured at the door. "Perhaps you would be good enough to attempt an egress?"

Miss Cardinal paused a moment to gather her resolve and then she stood up and walked steadily to the door. She looked back at me and then attempted to cross the threshold.

I confess, I was taken aback. I had seen nothing like this in any of my investigations. She was caught in the act of walking, one foot raised, as if trapped in an invisible spider's web of tremendous strength. I could see clearly that she was trying to complete her step and that there was some unseen force literally preventing her. I asked her permission and then attempted to push her through the exit. This proved to be impossible—she was not able to move forward at all. Yet, when I tried it, I was able to leave the room without hindrance. I gripped her hands and attempted to draw them after me, but they were completely immovable, though only in the forward direction. As soon as I told her to cease the attempt, she was able to step back into the room without a problem.

"Miss Cardinal," I informed her, "you have certainly shown me something novel."

"Then you do not know what is causing this?" she asked me, disappointment evident in her voice.

"On the contrary, I am certain I know precisely what is causing the problem. I simply have never seen it before."

She blinked and then looked hopeful. "Then you can cure this condition?"

"As to that, I am not so certain." I knelt down and examined the door frame from the hall side of the door, looking for something I was certain had to be there. After a moment, I discovered what I had anticipated—at the base of each side of the frame, two small sections of wooden paneling had been fixed to the door. They were colored so as to blend in perfectly with the existing frame and so would not be evident except to the sort of intense scrutiny to which I had subjected the frame. Miss Cardinal watched me in surprise as I pried the first of these loose from the door and examined it.

As I have said, the outside was camouflaged to blend in perfectly with the frame. On the inside, however, there was an inscription in some language unknown to me—and, I suspect, to most human beings now alive on our planet—surrounding an inverted pentagram. I showed it to Miss Cardinal.

"What in the world is that?" she asked.

"What is preventing you from exiting this room and preventing anyone else from entering during your ordeal," I informed her. "They are called wards, and these are exceptionally powerful ones written in a tongue that was ancient when our world was still a boiling ball of stone. They manipulate the lines of forces of what we call magic and what other intelligences consider their science. They were left here by your friendly Madame Palmyre."

Understanding flooded her features, making her for a moment less plain than she normally appeared. "I see why you knew she must have been here twice, then," she commented. "The first time she would have needed to ascertain the wood for the door frame, and the second time to place those—what did you call them?—wards."

"Correct." I smiled. "It was clear to me that something had to be keeping you in the room, and when I saw your reaction attempting to cross the doorframe, it confirmed my suspicions." I bent to replace the ward where it had been. When I straightened again, I saw the shock on her face.

"If you remove those wards, will I not be able to leave my room?" she asked. "The hour of eight approaches." I could see the terror she felt in her eyes and in the slight tremors of her body.

"Yes," I said gently. "You would be able to leave your room. But so might your nocturnal haunter. I do not understand the language the wards are inscribed with, and they might be all that keeps the horror confined to your room."

"I could not inflict my sufferings on my brother and his family," she said, sadly but firmly. "You are right to leave them in place, then, even though it means another night of agony for me."

"I am hopeful that this may not be the case," I informed her. I gestured to her bed. "My electric pentagram and the incantations I have used have their own power, and I do possess knowledge of my own—not as ancient or as dark as that of Madame Palmyre, admittedly, but it may suffice for us this night."

"Us?" Agnes Cardinal blinked. "But the same force that keeps me here will prevent you from lingering."

"Within my pentagram, I believe the spell ejecting strangers will not work," I said. "And I trust it will keep whatever evil manifests itself in your room from approaching you." As her face lit with hope, I held up a warning hand. "I cannot promise either without trial, but I am hopeful."

"Then so am I," she decided. "Mr. Carnacki, whatever befalls this evening, I offer you my heart-felt thanks for your efforts."

I had almost forgotten Miss Bolton was still present, so silent had she been, but she now stepped forward. "I, too, shall stay," she insisted, with a sniff. "I cannot leave Miss Cardinal without a chaperone."

"Then we shall face this together," I informed them. "First, I must stress this—on no account leave the protection of the pentagram. This has strength only within its confines— if you cross the electric barriers, then you will be subject to anything without. Second, if I appear distracted it will be because I am reciting protective chants to aid us. Try not to break my concentration."

The ladies both signified their understanding, and so we sat tensely awaiting the numerous clocks scattered about the house to mark the appointed hour. It was not long in coming, but the strain made it seem almost eternal. Miss Cardinal was upon her bed, and Miss Bolton was upon a chair within the confines of the electric pentacle. I myself paced up and down, knowing the weaknesses that might prove disastrous. A thousand thoughts and scenarios flickered through my mind, haunting me with possible outcomes. Given that Miss Cardinal had survived every other night, I felt it unlikely she would be harmed any more than usual if my precautions failed us. But as Miss Bolton and I were intruders on an event that its perpetrator seemed eager to keep secret I could not be assured of our own safety.

As the numerous clocks began to strike the hour, we all three stiffened. Now it would begin.

And, indeed, I immediately began to feel the effects of some strange force. It was as if a hundred unseen hands were grabbing at my, tugging me toward the door. Unheard voices seemed to cry: "Leave!" The pressure on me to move was strong and relentless—but not overwhelming. I fought back, struggling to remain rooted in place.

Miss Bolton gave a startled cry and rose to her feet. Shaking, she took a step. Worried, I cried out: "If you leave the pentacle, rush immediately out of the door! You should be safe outside of the room, but do not linger." This warning penetrated the shock, and she shook her head and then reseated herself firmly in the chair.

And then the urge to flee was gone. For a brief moment there was peace—the dreadful tension in the air stilled. But only for a moment.

This time it was Miss Cardinal who gave the warning cry. With a shaking hand, she gestured toward the window, and we both followed her gesture.

It is difficult to describe what we saw. Imagine that the world we see here about us as a painting. Then what we were watching was as if some unseen hand had ripped the painting and was pushing it aside, exposing another scene behind it. In front of the window was a tear in the picture of the world as we know it, and—from some nether dimension beyond—a separate reality was exposed. What that reality was is impossible to describe, because it was something no human eye was ever meant to see. Our senses are too feeble, too ethereal, to be able to grasp the substance of that world. There were colors and shapes and movement, but what any of them were I cannot say. Human mouths and tongues cannot form themselves about the words needed to describe those events. Suffice it to say that there was a second reality temporarily imposed upon ours, a reality that was utterly incompatible with our own realm of experiences. And it was a reality populated with life utterly unlike anything we have ever known.

One of these dwellers was waiting as the breach occurred. We never did see all of it, so I cannot describe the entirety. It sat, or squatted, or stood beyond the rift, and allowed only portions of its immense form to pass through into our world. Tentacles there certainly were, in profusion, writhing and questing as they came. Sections of a leathery hide were visible behind these, but it was impossible to focus on those. Whether the creature had eyes or other senses, I cannot say. The tentacles were the overwhelming substance visible, the more so as they groped toward us.

I have heard that octopi and squids of the seas of our gentle world use their tentacles as hands, able to manipulate them to seize prey and drag it into their maw. This unearthly thing used its appendages to do far more. They reached across the room, writhing and searching, clearly intent upon Miss Cardinal.

Now I was aware again of my companions. Since the tear in reality had occurred, I had barely thought of them, but now Miss Bolton screamed and promptly fainted. My first thought was that this would at least prevent her from attempting to leave the protection of the pentangle. Miss Cardinal was affected in a different fashion, drawing the bedclothes about her as if mere fabric could defend against those questing digits.

"That... that is the thing which has attacked me these nights?" she gasped.

"Evidently," I replied, my own voice far from steady.

"Little wonder my mind has refused to recall it, then," she observed. "Even now, I find it hard to see and understand. Can it... reach us?"

Her question was a good one, for the tentacles had reached the boundaries of my pentacle now and had paused. The tips quivered and moved slowly in the air as if they had come across something solid that barred their way. Then they reared back and struck forward—but recoiled as if they had struck a wall. There was a pause, and then another assault. Again, my protection withstood.

The being beyond the rift possessed intelligence and purpose. It probed and pushed and squeezed, the tentacles whipping about the room, surrounding the bed and striving to reach us—or, rather, Miss Cardinal. I could not be certain it even knew or cared that I was present. It had one objective in mind and focused all of its energies on achieving that end. Strange sounds that had to be the voice of that creature shook the room as it screamed its frustrations.

My incantations and protections held. I cannot describe the relief I felt as I realized this. I meant nothing to that being—if it could reach me it might swat me or squash me or even ignore me. To an intelligence that alien, anything was possible. But it possessed one single thought—to reach Miss Cardinal. To what purpose? Why should a creature from a realm so distant in space and time and imagination concern itself with a weak, terrified human victim? Why should it attack and torture her night after night?

I discovered that I had retreated into the center of the pentacle, which was filled by Miss Cardinal's bed. The edge of it struck the back of my knees, and I fell upon the edge of it.

Miss Cardinal grasped me, holding on as if her life and sanity depended upon that link.

"What is it?" she gasped. "What does it desire of me?" I simply shook my head.

The cries of the creature doubled in intensity and fury, and the tentacles lashed and slammed against the unseen barrier preventing them from reaching its prey. I was not thinking logically at that point—in that noise and amidst that insane activity I doubt if any human being could—but some thoughts penetrated the haze of terror and shock.

I recalled that the Bible mentions the early days of the Earth, and that in that dim and distant pass before we humans had built up our defenses that other creatures came to our world in search of women with which to mate. The Bible calls them giants, or *nephelim*, but we have other names for them. One that I knew was Baal. Was it possible that this thing that was attacking us might be one of the surviving *nephelim*, these untold ages afterward? That it still sought to mate with human women? Why it should wish so, I cannot say, but these were the thoughts running through my mind—as much as I was thinking anything at all coherently under that assault. The screams, the frustrations, the desperation to reach Miss Cardinal—all of these pointed to the possibility that my hypothesis was correct. It would explain why she was alive after facing such an inhuman being night after night, and why her tortured mind refused to allow her to recall any details of her encounters. Who on our warm and friendly planet would wish to remember the embraces of such a cold and pitiless demonic entity?

The night passed. I would describe it in more detail if possible, but there is little to say. Miss Cardinal and I clung to each other for comfort as the creature raged and thrashed impotently about. When the dawn came, the tentacles withdrew and the gash between the dimensions sealed itself. The terrible pressure we had felt and the raging fear both subsided and we were able to let our feverish grips on each other go. There was a bond of sorts between us, for we had survived a night such as—thankfully—few other humans ever had. Once again, I was grateful that my electric pentacle had proven to be so efficient.

Miss Bolton was still unconscious—indeed, she did not recover her wits until the family doctor had called and treated her. She then promptly gave notice and immediately quit the household, refusing to ever return.

Miss Cardinal and I were both strained from the night's events, but there was no thought of sleep for either of us. We both knew that if we closed our eyes, we should see that living nightmare fresh and cold and clear again, so we sought to defer sleep as long as possible.

"You have saved me, Mr. Carnacki," she commented, as we sat to breakfast with her brother. I had removed the wards at her door once again to allow her to leave that haunted room and she had vowed to move to another before the day was through. "I cannot thank you enough."

"I have not saved you, Miss Cardinal," I replied. "Yet. I have merely postponed the evil for a single night. I am certain that the horror will return this evening to that room if I am not able to lay it. Accordingly, I intend to visit your Madame Palmyre today and see if I cannot persuade her to remove whatever spell she has cast upon you." I scribbled a note on the back of one of my calling cards and had the butler send it around to her hotel by one of the footmen. As I had hoped, I received a short note by return.

"*Six o'clock would be convenient. Madame Palmyre.*"

I showed it to Mr. Cardinal and his sister. "Tonight, then, should see the end of this—one way or another."

I arrived at the hotel shortly before six, carrying my equipment bag. Madame Palmyre had rooms on the third floor front, and I was escorted up. I was uncertain what I would find when I arrived, and was quite surprised when the lady greeted me.

She was tall and very beautiful, dressed in impeccable fashion and with little jewelry. With her was a smaller woman, fussy-looking, but clearly quite intelligent and obviously devoted to her companion. "My secretary and companion, Renée," Madame Palmyre introduced her.

I dropped my bag just inside the door, and gestured to it. "I apologize, but I've come straight from the Cardinal household, and had no time to return this home."

"The Cardinals?" Madame Palmyre did not seem surprised to hear the news. "And you came straight here? How... kind of you to call."

"This is not a social visit, I am afraid."

Her eyes gleamed. "I hardly thought it was, Mr. Carnacki, given your profession. Yes, I have heard of you— we have friends in common."

"Really?" I murmured. "I am surprised we have anything in common."

"Now you're being rude, Mr. Carnacki," she protested.

"Madame," I responded, "you have callously dispatched a demonic being to prey upon an innocent young woman, setting both her and her family into nights of terror. I hardly think I am being rude to a person capable of such sins."

"Sins?" She glared at me. "Mr. Carnacki, you English are capable of only pallid sins." She cast a scornful eye over me. "Judging from your waist-line, I was guess that a minor case of gluttony was as serious as you could ever achieve. Do not speak of that which you do not understand."

"I understand evil, Madame," I replied. "I understand wickedness. And I understand selfishness. What I do not understand is why you have inflicted such wanton cruelty on an innocent woman."

"Innocent?" She laughed. "Oh, I think not, Mr. Carnacki. If you read your Bible—and I suspect you do, from your attitude—then you know that we are all of us sinners, and there is not one innocent amongst us."

"You play word games with me when I wish a serious answer."

"I am being quite serious," she assured me. "Agnes Cardinal is not the sweet, gentle girl you take her for. Did she tell you why she sought my services?"

46

"She spoke of a love potion to be used on a man she admired."

"And did she bother to mention that this man is already married, with two children? I see from the look on your face that she did not." She smiled at me again, the smile of a cat stalking a wounded bird. "Miss Cardinal wished to destroy the lives of a perfectly fine family for her own selfish desires. How, then, is she innocent?"

"I see that you are not a believer in Gilbert and Sullivan," I replied.

She raised an elegant eyebrow. "Musical comedy? My dear Mr. Carnacki, perhaps you are not as dull as I feared. To which of their entertainments do you refer?"

"*The Mikado*."

"Ah!" She gave another of her delightful laughs. "Let the punishment fit the crime?"

"Precisely. Even if she did seek her own desires through compelling a man to desert his wife and family, that hardly merits long nights of torture."

"Go back to your Bible, Mr. Carnacki," she suggested. "The vengeful God within its pages aims to send all sinners to the eternal fires of damnation. All I did was to give Miss Cardinal a foretaste of what your God plans for her in any event."

"Whatever God may or may not plan for an individual—and one who may yet have remorse for her sins—does not give you the right to assign punishment of your own."

"Perhaps not," Madame Palmyre agreed, casually enough. "But it suited my purposes. And it still does."

"You condemn her to Hell far too casually," I protested. "I have come to ask you to remove the spell upon her that brings that... hideous creature to her every night."

"Ah, I see that you have met Baal yourself, then?"

"Miss Cardinal and I spent the night frustrating his desires."

She laughed again. "Spending the night with an unmarried lady? Mr. Carnacki, you are getting positively naughty!" Then she turned serious. "But frustrating Baal is never a good idea—it merely makes him more determined to achieve his desires. His attack tonight will be even more ferocious—and you are here, with me, and not there to protect Miss Cardinal." She shook her head. "I fear she may not survive the next attack."

"I am here to appeal to you to prevent any further attacks," I informed her.

"It would not be in my best interests so to do," she replied. "You see, I have been the object of Baal's interests in the past."

I began to understand. "I see. And to avoid them in the present you needed a scapegoat with which to keep him occupied."

"Quite so. And I am afraid that Miss Cardinal is still of use to me in that role, so I must reluctantly decline your request." She glanced at the clock on the sideboard. "It is nearing six thirty, and I am due to take my dinner now. It has been a pleasure meeting you, Mr. Carnacki—you amused me, and few people can do that. If you would be so kind as to leave?"

I sat myself in one of the chairs. "I do not aim to leave here until you have agreed to my request," I said, stubbornly.

Her eyes flashed with anger—she was not one used to having her desires denied. "Now you begin to annoy me, Mr. Carnacki," she said. "Very well—if you will not leave, then I shall." She crossed the room and then halted in the doorway. A look of surprise and then concern crossed her face as she discovered she could not approach the door. She turned back to face me, coldly. "What have you done, you wretched little man?"

"I have told you a small falsehood," I replied. "I did, in fact, have the time to go home before I came to see you. And there, in the Aadrach Testament, I found the warding spells you cast upon Miss Cardinal to bind her within her own room." I smiled slightly. "I rewrote your spells a trifle and brought them along with me."

To my immense surprise, Madame Palmyre broke into peals of genuine laughter. "Why, Mr. Carnacki, it appears that

I have underestimated you—you are capable of more imaginative sins than I had expected."

"I take that as a compliment."

"It was meant as one." She inclined her head slightly. "But you do understand what this means?"

"It means that Baal will be visiting here this evening instead of the Cardinal residence," I answered.

"It means I am to miss a very fine meal," she answered. "Well, there is always tomorrow—if we survive the night."

"Baal will be coming here?" her secretary asked, anxiously. I could tell from her tone that she had witnessed that being before.

"Thanks to Mr. Carnacki's interference, yes." Madame Palmyre shook her head and then turned back to me. "I do hope you have some sort of a plan for dealing with him. While he will not have the same interest in you as he will have for the two of us, he will not leave you untouched." Despite her brave words, I could hear the fear in her voice. "And he will be angry when he arrives."

"I have a few small weapons," I told her. "And you have your witchery. I had thought we could join our forces together and defeat him."

"You have a high opinion of yourself!" she scoffed. "And of me, it would seem. Mr. Carnacki, Baal is unborn and undying. We are *nothing* in his eyes, beyond sport and perhaps food. Neither we nor any human can hope to defeat him."

"Then perhaps we can simply close the rift that he uses to get from where he dwells to our world?" I suggested.

She considered the idea a moment. "There is a possibility of reversing the spell that calls him to the wards," she agreed slowly. "But it will take time and energy and concentration on my part. I cannot defend myself against his amorous advances and cast the spell at the same time."

"Then allow me to protect us all," I offered.

She gave me an odd look. "Mr. Carnacki, the bindings in my spell only keep us women here in this room. You could leave at any time quite safely."

"I know," I replied. "And whilst the thought has its appeals, unlike you I cannot condemn anyone to suffer at the hands of Baal without attempting to help."

"Ah!" She threw up her hands in disgust. "Now you have quite spoiled my opinion of you—you have an idiotic nobility ruining your soul."

"I find it quite touching and heroic," Renée offered.

"You would." Madame Palmyre shook her head. "Well, if you are to have a visitation in an hour or so, we had better get busy. I suspect the management may well ask us to never return again. And they have such an excellent kitchen, too."

Despite her mocking words, she proved to be a very efficient and careful worker as we prepared for the manifestation of Baal. She consulted texts she carried in her luggage, but much of her preparation was from memory. As I set up my electric pentagram, she paused to examine it.

"An interesting juxtaposition of science and magic," she commented. "If we survive this, I shall have to discuss your researches with you. You are proving less dull by the minute."

We worked carefully but swiftly as the appointed hour approached. Renée fetched books and special inks and paper for her mistresses' wards and spells, and watched us, enthralled, as we prepared. Finally, we were finished, and with barely ten minutes to spare. The three of us took our places inside the pentagram and waited.

"You interest me, Mr. Carnacki," Renee finally observed. "You manage to meld two very different disciplines—science and magic—with apparent ease."

"The ease if only apparent," I replied. "Perfecting my instrumentation has been a matter of long and careful research." I managed a rueful smile. "And a considerable number of failures."

"It had better not fail us this night," Madame Palmyre said sharply.

"It stood the test yesterday," I pointed out.

"But today Baal will be angrier and stronger," she snapped. "Make no unwarranted assumptions!"

At that moment, the hour struck. We glanced at one another, and then felt the tension in the air that signaled the approach of the horror. The compulsion to leave the room struck at me, but I was able to fight it down. Then the lights dimmed as something fed upon the electrical power, drawing it to itself. Again came that slashing in the air as a second world intruded upon our own.

Madame Palmyre was quite correct—this time around Baal was stronger and more furious than ever. The tentacles whipped from the gash, assaulting my shield. They battered against the invisible force generated by the pentacle, writhing, grasping, tearing—but unable to secure a purchase. A stench that burnt the lungs issued from the vent, along with screams and howls of rage and fury.

I recited from the texts again, struggling to retain my composure under the dreadful strain, in order to keep our protections fresh and effective. I was barely aware of Madame Palmyre beside me, muttering and gesturing in her own quest for serenity amidst insanity. The rest of the hotel must have heard the noises and felt the building shake from the attack. I discovered later that the management had believed the building subjected to an earthquake and evacuated it. Thankfully no member of the staff was foolish enough to try opening the door to this room.

Baal raged. Why it should desire to mate with human females is beyond my understanding. Perhaps it was simply some primal drive even Baal could not fathom. But it was clear that frustrating its urges was driving it mad with both desire and anger. Again and again those tentacles struck out, seeking one or other of my companions. If they had been able to connect, neither woman would have been able to survive. Thankfully for us all, the pentagram held fast. But the strain on me was terrible. As you have all noticed, the struggle left me drained of almost all of my strength. Even now, days later, I am not fully recovered. But I held.

And Madame Palmyre came through in her own fashion. I was gradually aware of her voice rising louder and louder, her calm manner giving way increasingly to triumph as she cried out the words of those ancient texts, words that seem to tear from her throat in a voice no human could form. Stronger and stronger she spoke, the beats and stresses in her voice rising and ringing about us.

Baal screamed, and redoubled its efforts, clawing at us—again, without effect. It could not know how close to total collapse I was as I struggled to remain alert and erect, fighting to keep the shield intact. When it seemed as though I could withstand no longer, Madame Palmyre's voice rang with triumph, and she pronounced the final sibilant syllable of her spell.

The gap slammed closed—so fast that Baal was unable to react in time. Three of the lashing tentacles were severed and dropped to the carpet, oozing ichors and writhing for several minutes.

The three of us collapsed also, within the protection of the pentangle. Both women were shaking from strain, exhaustion and shock, and I knew I must look the same. Madame Palmyre finally managed a small, feeble smile. "I suppose the kitchen is probably closed by now?"

The tentacles were composed of some alien ectoplasm, and they dissolved in moments, leaving nothing but a dire stain on the carpet and a stench in the air. When we were certain that the creature was indeed banished back to its dark realm, we exited our protection. I dismantled my apparatus and returned home.

Miss Cardinal has not been bothered again by any nocturnal invaders and has, she assured me, given up her interest in the married man that caused these events. Madame Palmyre and Renée were asked, politely but very firmly, to vacate their suite in the hotel. They plan to return to France shortly. I myself have just about recovered from my ordeal, as you can see. Now (he concluded), I must ask you all to leave because I am expecting a female visitor.

As I have said, my friend Carnacki is a man of unvarying routine. One of his points of insistence is that he will answer no questions once his tale is concluded. He made no exception to his rule this time. We all departed, not knowing who that female visitor was to be.

Jean-Marc had asked me a couple of times to consider using Simenon's immortal Maigret in one of my tales, but this was the first time I felt he was right for one of my tales. Alas, he only gets a small role, but it is important. I even threw in a cameo by The Saint. Leslie Charteris's devil-may-care buccaneer was an early love of mine, thanks to the Roger Moore TV series. That led to my discovering the novels – which I liked even better. Though the later Saint stories with him as an international adventurer were fun, my favorite period was when he had his own little gang of madcap companions in the Thirties, so that is the incarnation I used. The main character in this tale, though, is J.G. Reeder. I'd discovered the works of Edgar Wallace at about the same time as The Saint. They had the same bizarre approach to crime stories – The Four Just Men are not far removed from the early Saint, who was quite happy to knock off anyone he thought made this world a slightly worse place in which to live. But for me, my favorite Wallace creation was Mr. J.G. Reeder – a wonderfully gentle, sorrowful chap who happened to have a "criminal mind" that helped him to predict and apprehend villains. (And also the star of his own Sixties TV series, though not as popular as The Saint.) It wasn't until recently that I discovered I hadn't merely stolen The Saint from Charteris, but also the title of this story...

The Benevolent Burglar

Paris & London, 1930

It was one of those beautiful days that made one glad to be French and in Paris. The sky was a cheery blue, flecked only by fleeting soft clouds, allowing the sun to cast a pleasant warmth on the city. It was still early, so the streets weren't crowded with the inevitable tourists, nor workers heading to and from their jobs. It was the rare kind of day that Maigret enjoyed too infrequently.

He doubted that he'd enjoy this one for much longer, so he walked at a slower pace than normal, dragging out the time he had virtually alone. The streets here wound rather vaguely in the direction of the river and there was the far-off sound of the boatmen mingled with the rumbles of traffic. He had grown up with the motor car, but he still cast nostalgic thoughts back to the days when horses and not internal combustion engines roamed the cobbled streets. It was foolish, he knew, but days like this made one a trifle foolish.

Maigret found himself approaching the small café where the rendezvous was slated and he sighed a trifle in regret; his pleasant walk was ending and work was about to commence. Honoré was already there, slouching a little in his seat outside, the inevitable croissant thickly buttered and half-eaten on a small plate in front of him. He was sipping at a thick, Turkish coffee and fumes rose from the omnipresent Gauloise loosely held between his lips. He looked up and nodded as Maigret approached and then took the other chair at the small table. The waiter, who had been somnolently lounging in the doorframe, approached. Maigret quietly ordered a coffee of his own, though he doubted he'd actually drink it. But Honoré always seemed vaguely insulted if Maigret ordered nothing, and it was important to keep the bulky man happy.

"You're a good man, Maigret," Honoré said, staring off into the air, "for a policeman."

"Detective," Maigret corrected him, automatically. "Or Commissaire, if you want to be technical."

"I don't," Honoré replied, blowing smoke. "Policeman is quite close enough for my sensibilities. But either way, I find I like you, Maigret. You're not dull or plodding, like so many policemen. You're more interested in justice than mere laws."

Maigret might have been offended, but he knew the other man was not being insulting intentionally. If the truth be told, quite a lot of his time *was* dull and plodding, because that was the nature of police work. It was only in fiction that leaps of intuition and deduction worked; in real life it was generally boring leg-work that paid off. But all he said was: "I try to do the best I can."

"I know," Honoré said. "And it is because of this that I feel I can talk frankly with you." He glanced around them. "Is it safe to talk, do you think?"

Like many an informer, Honoré was worried about being seen and heard passing along information; it was a fear that Maigret understood, because if an informant was uncovered, his life expectancy would have alarmed any insurance salesman. Maigret glanced about also, but saw nothing to alarm him. There was an Englishman two tables over—quite unmistakable by his refusal to alter his lifestyle in any way to accommodate a foreign country; he was dressed in a suit and tie, despite the warmth of the morning, with highly polished shoes, perusing his copy of *The Times* of London and sipping from time to time at the inevitable cup of tea. In the other direction was a pair of young lovers, murmuring gentle endearments to one another and ignoring the rest of the world entirely. Maigret envied them, remembering his own days of courtship.

"I can think of no place safer," he finally announced.

Honoré shrugged. "Nor I," he admitted. "Why should two friends not meet at a small café to share coffee and conversation?" As if on cue, the waiter appeared with Maigret's drink. When he had placed it on the table, he returned to leaning on the door frame. He would be able to hear nothing from that distance if Honoré continued to speak in hushed tones. The large man seemed to be in no hurry to divulge what he had called Maigret here to hear, however. He blew more smoke, and then crushed his cigarette out. Instead of speaking, however, he promptly lit another. As he extinguished his match, he finally looked Maigret directly in the eyes.

"You have heard of the Black Coats, of course," he stated.

"Which policeman has not?" Maigret answered. "That criminal organization is blamed for a great many crimes—

though it is hard to say how much of that credit is truly due them."

Honoré smiled. "And they are *not* credited with a great many more crimes that they *have* committed."

"You are not a member." Of this Maigret was certain— In all of his memory of all of the cases he had conducted or read about, not a single person had claimed to ever belong to the gang. Especially not the ones who did.

"I am not the sort of man that they would recruit," Honoré answered. "I am a thief when it suits me, that is true. But it is a hobby rather than a vocation, and I do not do well when given orders. I do not join gangs, and gangs do not ask for the dubious pleasure of my company. But they do, from time to time, ask for the loan of my skills. If they ask on the right day and in the right way and with the right remuneration... Sometimes I say yes."

"You said yes recently, I take it?"

"Off the record, I did." Honoré trusted that Maigret would not insist on being accompanied to the CID to research the matter and Maigret knew that he would get more in return for being discrete. "In the Third Arrondissment. I doubt you'll have heard of the work. It was not the sort of job that would be reported, so you are not neglecting your duty by not questioning me on it. But in the course of the... work I met a few members of the Black Coats." He glanced around the street again, but there were no new intruders in their space save a distant pedestrian carrying groceries home. "Generally speaking, if they do not bother me, I do not bother them. But these men were not like you, my friend—they were cold and cruel and arrogant, and I did not take to them. They treated me as if I were a cheap hireling and not a skilled craftsman and I tell you—this kind of treatment I do not like."

"No man would," Maigret answered carefully. It seemed that Honoré's pride might be quite useful, so it didn't hurt to feed it a little. "It is painful when one's abilities are looked down upon."

"Quite so." The informer beamed. "I knew that you would understand, Maigret—you're a good man. So I resolved to pay their insults back, and I do so to you. These arrogant men, these Black Coats—they spoke of their Treasure…"

Maigret took out his pipe and fussed with it. "Their Treasure?" he asked. "What might that be?"

Honore shrugged. "It might be anything—I do not know. But they spoke of it with reverence and some awe. If it is money, then it must be a lot of it. But it may be something that simply has great value to them. I did not ask questions, which would have drawn their attention to me, and one does not wish to be noticed by such men. Needless to say, they do not trust their Treasure to a bank; after all, they are responsible for breaking into more banks than the rest of the Parisian underworld added together. Instead, I gather, they move this Treasure of theirs around from place to place at seemingly random intervals in order that nobody should know where it is at any moment." He beamed. "But I know. At least," he amended, "I know where it *will* be on a given date. It will remain there for one day only before moving on again to a place I do not know. But for this one day—its location is known." He looked earnestly at Maigret. "My friend, I will tell you where it will be and when. It seems to me that you may be able to pay back the insult these men have given me by taking their Treasure and inconveniencing them. And it will do you no harm if you are the sole officer who can bring about such a devastating strike against the Black Coats, will it?"

"No," Maigret said slowly. "It would do me a great service."

"And you, my friend, are one man who knows how to repay a kindness," Honoré said. "Which is why I tell you these things. I know you will not forget poor Honoré, or fail to treat him with respect."

"I should certainly not forget such a deed," Maigret replied. "To strike a blow like that against the Black Coats—there is not a man on the force who would not give his right arm for such an opportunity."

"There is, however, a complication," Honoré admitted. "It is one that is not beyond your powers to resolve. But the Treasure will not be in France—it will be in England. Ebbington House, just outside the town of Turley, to be precise." He looked over the rim of his coffee cup at Maigret. "But you are a pleasant companion; I am certain you must have friends in England who would be willing to help you."

Maigret wasn't quite as certain as his informant. There was no formal accord between his department and Scotland Yard, nor, indeed, between their two countries. A man might be wanted for a crime in England, but be completely free to walk the streets of Paris unmolested by the police, or vice versa. The English police, then, might consider the fact that the Black Coats were not wanted in England as leaving them out of any possible course of action. The Treasure undoubtedly consisted of the outcome of many crimes—but if none of those crimes had been committed on English ground, then Scotland Yard could not become involved.

Officially.

He had met one or two officers from the Yard in the past few years that he had found amiable enough. There was a certain Detective Inspector by the name of Teal who had been hunting an English criminal by the name of Simon Templar... Templar had been wanted for murder in England, but living the high life in Paris, as he recalled. Teal had been quite frustrated that he could not arrest the miscreant, but there had been nothing that could be done about it as long as Templar was on French soil and committed no crimes in Paris. Maigret had been apologetic and wished the Inspector well... Would Teal hold that unavoidable failure against him, or would he be willing to try and aid him? It was impossible to know in advance. But, still, that was his problem, and one he would do his best to resolve.

He placed the pipe back in his pocket without lighting it. "And the date the Treasure will be there?" he asked.

Honore smiled...

There had been a faint noise in the background that now grew louder. Maigret had dismissed it, but now it was getting intrusive. He glanced around to see a motorcycle heading toward the café down the otherwise quiet street. It looked to be one of the German DKW models, quite modern. The rider was bundled up, in cap, scarf and heavy coat. Oddly, he did not wear gloves. Maigret noticed this all in passing and then turned his attention back to Honoré. As long as the rider obeyed the speed limit, Maigret had no interest in him. He always felt that motorcycles were noisy, unpleasant devices and preferred an automobile for travel.

Honoré, however, seemed to be fascinated by the machine. He had still not spoken, but his mouth was open.

There was a bang from behind, presumably the noisy motorcycle backfiring, and then Honoré had two open mouths, the newer of which was filled with blood. Time seemed to have slowed for Maigret as he started to stand and turn, looking over his shoulder toward the rider.

The man had a large pistol in his hand, and the barrel of it was moving away from pointing at Honoré to aim in Maigret's direction. Maigret was unbalanced and knew he would not be able to dive out of the line of fire in time. His only hope was that the bumpy ride over the cobblestones would make it difficult for the assassin to shoot straight.

It was not much of a hope, considering the accuracy of the man's first shot. He was a professional killer, that was quite clear, and the gun was almost centered upon Maigret's head.

Out of the corner of his eye Maigret saw the English gentleman two tables away jump to his feet, clearly startled by the shot. His foot caught the chair opposite him as he did so, sending the cast-iron seat clattering into the road.

The assassin, concentrating on the difficult shot at Maigret, did not allow himself to be distracted by this movement. It was an understandable response, but quite the wrong decision. The chair landed in front of the DKW's wheel, and the bike hit the iron chair at a good fifty miles an hour.

The bike upended, flinging the startled rider into the air. The gun went off again, the bullet narrowly missing the two lovers. The man had leaped to cover the pretty girl, keeping her safe, but the bullet missed them by several feet.

Maigret was on his feet now and already moving toward the falling killer. The motorbike hit the cobbles and slid across the road, finishing up on the far curb, still spinning its wheels and making its horrible racket. The rider hit the stones face-first, bounced and then slammed down harder. The snap of his neck was audible even over the row from his machine. No need to worry about further trouble from him, then. Maigret turned to Honoré as the Englishman hurried to join him.

"Is your friend...?" the man asked, clearly concerned. He had turned quite pale—obviously these sort of things were not a part of his daily life.

"We shall see," Maigret said.

Honoré had fallen, sprawling, from his chair. Blood was still flowing sluggishly from the hole in his cheek. There was no exit wound, so the bullet had probably remained within the skull. His eyes flickered slightly, and his arm moved feebly. "Twenty-third," he managed to croak, and then he died.

Maigret sighed; the man had been a crook and an informant, but he had been a likeable rogue. He had never in his life been violent, nor committed any crime that injured anyone. It might not be much of an epitaph, but Maigret was sorry that he was dead.

"My condolences," the Englishman said gently. "He was a friend?"

"Only in business," Maigret admitted. He glanced around and saw the waiter. The man had ceased lounging casually against the door jamb and was now flattened on the ground, shaking. "You!" he called. "Telephone the police immediately! Tell them to send men here." The waiter nodded, glad of the chance to rush inside the café. Maigret looked at the Englishman. "Thank you," he said. "Your actions saved my life."

The man looked embarrassed. "Well, I'd love to take the credit, but it was a pure accident. When I jumped at that shot, I knocked the chair over. You should be thanking the furniture, not me."

Maigret smiled slightly—a typically modest Englishman. "Nevertheless, it is you I thank, Mr…?"

"Tombs," he replied. "Sebastian Tombs."

A short while later, the modest Englishman ran into the two young lovers. "Brother," he murmured gently, "you may unhand Pat now. Your role is over."

The male "lover" smiled. "I was merely doing what any good thespian would, Simon," he replied. "I was throwing myself into the part."

"If you don't detach yourself immediately," Simon warned him, "I shall throw you into the river."

"I thought we were very convincing," Patricia Holm commented, making a slight adjustment to the way her golden hair flowed. "That policeman wasn't at all suspicious of us. It was almost as much fun as teasing Claud Eustace."

Simon lit a cigarette thoughtfully. "This Maigret is no fool," he warned her. "He wasn't expecting to be observed at this meeting with Honoré, which is the only reason he didn't detain us all for questioning."

"Did you hear enough, Simon?" Roger Conway asked. "We managed to catch some of it, but we were too far away for the man's last words."

"The twenty-third," Simon replied. He blew a smoke ring and watched it evaporate. "Children, this one could earn us a bundle of boodle. It is time for us to smite the ungodly…"

Mr. J.G. Reeder was a quiet, respectable man of very definite and mild habits, but he had three vices. Two of these were reasonably public, but the third—as far as he knew—was still a secret. The secret vice was that he read fairy stories. If booksellers looked at him oddly when he bought his latest volume he would invent some totally fictitious niece or nephew to explain his purchase—in truth, Mr. Reeder had no close relatives. Quite why he enjoyed fairy tales so much he was at a loss to explain, unless it was that their innocence and their firm grasp of good and evil was in distinct contrast with the everyday world he occupied.

Of his more public vices, the first was a tendency toward secrecy. Partly this was because he worked in a business where secrecy was considered a virtue, but it was mostly because Mr. Reeder rather enjoyed springing surprises on people. He knew this was an unworthy motive, but he acknowledged it because it was true.

His final and most public vice was the one he was indulging in at this moment in time. He had a predilection for smoking very cheap cigarettes when he was thinking. Almost everyone who worked with him had complained of their foulness at one time or another. Mr. Reeder apologized. He apologized most sincerely, because he knew that it irritated others. But the truth was that he needed those odiferous objects to help him think. He had experimented from time to time with smoother, more expensive cigarettes, but discovered that they were too distracting—he spent his time noticing the subtle flavors and the tastes of the various additives to the blends. Rather than help him think, they detracted from his studious ways. He knew that he needed the terrible smokes he employed precisely because they were cheap and easy to ignore.

At least, for *him* to ignore.

His visitor was attempting to be polite, but Mr. Reeder could see that the cigarette was bothering him. Mr. Reeder could hardly fault the Frenchman for that—the cigarettes bothered almost everyone who knew him. With a hidden sigh, he crushed the life from it in the overflowing ashtray on his desk and resolved to conclude the conversation unaided.

"You do seem to have a bit of a, ah, problem, Commissaire Maigret," he said, politely. "But I am not sure why you came to see me."

"It is a shame that we police cannot cooperate more fully between national borders," Maigret answered carefully. "The International Criminal Police Commission[1] is a step in the

---

[1] The forerunner to Interpol.

right direction, but your country has only recently joined it and…"

"The left hand still doesn't know what the right hand is doing," Mr. Reeder finished for him. "Yes, that much, um , I can see. But what do you expect me to do?"

"Expect? Nothing. Hope? Ah, well, that is another matter." Maigret shook his head. "I know that the Black Coats are a criminal organization almost beyond belief in their efficiency and income. But proving this knowledge is harder, and proving it to the point where Scotland Yard might make arrests on my behalf is beyond my small powers. Though I have information that some of their ill-gotten gains will be in Ebbington House in Turley on the twenty-third, I cannot establish this sufficiently for the law to act."

Mr. Reeder sighed. "Yes, I have often thought it a great shame that while we are handicapped by, ah, a need to follow the law, criminals are not. So, Scotland Yard cannot help you, and thus you come to me—to do what?"

"To be honest, I do not know." Maigret spread his hands. "I can do nothing; your police can do nothing… But it seems to me that it would be a greater crime for *everyone* to do nothing and that these Black Coats should get away with the proceeds from their illegal activities."

"I find myself compelled to agree with that assessment," Mr. Reeder admitted. "But if the police cannot act, neither can the Public Prosecutor's office."

"But can Mr. J.G. Reeder?" Maigret asked. "Chief Inspector Teal mentioned that you sometimes…" He searched for the correct English word. "Circumnavigate the problem."

Mr. Reeder sighed a second time. "It is true that I possess a criminal mind," he admitted. "And I am often tempted to, ah, bend the law a trifle to get things done. Sometimes the temptation is virtually overwhelming. But I do not think it a matter I should be, er, discussing with a policeman. Even one who cannot actually arrest me for my thoughts."

Maigret smiled. "Then perhaps, my friend, I should leave you alone with your thoughts. I am sorry to have troubled you."

"I am used to trouble," Mr. Reeder said, with a final sigh. "It is my lot in life." But he noted that the French policeman looked distinctly hopeful. He could only wish that this faith could be repaid.

Mr. J.G. Reeder did not possess many friends. In fact, one might count them on the fingers of a single hand and still find several fingers out of work. It was considered somewhat strange, then, that his one real friend was a man nobody would have expected him to have had anything to do with, and that on two counts.

Firstly, Mr. Larry O'Ryan was rumored to be a thief—or, more accurately—a safe-cracker. He had been arrested and tried once for this crime, but had somehow managed to evade being sent to jail due to a technicality. Mr. J.G. Reeder was morally certain that Larry had in fact committed two further thefts that also involved gaining entry to safes, but his moral certainty and his ability to prove the same were at quite opposite ends of the spectrum. Mr. Reeder, however, knew that the thefts in question were in fact from men who were more larcenous than Larry and far more deserving of punishment. Again, he could not prove this, but his moral sense was, once more, assuaged.

Secondly, Larry O'Ryan was a millionaire—twice over. Mr. Reeder lived very modestly in the Brockley Road; Larry's residence was immodest and in the country. Mr. Reeder was a confirmed bachelor, whilst Larry was happily married to the beautiful one-time Lane Leonard (who had contributed the second million to their joint account). Their life-styles were far apart, but, despite this, they met quite regularly for tea— which they both enjoyed—or classical music concerts—which Larry did not like, but endured for the sake of both Mr. Reeder and his adored wife.

It was over tea at the O'Ryan mansion that Mr. Reeder broached the reason for this particular visit. "Did you know," he said, as if reciting a fact he had discovered on the back of a packet of corn flakes, "that Ebbington House has recently installed a Monarch Security Steel safe?"

"I did not," Larry replied honestly. His interest in the company had declined since he had left their employ more than a year earlier, along with a set of duplicate keys that could open many of their safes. "More profits for Monarch, eh?"

"I imagine," Mr. Reeder agreed. "As you know, their installations are not, um, cheap."

"Nor as impregnable as they might wish," Larry agreed, catching the drift of his friend's conversation. "Did you know," he added, "that Ebbington House is actually little more than a hop, skip and a jump from here?"

"The fact has been brought to my recent attention," Mr. Reeder confessed. "And that brings me to a, ah, somewhat embarrassing question." He eyed the beauteous Mrs. O'Ryan but knew them both better than to suggest the rest of the conversation might best be continued with her absent. "I am reluctant to ask it, but ask it I must. Are you free on the night of the twenty-third?"

Lane glowered at him. "Mr. Reeder, I am ashamed of you!"

Mr. Reeder lowered his head. "I am ashamed of myself," he said. "Frequently. I should not have asked…"

"That is not why I am ashamed of you," she snapped. "I am ashamed that you think so little of our friendship and the debt we owe to you for our happiness together that you feel reluctant to ask a favor of us!"

"But this is not a little favor!" Mr. Reeder exclaimed. "If things go amiss, there is a distinct prospect that I might be forced to arrest myself for breaking and entering. And anyone else who accompanies me. Also, um, there is the possibility that the people I am planning on… visiting may have hostile tendencies."

Larry looked distinctly cheerful. "Life has been rather quiet of late," he observed. "No reflection upon you, my love," he added quickly to his wife. "But there are days when I sometimes pine for a little excitement again."

"Do you think you're the only one who likes to feel alive?" Lane growled. "I wouldn't miss this for the world."

Mr. Reeder was appalled. "I had not planned on asking for your aid!" he protested. "It would trouble my conscience greatly if anything were to happen to your husband as a result of my request—but should anything befall you…"

"Anything worse than my uncle had planned for me?" she asked drily, alluding to her relative's attempt to rob and murder her. "That you and Larry saved me from? How could you even think I would not be there to help you both? Mr. Reeder, I am sorely tempted to blacken your eye." She made a fist and shook it in his general direction.

"And she'd do it, too," Larry said, proudly. "That's my girl."

Mr. Reeder was a realist, and he knew when he was facing a foe he could not defeat. "Very well," he agreed. "But you must undertake to do *exactly* as I instruct."

"You can tell you're not married," Larry muttered, "if you think *any* woman will do exactly as she is instructed."

"When you two children are *quite* finished…" Lane said, glaring at each in turn. "Mr. Reeder, I assume you have some sort of a plan?"

"It's rather vague at the moment," he confessed. "I have not yet reconnoitered the ground, so to speak and until I have, I would not, um, venture a fixed plan."

"But with my skills and my keys," Larry observed, "I am assuming a little burglary is being planned."

"Strictly in the name of justice," Mr. Reeder added, hastily. "The proceeds will be turned over to the French police to see if they can match them up with any known missing property. I doubt the current owners will file a complaint about the, ah, robbery."

"About the house," Larry said. "I'm assuming there are guards."

"One or two," Mr. Reeder replied. "The Black Coats do not wish to draw the attention of other, um, criminals to the place. I suspect there will be some sort of security system in place, so we will have to scope out the lay of the land first. We have three days until the twenty-third, when the treasure will arrive."

"How certain are you of this information?" Lane asked thoughtfully.

"You have, sadly, put your finger on the main problem we face," Mr. Reeder admitted. "The information comes via an informant who was murdered, presumably in a vain attempt to stop him talking. But I cannot help thinking that he may have been murdered *after* he talked in an attempt to underline his testimony, so to speak."

"In other words, that the information is false, but that the Black Coats wish us to believe it to be true." Larry rubbed his chin. "It would be a clever diversion if the treasure was really going to be somewhere else instead. But how can we know?"

"Only by going ahead as if the information is correct," Mr. Reeder said. "I have little other choice."

"Well," Lane said, in a far-off voice, "I for one am quite intrigued to see what this treasure might possibly be." She smiled at Mr. Reeder. "I just hope it isn't so fascinating that I'm tempted to keep any of it for myself." Seeing his aghast expression, she added: "Oh, don't worry, I'm pretty certain I can restrain any larcenous impulses I might feel. At least, you'd better hope so…"

Mr. Reeder and Larry were both flat out in the grass, elbows down and binoculars propped up in their hands when Lane slipped in beside them. They were studying Ebbington House carefully, and Lane noted an air of frustration. She glanced at the edifice herself: early Elizabethan, obviously, with a lot of additions in varying styles seemingly attached to the main part of the house at random. It was a quaint, early English mess.

"So," she asked cheerfully, "what have you boys decided?" Not many people would have used the word *boy* to describe Mr. Reeder, who was distinctly middle-aged.

"This is a tough one," her husband answered. "There would appear to be three guards at all times, one of whom has a dog with large teeth and an unpleasant attitude. They patrol the grounds about the house. According to the delivery records, the safe was installed in the main study. It is some twenty feet deep, eight high and eight across. Whatever the treasure is, it sounds to be fairly large."

"Quite," Mr. Reeder agreed. "So we somehow have to navigate the open grounds in front of the house, avoid raising the suspicions of the guards and their canine assistants, break into the house, make our way to the study and then break into the safe. After which we, er, have to carry half a ton or so of treasure back out without being observed."

"We'd need a lorry of some sort parked nearby," Larry added, "but not so close it would be spotted." He shook his head. "It all sounds perilously close to being impossible."

"Nonsense," Lane said, firmly. "I'm quite sure that is what these Black Coat people are counting upon to dissuade anyone from attempting what we shall manage." She looked at her husband. "Are you sure you can break into the safe?"

"In all modesty, yes," he replied. "I helped build the things, so I know a few tricks that the average safecracker wouldn't. It'll probably take me an hour, but I know I can manage it."

Lane smiled. "I'm so proud of you, my darling," she murmured. "How many wives have husbands like you?"

"Thankfully few," Mr. Reeder interrupted. "Or else my job would be considerably harder than it already is. But breaking into the safe is, um, the simplest part of the problem."

"Well, it's the only part I can't assist with," Lane informed him. "I've already worked out the rest of it." She rather enjoyed the look of pure astonishment on Mr. Reeder's face.

"But you haven't even studied the place!" he protested.

"Oh yes I have," she retorted. "Where do you think I've been? I was in the village taking tea with Mrs. Oswald Murphy."

"I wonder what they slipped into the tea to make you so sure of yourself," her husband muttered.

"It wasn't the tea that matters," she informed him, "but the conversation. Mrs. Murphy is the head of the local Conservation Society. She has been pressing for the preservation of Ebbington House as a national monument. It seems it is an excellently-preserved example of the builders' arts dating from the Elizabethan period. The Society did a thorough survey of the house five years ago and have been struggling to raise funds for its purchase ever since. I am strongly tempted to send them a cheque to aid them in their work."

"That's all very noble," Larry replied, "and I certainly have no objections if they really wish to preserve that monstrosity. But are you going to get to the point of your brilliance?"

"During the Elizabethan age," Lane explained, "people got very upset over whether you were Catholic or Protestant. The upper hand went from one to another at the drop of a monarch. Most of the nobility were Catholic, and it was sometimes very dangerous to be identified as such. Having a priest about the house tended to get you labeled as a traitor. But the nobles liked having their pet priests about to say Mass in their private chapels, so they built bolt-holes and secret passages in order to smuggle said priests in and out of the house unobserved." She saw the light dawn on her companions.

"And Ebbington House has such a bolt-hole," Mr. Reeder ventured.

"It does indeed," she agreed. "Mrs. Murphy was quite specific about it. She helped to clean the mechanisms to open and close it during that survey five years ago. It starts in the study where the safe is and comes out in the stables."

"And you got the information from her," Larry said, grinning cheekily. "My love, you are a wonder." He gave her a quick kiss. "Well, now we can get in and out without being seen. But we still have the problems of transporting the treasure."

"No," Mr. Reeder said thoughtfully. "We don't have to transport it at all." Lane and her husband stared at him in complete confusion. He smiled. "All we have to do is to move it into the bolt-hole. The Black Coats have the lease for only three days, and they must vacate. We can simply wait until they are gone before bringing in the necessary lorry and then removing the loot."

"What about the dogs?" Larry asked. "We can dodge the guards to get to the stables, but the dogs will most likely sniff us out."

"Aniseed," Mr. Reeder said, promptly.

"I beg your pardon?"

"Dogs love aniseed," Mr. Reeder explained. "They go crazy for it. All we need to do is to spill some on the far side of the house and, ah, the dogs will go for it. They will ignore us completely."

Lane smiled in satisfaction. "Then I do believe, gentlemen, that we are ready for our burglary tomorrow night."

Mr. Reeder was pleased that the night had turned out to be rather overcast. From the same vantage point he had used to initially survey Ebbington House he could now see only the lights of the house and beyond that merely shadows and vague shapes. It would make slipping into the stables a lot easier for them.

Beside him, dressed all in black, Lane fidgeted nervously. "Where's Larry?" she muttered. "Shouldn't he be back by now?"

"Patience, my dear," Mr. Reeder advised. "It is better that he doesn't rush and perhaps stumble and break a bone or, ah, two." Larry was off planting the aniseed lure to attract the dogs to the side of the house they would not be approaching.

"Once he returns, we can make our way down." Mr. Reeder knew that in this kind of mission waiting was almost as important as acting. One premature move could spoil an elaborate plan. Lane, not having been raised with a strain of larceny in her soul, could not quite grasp this. He could only hope her eagerness to be a part of this venture wouldn't put them all in jeopardy.

There was no more than a slight rustle in the grass—any casual observer would have put it down to a vague gust of wind—and Larry was back with them, grinning. "Once the dogs get around that side of the house, they won't be returning in a hurry," he promised.

"Then we shall allow them ten minutes," Mr. Reeder decided. Lane looked as if she might be wanting to say something, but then she wisely snapped her mouth shut. Mr. Reeder liked and admired her more the longer he knew her.

Once the ten minutes had passed—Mr. Reeder timed it precisely on his pocket watch—they moved cautiously out and down the hillside toward the house below. There were lights ablaze outside the front and rear of the house, and he could see two guards in place. There was no sign of the one with the dog. With luck, he was off on his rounds and not close to the stables. There was, after all, no reason why the guards should be concerned with the outer buildings on the estate when the treasure was ensconced in the main house. The stables were as old as the house, but had been rebuilt a number of times over the centuries. The last owner had evidently used them, but now they appeared to be mainly applied to the storage of landscaping tools. That was a stroke of luck, as it meant nobody was likely to be in need of a rake at this time of night.

"This way," Lane said, confidently. "Mrs. Murphy was quite detailed in her descriptions." She entered the third stall, which now was clear of hay or tackle, and held only a wheelbarrow and tarpaulins neatly stacked. There was a feed bin attached to the end wall, and Lane felt beneath it with a grin. A moment later there was the sound of a catch being released, and the entire wall swung gently toward them. Larry gripped the edge and pulled it open. There was just sufficient light to see a tunnel sloping downwards away from them.

"Come on," Lane whispered, and started down the way. Larry gestured for Mr. Reeder to follow her, and then he pulled the wall closed behind them. There was a moment of utter blackness before Mr. Reeder switched on his electric torch. Two pale, excited faces blinked back at him.

"Excellent work," he complimented the young woman. "Now, let us perambulate."

They walked down the passageway, which had been constructed of ancient bricks and which dropped about ten feet under the earth. It had a musty, earthy stench to it—not pleasant, but bearable. There were no side passages and no turns; it was arrow-straight to the house. Whoever had built this had chosen the simplest, straightest way. They reached the end of the passage inside of five minutes. Like the entrance, this end was simply a section of wall on a hidden pivot, with a catch holding it in place.

"Plenty of room in here to hide any amount of treasure," Larry observed. "So far, so good."

"This was the simple part of the plan," Mr. Reeder replied. "Now comes the most difficult part." He clicked off the torch as Lane triggered the catch to open the wall. With barely a sound, the section swung out and they slipped through into the study.

The lights were on in here and the curtains drawn open. If any of the guards walked past, they were bound to be able to see straight to the safe, which stood alone in the center of the room. It was twenty feet by eight by eight, and had obviously been installed in sections as none of the doors in the house were large enough to bring it in constructed. The walls were of steel and the door had a heavy, impenetrable looking lock.

"Nice," Larry murmured in appreciation. "They've spared no expense on this. It's almost unbreakable."

"But only almost?" Lane asked.

"Yes, my love—only almost." He pulled his bag of tools from his knapsack and glanced at Mr. Reeder. "I estimate it will take me about an hour to get into this. You'd better keep watch at the window and call out if you see any guards coming this way on their rounds."

"Of course." It was what Mr. Reeder had planned to do all along.

"And what can I do?" Lane asked.

"Apart from telling me how wonderful I am?" Larry grinned. "Take the bag and go around the side of the safe. If any guard looks in, you and the tools will be out of his line of sight. I'll tell you what I need and you pass it to me. That way, if I have to hide, I'll be unencumbered."

"Righto," Lane said, with a grin. She was clearly enjoying her first foray into a life of almost-crime. Mr. Reeder sighed silently and went to his position by the window. He could only hope that she wouldn't be cured of her mistaken belief by an influx of armed men. He hadn't mentioned it to his companions, but there was a loaded revolver in his coat pocket. Mr. Reeder disliked using guns almost as much as he disliked being shot at.

For a while there were no sounds in the room save for the noises that Larry made working on the lock. Mr. Reeder glanced at his companion from time to time and could see the furious look of concentration on the young man's face and the sympathetic glances cast at him by his wife. For the most part, though, he focused all of his attention on the grounds beyond the windows.

Twice he gave a low call to alert the others to the presence of patrolling guards. Both time they all ducked from sight and waited until the patrols had passed on. Thankfully there was no sign of the dog handler—hopefully, he was entangled in deep brambles right now with his animal seeking the intoxicating taste of aniseed.

The thought made Mr. Reeder wish he'd brought along some humbugs to suck. It might have helped him pass the time with less strain. Instead he could only think of all the possible things that could go wrong with their plan. Most of these thoughts led to guards shooting the three of them to death. The rest led to his being brought up before the beak on burglary charges and being sent to prison for the rest of his life. None of them were in the slightest bit comforting.

"Almost there," Larry said, softly. He chuckled. "I have to hand it to the development boys—they've come up with a winner in this design." There was a soft click, and then he turned the handle, without any effort. Mr. Reeder took a final look for guards, but the coast was clear. He slipped over to the vault.

Larry looked at him, a slight grin on his face. Lane beamed proudly at her husband. Mr. Reeder gave a polite smile. With a flourish, Larry opened the door and the three of them stared inside.

"I don't believe it," Larry finally said.

"I'm afraid I do," Mr. Reeder murmured.

The vault was completely empty. The only thing marring the polished metal walls was a large, crude stick figure in chalk opposite the door. It showed a man with a slightly-tilted halo above his head.

"Simon Templar..." Mr. Reeder breathed.

Bob Morane is a popular French pulp hero from the 1960s who, sadly, has appeared in very few English translations. One of these was The Dinosaur Hunters. *How could I resist a tale of "let's go and bag ourselves a T Rex"? I've always loved stories about time travel, from Doctor Who to H.G. Wells to DC Comics' original Rip Hunter, so I just adored this story as a kid. I reread it before writing this tale, and still love it. And since that story involved time travel, who better to show up again than Doctor Omega? And—to make Jean-Marc happy!—Maigret is once again involved.*

Time to Kill

Paris, 1960

"I have a dead body on my hands that I can't explain."

Bob Morane looked at his bank manager, André Durand-Mareuil, and merely raised an eyebrow.

His friend Bill Ballantine, on the other hand, whistled loudly. "Crikey! That must be a bit hard to explain to the police," he commented.

"Quiet, Bill," Bob admonished the burly, red-headed Scotsman. "I have a feeling Monsieur Durand-Mareuil is going to fill us in." They were in Bob's apartment on the Quai Voltaire in Paris, and his landlady had served tea just before announcing the banker. Bob offered the banker a cup of tea, but Durand-Mareuil shook his head.

"There really isn't that much to... ah... fill in," he said, sadly. "And Mr. Ballantine is quite right—it is difficult to explain to the police, and to my bank's Board of Governors. They're not at all happy about the matter, I'm afraid."

Bob rather liked Durand-Mareuil—he'd always been very helpful in the past when he had faced urgent needs to raise funds to gallivant all over the world in some of his more extreme cases, and he felt sorry for the man, who clearly hadn't managed to get much sleep.

"Well, why don't you tell us what you can?" he asked.

"You may already have heard some of this," Durand-Mareuil replied slowly. "The victim was Albert Carrigan."

The name was indeed familiar. "The millionaire?"

Bill sat bolt-upright in his chair. "I read something about that in the papers yesterday! He was shot to death in a bank…" He realized what he was saying. "Oh—*your* bank…"

Durand-Mareuil nodded sadly. "My bank. More specifically, inside my security vault."

"I can't see the problem, then," Bill said. "Whoever did it must have been seen by dozens of people."

"Nobody saw him. Nobody *could* have seen him."

Bob had been in plenty of interesting moments during his time in the Military, and even more in his days since, as a kind of freelance adventurer. He could always tell when something interesting was on the cards, and his intuition was signaling strongly now.

"Perhaps you'd care to explain that rather cryptic comment?"

Durand-Mareuil frowned slightly. "I don't think you've ever been in the bank's security vault, have you?"

Bill laughed. "We've never had the kind of money to need to."

"Quite. Well, it's where all of the safety deposit boxes are kept. Many people store jewelry, stocks and bonds, that sort of thing in our boxes. Mr. Carrigan has—*had*—several with us. He would come into the bank once a week, on Wednesday afternoons at two o'clock precisely."

"He'd been in that habit for some time?" Bob asked.

"Oh, indeed—since before my time, in fact, so over five years."

Bill chewed his lip. "Always dangerous to get into predictable habits."

"Quite so," the banker agreed. "Last Wednesday, Mr. Carrigan came into the bank as usual, and, as always, I accompanied him into the vault, along with one of my security guards. Mr. Carrigan and I opened the door to the box he wished to use. The guard and I then left the room, and the guard closed and locked the door."

"Forgive me a moment," Bob said, "but allow me to ask an obvious, if foolish question: there isn't any other way into the vault, I take it?"

Durand-Mareuil shook his head. "Just the one door, which the guard locked. He remained outside the door for thirty minutes. Mr. Carrigan always stayed for precisely that length of time. I returned when the time had elapsed, and we opened the door together. And inside, we discovered the body of Mr. Carrigan. He had been shot once, through the heart, and was quite dead."

"Crikey!" Bill muttered. "That must have been unsettling. Did he shoot himself, then?"

"He couldn't have done, because there was no gun in the room."

Bob hesitated before asking the obvious question. "I don't like to cast doubt on anyone, but how trustworthy is that guard?"

Durand-Mareuil smiled bleakly. "Yes, the police wondered about that, too, obviously. Their initial theory was that my man had opened the vault door, shot Carrigan, and then closed the door again."

"That *is* the logical conclusion," Bob agreed. "But I take it that was also impossible?"

"I'm afraid it was. You see, the security vault is adjacent to the cash vault. Our chief cashier is locked within that vault while the bank was open—there is a barred door, and his desk is immediately behind it. If any money enters or exits the vault, he and the guard have to open that door together. So while he waited for Mr. Carrigan to finish, the guard was seated just outside this door and in the full view of my chief cashier the entire time. Both men insist that the security vault door was not opened again until I returned."

"They could be in cahoots," Bill suggested.

The banker shrugged. "But to what end?" he asked. "The two men do not socialize; they do not even know where the other lives. Both have worked for the bank for more than a decade, and have always been steady, reliable men, otherwise they would not have been in the positions of trust they occupy. Neither of them have any reason to kill Mr. Carrigan."

"Couldn't they have stolen something from the strong box?" Bill asked. "Some fabulous jewel, or something?" He sounded quite excited.

Durand-Mareuil shrugged again. "It is always possible," he agreed. "The bank has no record of what was kept in the box, of course. But as soon as we discovered the body, I telephoned the police. I remained with the guard until they arrived. Before either the guard or the chief cashier were allowed to leave the bank at the end of the day, they were both thoroughly searched." He coughed, embarrassed. "As was I myself, and quite rightly so. The security vault was checked, and the cash vault. Nothing out of place was discovered anywhere. As far as they were able to ascertain, the motive for the murder was not robbery."

Bob smiled widely. "Monsieur Durand-Mareuil, you couldn't keep us out of this now if you tried." He grinned at Bill. "A classic, eh? A locked room mystery. No way for a murder to have been committed, no possible killer."

"And no clues, either, it sounds like." Despite his pessimistic comment, Bill's grin was just as wide as Bob's. "Sounds right up our street."

The banker's relief was evident. He pumped Bob's hand enthusiastically. "Thank you, thank you. Are you able to accompany me right now? The sooner this mystery can be cleared up, the happier my Board of Directors will be."

"I can't guarantee I can solve it," Bob said, "but I think Bill and I can spare some time, eh?"

Bill nodded. "I'll say." He rubbed his large hands together. "I can't wait to take a peek at the scene of the crime." He looked anxiously at Durand-Mareuil. "We *can* see it, can't we?"

"I've already spoken to the police. They have it sealed off for the time being, running fingerprint tests and such like, but they have agreed to allow you access as representatives of the bank. You will, of course, be recompensed for your time."

Bob smiled. "I think this mystery in itself is going to be payment enough," he said.

"But we accept your generous offer," Bill added, hastily. "Er—it *will* be generous, won't it?"

"Quite so."

"Jolly good."

The bank was just around the corner, so it didn't take them long to walk there. The main floor was conducting business as usual, though there were a couple of policemen watching over things. The handful of customers in the bank were trying not to be caught staring at the officers. The policemen nodded politely to the manager as he led Bob and Bill toward the stairs that led down toward the basement vaults.

As he did so, Bob had a curious sensation that he was being watched. He'd learned never to ignore his instincts, so he glanced around. One of the customers as the central table, standing with a deposit slip in his hand, was looking directly at him. He was an elderly man, with long, white hair (and an errant curl giving him a slightly wild look), carrying a gnarled walking stick under one arm. Bob had never seen him before. He frowned. The man didn't seem to be bothered to be caught staring, and inclined his head slightly in acknowledgment before bending to fill out the form.

Odd. But probably not relevant to their case.

The bank was one of those grand old buildings, filled with artistic flourishes. There were chandeliers on the main floor, and pedestals with fresh flowers. The stairs leading down were wide and marble-covered. There was a bank guard stationed at the head of the stairs, clearly to ensure nobody without official cause got to descend, but he knew Durand-Mareuil, naturally, and stood politely aside for them.

Bob looked carefully around as they walked down. At the foot of the stairs, there was a small area illuminated by another ornate chandelier. Directly in front of them was the cash vault. The barred door was of steel, some six feet tall and about eight across. It looked quite impressive. Behind it, he could see the chief cashier's desk—an ornate wooden affair, with ball and claw legs. The man himself was seated at it now; he was a fiftyish, greying man with the look of a goblin. He was clearly trying to get his work done and ignore two more policemen stationed in the hall.

Outside that door was a small desk and a chair. The bank's security guard was seated there, trying to look uninvolved, though he was clearly uncomfortable. Bob could see that Durand-Mareuil's comments had been entirely accurate: the two men would have been in full view of one another the entire time Carrigan had been in the vault. Unless they were working together, then it was impossible for either they or any other person to have entered the vault to kill the millionaire.

Bob finally turned his attention to the security vault itself. At the moment, the vault door was wide open, but it was a standard door, some six inch thick metal. Nobody could have shot Carrigan through the door, and nobody could possibly have opened it without being seen. All that was left was to enter the vault and look around to see if they could find anything that the police might have missed.

"Who is the officer in charge of this case?" Bob asked.

"Need you ask?" came a familiar voice from inside the room. "A case that is inexplicable and potentially career-damaging if I fail to solve it? Who else would they give it to?"

Bob's face broke into a broad grin as he walked into the vault and shook his old friend by the hand. "Commissaire Maigret!" he said, delightedly. "I don't know why they bothered to consult with me. I'm sure you must have the case completely solved by now!"

Maigret grunted. He had his pipe firmly clenched between his teeth though it wasn't lit. "Oh, I have it all solved, my friend," he agreed. "Except for who did it, and how."

Bob knew Maigret's methods of old. "Don't tell me that you don't have a suspect already."

Maigret shrugged. "Indeed I do—the dead man's nephew, Donald Carrigan. He's absolutely the perfect suspect: he likes the high life, he gambles on cards that he plays very badly, and is in a large amount of debt. He stands to inherit millions from his uncle's death."

"And yet?" Bob prompted.

"And yet, he has an unshakable alibi," Maigret said sadly. "At the precise time of the murder, he was losing money at baccarat in the casino at Royale-les-Eaux. There were dozens of witnesses to this fact. He was quite certainly not in Paris at the time of the killing, and, in fact, will not arrive back here until later today—accompanied by Janvier."

"I see your problem," Bob murmured.

"And I am afraid I see yours." Maigret waved his hand about the room. "Feel free to search for clues. If you uncover any, I would be most grateful, because my men and I have found nothing of significance."

"What about the bullet?" Bob asked. "Did you recover that?"

"Yes," the Commissioner said. He took his pipe out of his mouth, looked at it, saw that it was empty, and then replaced it. "Like everything else in this case, it is a puzzle. It is of no known manufacture, and has a rather unique set of patterning on it. It was fired by no gun either I, or anyone in my department, can identify." He shrugged. "As if there were not enough problems with this case."

Bob glanced about the room. It was about twenty feet by sixteen, and the ceiling was about ten feet high. There was a table and single chair, closer to the left-hand wall than the right, but no other furniture. The room was illuminated by another of those omnipresent chandeliers—rather brightly, in fact. Three of the walls were lined, floor to ceiling, with small doors that each had two key holes, and behind which the owners' safety deposit boxes resided. The fourth wall contained only the large security door. The walls either side of it were bare.

"Let's eliminate the absurd first," Bob suggested. He tapped the bare wall. "I take it that there's no possibility of a hidden panel behind this?"

Maigret looked over at Durand-Mareuil, who shook his head. "The walls consist only of two inches of covering over four inch steel."

"I really didn't imagine that there were secret passages, but it's as well to be certain." Bob shook his head. "There doesn't seem to be any other way into this room."

"What about the ventilation system?" Bill asked, cheerily. "In the movies, people are always crawling about them."

Maigret smiled dourly and pointed with the stem of his pipe at a rather small grille set in the ceiling about six inches in from the wall. "It's six inches across. Feel free to try and fit inside it." He eyed the burly Scot with a faint smile.

"OK—not that way, then." Bill thought for a moment. "But what about the gun? *That* would be less than six inches long. If the killer had somehow rigged a gun with a remote-control device so he could place it in the vent and then fire it…" He looked rather pleased with this suggestion.

"Well," Maigret admitted, "that's certainly an idea that had never occurred to the police." He didn't look impressed, however. "The problem with that idea, my friend, is that the vent is *behind* the table where Mr. Carrigan sat, and he was shot from the front. Horizontally, not vertically. The gun must have been placed about…" He walked to the right hand end of the room and stood in one corner. "Roughly here." He used the stem of his pipe to demonstrate. "Just at the level of a man standing here, holding a gun."

Bob scowled. "I've run into some pretty rum things in my time," he said slowly. "And I can think of only one solution that *might* answer all of the problems." He gave a slight laugh. "The only trouble is that it's even more absurd than the crime—at least on first glance."

"And what is that?" Maigret raised an eyebrow.

"That there really was a man standing there with a gun— but nobody could see him."

"An invisible man, you mean?"

Bob shrugged. "I know it sounds impossible, but, well, Bill and I have witnessed any number of things I'd have thought were impossible. Technology seems to be advancing so swiftly these days…"

"I agree, it sounds foolish, but let us consider it," Maigret said. "Let us postulate the existence of an invisible man…"

"With an invisible gun," Bill said, helpfully.

"As you say, with an invisible gun. He walks through the bank unseen and down into the vault area. When Monsieur Durand-Mareuil here opens the door, he somehow manages to slip inside and waits in the corner. When he is alone with Carrigan, he shoots the victim and then waits for the vault door to be opened and slips out again. Unseen the entire time."

The bank manager shook his head. "Even granting such a silly idea," he glanced apologetically at Bob "we would have *felt* someone brush past us, for the door is not large, and was closed behind us when we entered. I had to open it again when I left, and closed it immediately behind me."

Bob sighed. "Well, it was just a thought." He shrugged. "In that case, I'll admit that I'm completely baffled for the moment." He saw Durand-Mareuil's face fall. "Cheer up, sir! I'm only baffled for the moment. Ideas often come to me later. If you're quite done here, Bill, what say we go back home and think for a while? It's about lunch time, as my stomach is reminding me."

Bill, never averse to the idea of food, nodded his agreement, and they said their goodbyes. As they trudged up the stairs to the bank lobby, Bill turned to Bob. "So, what do you make of this?" he asked.

"Nothing, as yet," Bob admitted. "It seems to have no possible solution. But since we know that Carrigan *was* murdered, then obviously there must be an explanation of some sort. We simply haven't seen it yet."

They emerged onto the main floor of the bank. As they headed toward the exit, a figure moved to intercept them. Bob glanced at him, and realized it was the elderly gentleman who had been looking at him earlier. He held up his stick to block Bob's path.

"Please excuse my imposing myself upon you, Commandant Morane," the man said, politely. "If you would be so kind, I would appreciate the opportunity to speak with you."

Bob shrugged. The man seemed harmless enough, but he clearly had something on his mind. "By all means," he agreed.

"It's about the case that you're on," the stranger said.

And now Bob had him pegged: a retired gentleman with too much time on his hands who read the papers and fancied himself an armchair detective. "I think you'd better leave that to the professionals," he suggested, as kindly as he could—and, he had to admit, a trifle hypocritically, since he himself was hardly a professional.

"Advice you'd do well to take yourself," the man replied, testily. "Believe me, Commandant, this is outside the normal order of things."

"Look," Bob said, in a gentle manner, "I'm sure that you're very good at solving locked room mysteries in detective stories..."

"Your *locked room* isn't locked," the stranger snapped. "You've just come from there yourself."

"It's not locked *now*," Bob agreed, "but it was locked two days ago."

"A room is only ever locked in three dimensions," the man stated. "There are more—you live in four."

Bob smiled. "Don't you?"

"I dislike being confined." The old man reached into his pocket and pulled out a business card which he handed across.

Bob glanced at it. It bore only two words: *DOCTOR OMEGA.* "No phone number?"

"I am not reachable by phone. I... travel extensively." The old man touched the card. "If you need to contact me, tap the card against any piece of metal—the message will reach me wherever I am."

"Are you an inventor… Doctor Omega?"

"I am much more than that, young man." The old man straightened himself to his full height. "Now, if you wish to solve this case, all you need do is to meet me in the vault next Wednesday, shortly before two p.m."

"And then you'll explain everything?" Bob said, smiling.

"I shall do much better than that," Doctor Omega retorted. "You shall witness the murder taking place." His eyes twinkled as he added: "I suggest you bring a camcorder to record it for evidence."

"A what?" Bill asked.

Doctor Omega considered. "Oh dear—what's the day again?"

"Friday," Bill replied.

"No, no—I meant the *year*."

Bill laughed. "You don't know? It's 1960."

"Ah, quite so, quite so." He tapped Bill's chest with his walking stick. "Then I suggest you bring one of those Super-8 film devices." He inclined his head. "Good day, gentlemen."

"You're not going to tell us your theory?" Bill asked him.

"Theory? I have no *theory*, Commandant—just the truth. And there would be no point in my attempting to explain *that* until you have seen what will happen on Wednesday next. Until then." He spun about and marched from the bank.

"Well," Bill said, laughing, "I don't know how you do it, Bob, but you do manage to attract the weird ones."

"I'm not so sure he's crazy, Bill," Bob said slowly. "One thing he said makes a strange kind of sense."

"Well, you're ahead of me, then," Bill confessed. "I thought he was just rambling—a senile old man. Means well, but…" He tapped his temple. "Not all there."

Bob sympathized with his friend's view, but shook his head. "It's that business about us living in four dimensions, and the door being locked only in three…"

"So?"

"Don't tell me you've forgotten about our little adventure with Professor Hunter's time machine!"

Bill shuddered. "How could I ever forget that? Being chased by dinosaurs…" His eyes widened. "You mean he's suggesting that somebody used a time machine to go back and kill Carrigan?"

"Something like that, I imagine. Though there isn't enough room inside that vault for one of Hunter's machines to fit. And I can't imagine anyone simply sitting still when a time machine appeared and a man climbed out—and Carrigan was killed sitting at that table…" Bob shook his head. "And there's something else…"

"What?"

"Doctor Omega, as he calls himself, knew my name and my rank. We haven't mentioned the latter to anyone. And he obviously knew we've had experience with time travel. How could he possibly have known all that?" He couldn't make sense of it himself—yet. "I have a strong feeling that we're going to run into the good Doctor again—probably on Wednesday…"

Over the next several days, Bob and Bill had plenty to occupy their time. Bob tried to puzzle through the facts of the case, but got nowhere. More than once, he'd picked up the business card Doctor Omega had given him and then, sighing, put it down again. On the Monday morning, he'd called in at the prefecture de police to see Maigret and ask about the case.

The Commissioner shook his head. "I'm afraid we know no more than we did on Friday. I did meet with the nephew…" He lit his pipe and took a few puffs. "Every instinct I have tells me that he is the guilty man, and yet he has thirty-seven witnesses who saw him at the moment of the killing and who can testify to that in court."

"Could he have hired an assassin to shoot his uncle?" Bill suggested.

"Of course—anyone might have. But we still have that same problem—*how* did anyone kill Mr. Carrigan in a locked room?" He gave Bob a weary smile. "I am almost ready to believe in your invisible man, my friend."

Bob gave a short laugh. "And I am about ready to believe in something even more fantastic," he admitted. He told the detective about his meeting with Doctor Omega, which made Maigret sit up.

"That would explain this, then," he said.

Reaching into the basket of papers on his desk, he extracted an envelope. From it he took another of Omega's business cards, and a brief note, which he handed across to Bob. It read:

Please be so kind as to meet me in the bank security deposit vault shortly before two p.m. on Wednesday. Commandant Morane and Mr. Ballantine will be present.

"Sure of himself, isn't he?" Bill remarked.

Bob smiled. "I think he's relying on our curiosity, Bill. But he's right—I wouldn't miss this for the world."

Bill scowled. "Do you really think he can deliver what he promised?"

"We'll know in two days," Bob answered.

On the Wednesday, Bob and Bill arrived at the bank at one thirty. Durand-Mareuil was in the lobby, pacing nervously, when they arrived and hurried to meet them.

"Monsieur Morane! Thank goodness you are here! Such goings-on in a respectable bank!"

"Steady on," Bob said. "What do you mean?"

"The police are here again, and have asked me to keep the general public out of the vault for the next hour or so. And there's a strange old man prowling about—he's one of our customers, to be sure, but he's behaving very oddly. And he seems to want to give orders, too."

So, Doctor Omega was here! Bob clapped the bank manager on the shoulder. "Whatever the Doctor told you, I suggest you do. Bill and I are going down to the vault now also, so we'll keep an eye on everything."

Durand-Mareuil looked like he was going to erupt again, so Bob added: "And, relax. With a little luck, we'll have unmasked the killer within the hour, and everything will be able to return to normal. Come on, Bill."

And he hurried down the stairs before the nervous man could protest again.

He could see why Durand-Mareuil was so nervous—there were about a dozen uniformed gendarmes in the basement. Several of them were carrying chairs into the security vault. The others allowed Bob and Bill to pass after checking their credentials.

Inside the vault they found Maigret directing the traffic, with Doctor Omega standing in the background.

"What's going on?" Bob asked.

"Your friend here," Maigret said, pointing at the Doctor with his pipe stem, "says we have to simply observe. In that event, I aim to be comfortable and not simply stand about waiting." Once the four chairs he had required were in place, he waved off the gendarmes. "You two stay here," he directed. "The rest of you, upstairs, and give us some room."

When the room was clearer, he flopped into one of the chairs. "That's better." He glanced up at Doctor Omega. "Now, are you going to explain any of this?"

The old man shook his head. "Not quite yet, my good man—I fear that you would not believe my tale. Once you have seen what is to happen—what *has* happened—ah, *then* I promise to explain everything."

"Now, just a minute," Bill began to protest, but Bob held his arm.

"Let him have his minute, Bill. If he can explain this mystery, I think he's deserved it."

Doctor Omega beamed. "Thank you, my young friend. Now, did you bring your movie camera?"

Bill unslung the bag he was carrying over one shoulder. "It's right here, Doc."

"Good, good. Now, if you set it up here and aim it in this direction…" Then he glared. "And don't call me *Doc*." He indicated a place behind the chair set at the table. He watched as Bill took out a folding tripod and extended it to take the cine camera. "Right! How much film is in there?"

"About twenty minutes."

"Then do not start recording until our killer approaches the table," the Doctor instructed. "Until then, we shall simply wait."

"I'm glad I thought of the chairs," Maigret muttered. He nodded to the one beside him, and Bob sat down also. Bill joined them once he'd finished setting up his camera. Maigret gestured to the fourth chair. "And you, Doctor?"

"Not for me, no. I shall sit here." He settled himself in the chair at the table. "Where our unfortunate victim sat exactly one week ago."

"That's a bit morbid," Bill muttered.

"Now," Doctor Omega said, firmly, "whatever happens, I wish to assure you that I am perfectly safe. Do not interfere with what you are about to witness, any of you. This must play through precisely as it happens."

Bob felt his excitement rising. He had no idea what was to happen—though the Doctor clearly did—but he sensed that it was the final event in a chain forged a while back. It was for moments like this that he lived for—the excitement, the uncertainty, the mystery…

They didn't have long to wait. At five minutes past the hour, there was a noise in the outer hall, and then a man stepped into the vault. He stopped dead as he saw everyone present. Maigret gave a smile. "Donald Carrigan," he said, softly. Bob raised an eyebrow—the prime, impossible suspect.

"What is this?" Carrigan asked the vault guard, who had accompanied him. "I must be alone in here." He held up the small case he was clutching. "That is my right! Clear these men out of here!"

Doctor Omega turned to regard him. There was a faint smile on his lips. "I am sorry, Mr. Carrigan. If you are uncomfortable with an audience, perhaps you would care to come back later?"

"Yes. No. Yes." Carrigan the younger stood stock-still. He was starting to sweat. "Get out, all of you! I must be alone!"

"Mr. Ballantine," Doctor Omega called, and gestured at the camera. Bill hopped up and started it going.

Maigret stood slowly up. "I am Commissaire Maigret," he said. "I am afraid you cannot order me to go anywhere." He sat firmly down again. "I stay."

Bob grinned. "I've nothing better to do this afternoon."

Carrigan was sweating profusely now, and clutching his case tightly. "No," he moaned. "No—I *must* be alone."

"That is not going to happen," Doctor Omega stated. He glanced at his watch. "You have only three more minutes—you had better get busy…"

The young man was moving in a very jerky fashion, like some reluctant puppet being drawn by unyielding strings. He walked, shaking to the other side of the table, where he placed the case with trembling hands. He was sweating a stream now, and his eyes were wild and terrified. It took him three attempts to open the clasp on the case, and his hands trembled as he drew out an odd-looking gun. The part he clasped looked like a normal pistol, but attached to the barrel was a bulky tube-like structure that looked like an over-fed silencer. There were pulsing lights on it, tinier than any Bob had ever seen before.

Carrigan raised the pistol and pointed it directly at Omega's heart.

Bob gave a cry and jumped to his feet, but the old man's hand slashed out. "Stay!" he commanded. "Remember what I told you! I assure you, I am in no danger."

Shaking horribly now, Carrigan was forced to use his other hand to steady his grip on the pistol. Then, with a wild cry of terror, he fired.

Bob was terrified for a second, expecting to see Doctor Omega to collapse, dead. Instead, absolutely nothing happened. There was no sign of a bullet, and the old man was obviously totally unharmed. It made absolutely no sense.

With another cry, Carrigan dropped the strange pistol to the floor. "You fiend!" he hissed. His hand, no longer shaking, thrust into the case, and he pulled out a second pistol, this one a normal-looking Luger. He raised it and pointed it at Doctor Omega. "I don't know how you did that..." he began.

Bob saw the look of fear on the Doctor's face and realized that this was obviously not part of the old man's plan. He sprang forward and delivered a forceful blow to Carrigan's stomach. The man gasped, and folded as Bob wrenched the gun from his hand.

"Thank you, my friend," the Doctor said, wiping his brow with a handkerchief. "I must confess, I did not think he would have a second gun."

"Just glad to help," Bob said.

Maigret motioned to his two gendarmes, one of whom grabbed hold of Carrigan, who was still whooping for air. "It's nice to see that my instincts were not wrong," he said. He glanced at Omega. "I have a strong suspicion that I really do not want too clear an explanation for what I have just witnessed."

The Doctor smiled. "Probably not." He indicated the movie camera. "You have film of Mr. Carrigan there firing the gun. It has his fingerprints on it, and your ballistics department will be able to match the bullet to that gun—which has only the one bullet missing, the one that killed his uncle a week ago. I believe he will confess his guilt rather than go to trial, so that should prevent any necessity for a clearer explanation of what happened here." The second gendarme had carefully picked up the gun. Omega pulled on a pair of white calfskin gloves. "Ah—if I might?"

The policeman looked at Maigret, who nodded. Omega took the pistol and unsnapped the odd device on the end of the barrel, and then handed the pistol back to the officer.

"It's probably better that this not be left here," he said, gently.

Maigret nodded. "I have my killer," he said. "I have my evidence. I will sleep better without an explanation." He picked up Bill's camera. "I'll return this to you later," he promised. He nodded, and the gendarmes preceded him, dragging the shaking Carrigan.

Bill turned to Doctor Omega. "Well, may *he* doesn't want an explanation, but I do! What just happened here? And why on Earth did Carrigan fire that gonzo gun with so many witnesses present?"

"The inexorable force of Temporal Destiny," Doctor Omega replied solemnly. Seeing Bill's blank expression, he chuckled. "Invite me home for tea, and I shall explain everything," he promised.

A short while later, the three of them were seated comfortably in the apartment on the Quai Voltaire with a fresh pot of tea and some small cakes, courtesy of the landlady. Bill couldn't keep his calm any longer.

"All right!" he exclaimed. "We have tea! We have cakes! Now may we have an explanation?"

Bob couldn't help laughing at his friend's vexation. "Well, the first thing is that our friend here is obviously a time traveler."

Doctor Omega smiled. "I knew you would deduce that, my boy. Capital! Yes, I am indeed a wanderer through the dimensions."

"A time traveler?" Bill said, looking surprised. "How do you know?"

"From what he said. Don't you remember? He said that *we* travel in four dimensions—not himself. And the fourth dimension is time. And he didn't know the year, or what recording capabilities we had."

"I thought he was just cra..." Bill caught himself in time and shut up.

"Yes, well," the Doctor said, shifting uncomfortably in his chair. "Anyway, onto the explanation I promised you. As a wanderer through the dimensions, I have the capability of detecting other time travelers. My ship arrived here just over a week ago, and my instruments detected a waning temporal field, so I investigated. It was not far from Royale-les-Eaux, and I found a dying man." The old man frowned. "He was a member of a rather... ah... unpleasant organization. There was—or, from your point of view—will be... It's very difficult discussing temporal matters—languages these days aren't formulated to speak of things that haven't yet happened for you, but are in the far past for someone from the distant future... Oh well, in about three hundred years, there will arise a dictator who will make Hitler and Stalin look like amateurs." He paused. "You *do* know about Hitler and Stalin, right?"

"Yes," Bob said, grinning.

"Oh, good. As I say, I sometimes lose track... Well, this dictator-to-be was killed under mysterious circumstances, so this... temporal group decided to send a man to assassinate him. But they did so rather cleverly. The dictator was—as all such men are—paranoid, and was surrounded by bodyguards constantly. The group realized, though, that *after* his death there wouldn't be a guard. So they built a weapon..."

"That gun!" Bill exclaimed.

"Precisely, young man—that gun. It was programmed to shoot a single bullet exactly one week into the past. The idea was that the assassin would arrive one week after the dictator's death and fire the gun, thus killing the man one week earlier."

"But something went wrong, I take it?" Bob interjected.

"Indeed. When the would-be killer arrived, he was set upon by a group of soldiers who stumbled upon him accidentally. The man was shot and mortally wounded before he could perform his task. He did, however, manage to trigger his return device. But that, too, had been damaged by firing, and it malfunctioned, dropping him onto the road near Royale-les-Eaux some ten days ago.

"He was found by Donald Carrigan, who was driving to the casino. Carrigan found the man delirious, and heard this fantastic story about being a time traveler and owning a gun that could fire exactly one week into the past. Now, Mr. Carrigan is an amoral and lazy young man, with no love for anyone but himself. He left the dying man, but took his weapon. Obviously, he then hit upon the plan to murder his uncle.

"He would create a perfect alibi for himself for the time of his uncle's murder. He knew of his uncle's habit of visiting the bank vault every Wednesday at exactly the same time, so there was his chance! All he would have to do was to go to the bank one week after his uncle's murder and fire the gun…"

"And the bullet from it would travel a week back in time and kill his uncle!" Bill said, excitedly.

"Correct." Doctor Omega steepled his fingers and stared over them at his friends. "Unfortunately for him, though, I, too, discovered the time traveler before he died, and also heard his rambling tale. Naturally, I did not know the name of the man who took the gun—merely that someone had, with the intention of using it. Then, I read a few days later of the most mysterious death of Mr. Carrigan and understood immediately. I presented myself at the bank, and the rest you know."

"Except for the most important bit!" Bill exclaimed. "I get that Carrigan the younger came to the bank with the intention of shooting the gun that killed his uncle—but, when he saw us, why didn't he leave? Why did he stay and reveal his own guilt?"

"Because he was an amateur messing about with time!" Doctor Omega explained. "Such matters should be left strictly to the professionals. You see, my boy, time is unforgiving. Albert Carrigan was murdered last Wednesday shortly after two o'clock. The gun that did it *had* to be fired, then, today at precisely the same moment. It was the only thing that could happen. And though young Carrigan struggled mightily against it, the force of temporal destiny drove him to commit the crime—even with all of us present as witnesses. The crime *had* been committed—therefore it *had* to be committed."

"I think you've strained my brain," Bill complained.

Bob smiled. "It is a bit hard to grasp," he agreed. "And it's lucky Carrigan didn't work out how to change the settings on the gun—that would have messed everything up, wouldn't it?"

Doctor Omega chuckled. "It might have," he agreed. "But, as I said, he's a very lazy young man who would much rather steal and kill than work. I knew he wouldn't take the time to attempt to understand the weapon he had."

"Still, it took some nerve to sit in front of that gun while he fired it," Bob commented.

The old man chuckled. "I have faith in the workings of time, my boy. Now, if I might trouble you for another of those excellent little cakes…?"

Carnacki again. And, since the period was right, why not add in Dr. John Watson and Inspector Lestrade? (And, before you ask—yes, I am rather deliberately avoiding using the Great Detective himself; these days, he has been overdone rather, wouldn't you say? But perhaps one of these days...) Jean-Marc's influence brings in more French characters. Irma Vep (just in case it's not obvious, scramble the letters of her name) and Les Vampires, *a movie serial created by Louis Feuillade in 1915. As for the plot itself – it's a pure fantasy, but, once again, there are a few real characters involved...*

The Gutter God

London, 1888

When my friend Carnacki issues a dinner invitation, none of the recipients would willingly stay away. Only the direst of emergencies would prevent attendance. One reason is that Carnacki's feasts are utterly superb—the finest restaurants in either London or the continent cannot compare to the viands he serves. And yet the food is the least of the reasons we attend. It is the post prandial conversation that is the largest lure.

I say "conversation," but it is rare that any of us join in. We simply sit and listen to Carnacki tell us of his latest cases. For he has a somewhat unique occupation, one that provides him with thrilling and barely believable anecdotes.

Carnacki is a ghost-finder.

I do not mean to imply that he is a spiritualist or some sort of a psychic medium—though he has some abilities in that field—but that he investigates cases that would appear to involve the supernatural. Most frequently, of course, the so-called hauntings turn out to be fakes—though even those cases often have their interesting and entertaining sides—but there are times when he encounters something genuinely preternatural. The tales he tells of those encounters are frequently chilling, but are always unfailingly fascinating.

At this particular dinner, though, the general conversation, for once, centered about a rather different topic, and Carnacki sat through the discussion of the Whitechapel Murders with a slight smile on his face, but a very different expression in his eyes. When we sat down after the meal to brandy and cigars, we gathered in a semi-circle about him as usual, and waited to see if he could provide a tale one half as interesting as the one we had been discussing.

As ever, he did not fail.

I perceive that you are—understandably—all intrigued with the tales of the events in Whitechapel (he began). This foul stain on humanity who calls himself Jack the Ripper. Allow me to make a prediction that the trail of blood is almost complete, and that the police will not be able to arrest the perpetrator of these dreadful slayings. I can see the look of surprise on your faces, but I assure you that I do know whereof I speak. Allow me to enlighten you.

To understand these events, I shall have to tell you of an encounter I had almost two years ago. To call it difficult to believe would be an understatement; at the first, I was extremely reluctant to accept the truth of it myself, especially since it concerned one of the most degraded and disgusting creatures I have ever encountered.

I was, at the time, involved on a case which is quite immaterial to this tale. Suffice it to say that I had been hired to find a young lady of good breeding who had inexplicably vanished into Whitechapel. Her story has its interesting elements, and I may go further into it at some other date. What matters here, though, is that I was led to the sordid backstreets of one of the poorest and most blighted areas of our otherwise fair city. You can really have little idea of how terrible the conditions are, or how degraded the inhabitants have become. There are public houses on every corner, though I would hesitate to call the liquids that they purvey there as either refined or refreshing. They sell gin, mostly—the coarsest and most potent that they can manage. A pennyworth of that... liquid serves to help blot out the realities of the sordid life in those filthy, inhospitable streets.

The inhabitants of Whitechapel, for the most part, are the dregs even of the lowest layers of our society. It is almost impossible to understand how terrible and neglected their lives are. They lack the basic requirements of food and drink, their clothing is scarcely better than the rags our servants use to clean our floors, their children little more than the savages in either their demeanor or their education. The men take whatever employment they can, without questioning its purpose or legality, and the women... well, their lives are worse. They have very limited avenues of employment, and so many of them turn to selling their somewhat dubious charms to anyone who will pay them. I find it difficult to judge them for this choice—if, indeed, you can call that business a *choice*. It is a degrading and dangerous life, and many find themselves cheated, beaten or worse. The deaths of those poor unfortunates we read about in the newspapers are the rule and not the exception, sad to say. The only reason that these deaths are even remarked upon is because of the sheer brutality involved. The fates of the women who are merely beaten or killed cleanly do not merit a mention.

Obviously, then, my mission to find out why a well-bred woman would venture into such a place was quite urgent, but it also required some care. I could hardly walk among the inhabitants of those wretched streets in evening dress—it would mark me out instantly, and make a target out of me; certainly for robbery, and perhaps even worse. So I went in a careful disguise that made me look like one of them. If you had seen me as I was then, you would have crossed the street to avoid me—or, even, called a constable on me! But my disguise was suitable for where I was heading.

I eventually came upon one of the public houses on a small, grime-laden street that I shall not specify, and there I chanced across the most amazing figure. On the surface, he seemed indistinguishable from the many other wretched souls that filled those streets. His clothing was filthy rags, his body looked riddled with disease and his eyes were blood-shot and rheumy. To every appearance, he was a drunk living out the last of his days imbibing the cheapest, foulest gin that he could purchase.

And, yet—that was not the truth of it.

You cannot live the kind of life that I do without being able to detect notes of the odd or unusual, and this man reeked of both, along with the spirits he had imbibed. As I looked at him, I understood that this was no mere drunk. He was slumped, semi-conscious, against a wall of the public house that seemed barely strong enough to hold him up, let alone the building, but there was a strong sensation of *power* about the figure. I am sure that the very thought of this seems absurd to you, but it is true. And the truth was about to become stretched out of almost all proportion.

I bent over this man, studying him, and his hand shot out and seized me by the throat. His inebriation was not a pose, and his voice was slurred, his sentence structure twisted and difficult to follow. I shall not attempt to reproduce it—if I even could! —but will instead translate what he said into co-herent English. But do bear in mind that some of his sentences took several minutes for him to deliver and me to decipher.

"You trying to rob me?" he asked, and then peered my-opically into my face. "No... No, you're not simple thief, are you?" He released his grip, allowing me to breathe freely again (though I inhaled more alcoholic fumes than good, clean air). "You can see me, can't you?"

"Of course I can see you," I agreed. "It would be difficult to miss you."

"No," he countered. "You can *see* me. Do you know who I am?"

"No," I replied. "But I know who you are *not*. You're no simple alcoholic, are you?"

"You've the ability to see that much at least," he muttered. He waved a shaking hand. "Go away, and leave me alone—it would be better for your peace of mind." I had a strong feeling that he meant this quite literally.

But you all know me well enough to be able to predict that the last thing I was now able to do was to walk away from this mystery. I bent and examined him again. To the outer eye, he was nothing more than he seemed—another of those help-less drunks, laid out in the streets of our so-called fair city, beyond help and beyond redemption. But to the *inner* eye... he was nothing of the kind. I could feel the tingle of raw pow-er emanating from the man. I have, as you know, in my adven-tures sometimes encountered the truly supernatural creatures that exist on the fringes of what we term reality. There is no mistaking any of those for what they truly are, and there was likewise no mistaking this pitiful creature as a being of im-mense—and yet contained—power.

"What *are* you?" I asked him. "From which other dimen-sion do you originate?"

He laughed in my face. "Ah, ghost-hunter," he replied, "you have no understanding. I'll repeat myself—walk away, forget you ever saw me and let me get drunk in peace."

"You *know* me?" I asked.

"Never seen you before in my life," he replied. "But you have an unmistakable odor about you."

Considering the foul stench emanating from him, this was an uncalled-for insult, but I allowed it to pass; he could clearly detect my abilities as clearly as I could discern his.

"Explain yourself to me," I demanded.

"You had your chance," he complained. "I told you that you could walk away, but no, you wouldn't." He glared at me. "You consider yourself a truth-seeker, don't you?"

"It is my avocation," I agreed.

He spat on the ground. "*That* for your avocation." (It took him several attempts before he managed to stagger through the word.) "*This* is a truth you won't want to know."

"Try me," I suggested.

"I'm Bacchus."

I glared at him. "You've certainly been indulging in a bacchanalia."

"Bacchanalia?" He laughed, derisively. "You have no idea what you are saying."

I stared at the disgusting apparition before me. "You are Bacchus, the god of wine and drink? You appear to be taking your profession rather too much to heart." I did not—*could not!* —believe what he had said. And yet—there was still that inexplicable aura of true power about the man. If he *was* a man...

"You should be thankful that I'm drunk," he said. "Trust me, you would not dare face me if I were sober. Neither you, nor any other man in this entire blighted city." There was a cold ring of assurance in what he said.

"The gods of the ancient world were merely legends," I reasoned. "The embodiment of a primitive people's fears and desires."

"How terribly Victorian of you," he sneered. "Science rules the world, and superstition is banished to the outer darkness." He laughed. "You, of all people, ghost-finder, should know how narrow-minded that belief is. You've encountered the beings and powers that inhabit other spaces and times than merely this. How can you so blithely dismiss the existence of the gods, then?"

"Can you prove your rather fantastical claim?" I asked him.

"Why should I want to?" he demanded, belligerently. "I've told you who I am and asked you—for the sake of your own sanity—to leave me alone. Be a good little, timid mortal and do precisely that. Let me stay a solitary drunk."

"After what you have said, how can you expect me to do that?" I asked him. "I must know more."

"Of course you must," he sneered. "That's the trouble with you mortals—always trying to increase that meager supply of knowledge that you think encompasses all of reality. I have told you all that it is safe for you to know, so, for once in your life, do the sensible thing and walk away and forget you ever saw me. Go find the woman that you seek. You can find her at…" and he gave me an address.

"I didn't tell you that I was looking for a woman."

"No, you didn't. But I pay attention to what *isn't* said as well as to what is. You should learn to do the same."

"How do you know these things?" I demanded.

He pointed a shaky finger at his wretched self. "Bacchus, remember?"

"If you are indeed the Roman god of debauchery, then why are you here?"

"I'm debauching myself, of course," he said, as if that were the most obvious feature in the world.

"But *why*? And why here, in Whitechapel, of all places?"

"Because *here*, I'm nothing and nobody special," he growled. "To almost everyone who passes, I'm simply another stinking drunk. Even the vermin of society cross on the other side of the street. Here, I am nobody and nothing. Here I am *safe*."

"I shouldn't think you're that safe," I muttered. "If you manage to get inebriated and stay so, then you must have money. Aren't you likely to be manhandled by a passing pick-pocket?"

"Money?" He turned over a filthy hand and several gold-en coins rolled from his feeble clutch. I picked one up, and it was clearly a drachma, with Alexander the Great's head upon it, and apparently freshly minted. I stared at it, and then at him. "You mistake my meaning," he added. "I don't mean that I am safe from other people—I mean that *they* are safe from *me*."

"I don't understand."

"Of course you don't," he agreed, amiably. "That's fine. But what you *really* mean is that you *want* to understand –and that is a dangerous thing, my friend. But I can see I'll get no peace until I reach the point where you can accept no more, so I'll explain. Some." He considered for a moment. "What do you think happens to a god when people stop believing in him? When they stop worshipping him?"

I considered the point. "I should think he would shrivel up and cease to exist. Without worshippers a god is surely nothing."

"Nothing?" He barked a laugh. "You've a lot to learn about the gods, you small-minded creature. You seem like an educated man—haven't you ever read the stories of the gods?"

"Of course," I agreed.

"Then try and remember them," he snapped. "We gods don't *need* mortals. Never have, never will. Our power isn't dependent on some sniveling little jumped-up monkeys putting their faith in us. Our power is inherent—we were born with it, and it is a part of us. What sort of feeble gods would we be if we relied on humanity's beliefs to make us anything?" He eyed me with true disgust. "As if we rely on you arrogant idiots for anything!" He shook his head, which seemed to make him lose focus for a moment.

"Then what *does* happen when people stop believing in you?" I asked him. I realized that, somehow, I had slipped into believing his incredible claim, that I *did* accept this being in the gutter as one of the ancient gods of our world.

"We lose touch," he said promptly. "We lose our—for lack of a better word—our humanity. Recall the myths—how savagely and casually the gods behaved. We turned people into animals for slighting us, or trees, or a breath of wind. We annihilated cities, laid waste to the world. We fought and killed, and raped and maimed. Oh, we had power, and very few restraints. Remember those tales?"

I did indeed, and was somewhat surprised that I had forgotten them. The elder gods were indeed a selfish, arrogant and wretched lot at times.

"It was only our worshippers that kept most of us in line," Bacchus said. "We couldn't go around butchering you all if we had become addicted to your worship and your tasty sacrifices, could we? We were obliged to look after you, to keep feeding our needs. Ah, but once you forgot, once you slipped away from adoring us and burning offerings to us…

104

why, then, we were free to do whatever we wished with you again. No consequences, since you no longer believed in us."

"You're saying that the old gods are still around?" I asked him, astonished.

"Most of us, yes," he said, belching. "Mars is doing pretty well for himself these days. You may not worship *him*, but you serve him well enough. And Venus—that old lecher herself... Even in these Victorian days of hypocrisy, she's doing very good business" He waved his hand to encompass the inhabitants of Whitechapel about him. "Even if they only charge a shilling a time, these women serve her, and the men worship at her altar. As for me—well, there's drink enough to float the fleet that sank Troy, eh?"

"So we're worshipping you without being aware of it, you mean?"

"Something like that, yes."

"It doesn't explain why you're a drunk on the streets of London, though."

"Believe it or not, I actually *like* human beings. Oh, you can be a cantankerous, evil pile of excrement sometimes, but there are some of you who are half-way tolerable." He waved an unsteady hand about. "These... ladies of fallen virtue, for the most part, for example. They're not pretentious or hypocritical about what they do—they sell their bodies in order to remain alive... and have a tipple or two at my altar. They're quite refreshing, unlike the people in power in this benighted country of yours. Those politicians and the wealthy are just as bad as they've been throughout history, and they think that their hands are somehow cleaner because they cloak their evil behind a thin veneer of respectability. But their actions are less honest than those of petty thieves, prostitutes and villains that inhabit these disgusting streets."

I was not about to get into a political discussion with an inebriate—god or not—so I returned to my unanswered question. "But why are you drunk?"

He sighed. "I *told* you—I *like* these people. I'm saving their lives by staying drunk. Drunk, I can't harm them, only myself. But if I ever allow myself to get sober..." He shook his head. "You wouldn't like the consequences."

I confess, this self-proclaimed god intrigued me, and I was tempted to remain and converse with him. But I had a mission, a woman to try and save, and I reluctantly bade Bacchus farewell so that I could continue with my task. "Will I find you here if I come again?" I asked him.

He glared at me darkly. "It would be better for you if you didn't seek me out," he replied. "I rarely overstay my welcome, anyway, so I shall move on. Believe it or not, there are places lower than this that I haven't visited yet."

I left him and hurried to the address he had given me, remaining alert as I did so. It became quite clear to me that there were people guarding that domicile—if such a word could describe the filthy, disreputable place that I finally discovered. The guards were attempting to blend into their surroundings, but they were simple enough for me to identify. There were far too many of them for me to attempt a rescue, even assuming the lady I was seeking was actually ensconced within. I would need help, and that meant the Metropolitan Police.

Fortunately, I had made the acquaintance of a certain Inspector Lestrade—a simple, effective operative, who, perhaps, lacked imagination, but is an efficient and thorough officer of the law. I met him in his office at Scotland Yard—after changing back into my regular clothing, to ensure I wouldn't be arrested when I presented myself at that bastion of respectability! I described my problem to him, and he understood immediately.

"There's a new gang at work," he explained. "Frenchies, for the most part. Call themselves the *Vampires*, probably to throw a scare into the credulous, Mr. Carnacki. Like a lot of businesses these days, they're attempting to expand into the international markets, and they've got a toe-hold in Whitechapel."

"What do they do, Inspector?" I asked.

He shrugged. "Whatever may pay, I'm afraid—plenty of thefts, a bit of common extortion—you name it, they'll have a hand in it somewhere." He sighed. "There's been no ransom note for this missing lady you're after?"

"None."

"Pity; that would have made it simpler. In which case, I suspect she's been snatched as a part of a white slaving ring. She's of good breeding, and there's some who'll pay a good price to—ah—enjoy the favors of such a woman."

"She'd hardly cooperate, Inspector."

"She wouldn't be given a choice, I'm afraid, Mr. Carnacki. Putting it delicately, they have been known to addict their victims to opium or worse, till their poor victims will do anything for more of the drug. Anything..."

I shuddered at the thought. "Is there nothing we can do?"

"Of course there is." He managed a wan smile. "It takes a while for the addiction to take root, and she's only been gone a couple of days, so she's probably only on the periphery. If we manage to get her free, she'll need some medical attention, but probably nothing more."

"And she will be... untouched?"

"I'd say so," he said with conviction. "The... untouched bring a higher price, and these lads prefer their money to their bodily pleasures." That was at least slightly reassuring. "I'll put together a squad of men and we'll raid the house tonight. We'll probably only get the foot soldiers and not the generals, but we should hopefully be in time to save the young lady."

We made arrangements to meet up as close to the house as we thought we could get—considering how difficult it would be to conceal a host of London's finest. Lestrade warned me to come armed. I took my service revolver. Despite their name, the *Vampires* were not truly supernatural creatures, but merely unscrupulous men. True vampires would hardly draw attention to themselves by advertising their nature. This meant that I needed none of my usual equipment, so I could travel lightly.

The raid went off as Lestrade had planned. He's not the most imaginative of men, but he's very efficient when it comes to routine police work. He had the dwelling we sought surrounded, and then led the charge to close the net about the fiends we were after. They fought like the very devils, wounding several of the officers and killing one. A number of the gang were taken alive, but several perished rather than surrender.

Lestrade and I were amongst those who made it into the house. I was forced to use my weapon several times, but I could not wait and see the effect I may have had on those we fought. I hesitate to detail what we discovered when we forced our entry into that sordid dwelling, but we did discover the young lady I was after—and several others also. They were all in drug-induced stupors in foul rooms. Lestrade's assessment of the situation had been precisely on target. As I say, a most efficient officer.

The fighting was soon over. I discovered that I had suffered a very slight graze that I cannot recall receiving, and Lestrade's hat was rather the worse for wear; other than that, as I've said, a number of the police were wounded—mostly lightly—and one killed. But the bulk of the gang was captured. They were transported to the closest police station, and then the medical men came in. One of them, a Doctor John Watson, I knew slightly, and he examined my young lady before instructing her to be taken to a nearby hospital.

"You have been fortunate," he informed me. "The drugs are freshly administered to her, and, though she has been badly affected, I seriously doubt that addiction will have set in. Her family should be able to see her in the morning, and I would recommend a long recuperation, preferably somewhere with a little sunshine."

That was, incidentally, effected. At last report, the young lady is quite recovered from her ordeal. The effects of the drugs she was administered have affected her memory of her time as a captive, and she recalls very little of the horrors that she suffered—thankfully. Some of the other victims were not so fortunate, I am afraid to say, and two of the women had to be committed to an asylum, and there they remain. A foul business, from start to finish.

Rather naively, I had imagined that this was the end of the *Vampires*, but it turned out that it was, in fact, merely the first move in a longer game. We had severed a limb from the gang, but, like a hydra, two more grew back in its place. But it was some two months before my ignorance was completely exposed.

As you may imagine, I was reluctant to abandon the hope that I would find Bacchus once more. The inebriate had intrigued me, and I am ever the student seeking knowledge. I could only dream about what I might be able to learn from such a being. It might sound foolish of me, but I found myself growing more and more inclined to accept his claims of his divinity. Oh, I realize that he had offered me no proof of any of his claims, but he had been instrumental in the rescue. Of course, it was possible that he had simply overheard unguarded conversations between members of the gang who did not worry about some stupefied drunk in the gutter, but somehow I did not think this the case.

As a result, I found myself wandering in disguise whenever I had the time to spare through those wretched streets over and over, seeking out the foulest of public houses and gin-shops, hoping that at one of them I should stumble across Bacchus. For two months, though, I was completely unsuccessful. I examined many drunks—not a very cheering task, I can assure you—and was accosted more than a few times. My revolver saved my life more than once. I cannot count the number of women who offered to sell me the use of their bodies for meager amounts of money. Even had I been inclined to accept their offers, their squalid dress and unhygienic status would have revolted me.

And yet, I pitied them, even the foulest of the women or the most debauched of the men. They have so little, and their prospects are non-existent. They cannot improve their state, and there are but few who will help them. They are like the insects that scurry for cover if you turn over a rock in your garden—repulsive, but seeking only to live their lives. The police, for the most part, do not even venture into those streets, leaving its inhabitants to prey upon one another. There are a few churches that attempt to help, but such aid is so little and so ineffective that it makes not the slightest difference. I am aware that I sound like the most earnest of social reformers, but you could not spend time among these people without either hardening your heart to their misery or else feeling compassion. Fallen as they are, they are as human as the rest of us.

Everywhere that I went, though, I heard talk of the *Vampires*, and it quickly became apparent to me that we had effected but little damage to that criminal organization. Its influence was growing in Whitechapel, and its effects were terrifying.

I spoke with Inspector Lestrade about this, and he regarded me gloomily.

"There's not a lot we can do about it," he said. "The locals view the police force as worse than the gang. Those that won't help us out of fear of reprisals won't do it because they think we're after them. And I suppose we might well be. My friend Mr. Sherlock Holmes speaks often of a mysterious person he calls *The Napoleon of Crime*, but if you ask me, Mr. Carnacki, he's looking in the wrong place. This bunch is the real problem, not some hypothetical master-criminal. Confidentially, Mr. Holmes is a fair detective—almost good enough to be on the force—but he thinks too much, and sees things that aren't there. But, then, we all have our weaknesses, eh?"

I did not mention that I was looking for an ancient Roman god myself in those sordid streets. I am quite certain I know what his response would have been.

And then, as events turned out, Bacchus found me. I was on the hunt for him again when I was accosted by a disreputable middle aged woman of obviously slender to non-existent means.

"Mr. Carnacki?" I had no idea how such a woman would know my name, but I acknowledged that she had identified me correctly. "I've a message from *'im*," she informed me. "'E says as to how you should scarper from 'ere, soonest."

I knew that she could be referring to only one person. "I must see him," I replied.

She rolled her eyes. "'E said you'd say that." She shrugged. "Follow me, then, duckie."

And she set off at a pace I was challenged to match. I'm not entirely certain quite where she led me—the streets there are all alike, and there are many dark and twisting alleys—but our journey terminated, inevitably, before an extremely vile public house. Bacchus was seated in what they refer to as the saloon bar. He looked as blighted as before, but his eyes were no longer bloodshot, and he was clearly not inebriated.

"Carnacki, you damned fool," he said by way of greeting me, "I knew you wouldn't have the sense to listen to my warning." He turned to my companion. "Alright, Polly, you can go now—but be back within the hour—and don't be alone."

"You know me better'n that," she said.

She gave me a wink, and hurried off.

"You picked a poor time to seek me out," Bacchus growled. "I told you that you wouldn't like me if I wasn't drunk."

"And why are you not drunk, then?" I enquired.

"Because I'm off to war, Carnacki, and you have to be stone-cold sober to kill. Or, at least, I do. My army, on the other hand, is better off drunk." He waved a hand at the bar, and I realized something. I had noticed that it was rather full, of course, but now I saw that the occupants were almost all women. There was a barman handing out glasses of milky gin and buckets of foaming beer; there was myself, and there was Bacchus—if he could be called a man. Other than that, the place was filled with women in stages of intoxication. And they were clearly all of them women of little virtue.

"This is your army?" I asked, unbelieving. "And who do you fight?"

"*Les Vampires*, obviously," he growled. "The authorities bleat on about needing evidence to convict while that gang of cutthroats and cutpurses terrorize the area. I told you, Carnacki—I like these people. They're rough and crude, yes, but they are honest—well, as honest as they can be—and they don't pretend to respectability while hiding their vices."

"One of which is obviously drunkenness," I pointed out. "Your... *army* will be in no shape to be able to fight when you require them."

"Carnacki, you blasted fool, I had thought you an educated man. Does that not include a classical education?"

"Of course."

"Then how is it that you've forgotten about the Bacchae?"

The Bacchae... What a fool I was! I had indeed forgotten those stories for the moment. "Then..." I stared in horror at the prostitute brigade.

"Ah, your education returns! Yes—then..." He gestured at the women tossing back gin and beer. "Now do you understand why I ordered you to stay away?"

"I do indeed." I have to confess that a wave of fear washed over me. "Do I have the time to retreat?"

"I'm afraid not." He gave me a rather unpleasant smile, showing pure white teeth in that filthy visage. "Your only chance is to remain very close to my side. Disobey me this time, and even I will not be able to save you."

I really cannot describe the stress of the subsequent hour. As the women became progressively drunker, my fear rose, for they were changing. They were no longer women out to make a shilling or two by selling their dubious favors; they were becoming Bacchae... Worshippers of the god of wine and debauchery. His more than lethal followers...

And then the woman Polly was back, with more of her female friends, and they set to, aiming to get drunk as swiftly as possible. As they did so, I glanced outside. The windows had not been cleaned for a lengthy period, and it was difficult to make details out, but it was clear that the street outside was empty.

Bacchus noticed my gaze. "The word has been sent around, Carnacki," he assured me. "There will be none of my people out there—the only ones who will dare those streets today are the *Vampires*—and these." He nodded at his sodden followers.

I am uncertain how long I sat there, my terrors and imaginings increasing, but the women were growing less and less human and more and more inebriated. There was an unholy smile on the face of Bacchus as he regarded his army, and I realized that he was somehow drawing power and strength from these creatures. Eventually, though, that tortured period ended, and Bacchus clapped his hands once, loudly.

"It is time," he announced. "They come."

I had seen and heard nothing outside, but he clearly had senses that I lacked.

With a roar of rage and fury, the Bacchae began to pour into the deserted streets. Most were unarmed, but some snatched up cudgels or any instrument that came to hand. I was certain I was not imagining it, and that their teeth and nails had grown and become sharper... Their eyes showed none of their humanity, and their entire demeanor was more akin to a rabid dog than anything remotely human.

I remained close beside Bacchus, as he strode outside to commence his war. I knew only too well what would be my fate if I should lose him...

At the end of the grimy street, a second army started to filter in. These were the *Vampires*—well dressed, and well-armed. And—unfortunately for them—virtually entirely male. There was only one woman—elegantly dressed, as if for a promenade in Regents Park. Bacchus saw my surprise.

"She is their leader," he explained, with a sneer. "She is called Corvena Septimus[2]—at least, for the moment..."

---

[2] Yes, like "Irma Vep" (her daughter), her name is an anagram...

"A woman," I breathed. "In command of these wretch-es?"

"Not merely a woman, but also a mother," Bacchus replied. He smiled. "Prophecy isn't really my gift, but *in vino veritas*, you know. Her daughter will grow to be more than her mother, and she will remember this day as a warning. It is the day she will become an orphan."

There was the crack of pistols as the *Vampires* opened fire. Several of the prostitutes fell, but that did not discourage the rest. Even those wounded screamed and pressed forward.

I cannot describe what followed. It would revolt the mind, and my memory strives within me to blot it out. The Bacchae had but a single thought—to annihilate their enemies. They used whatever weapons they had—primarily teeth and claws—and they simply tore their foes apart. It did not matter how many of the Bacchae fell—the remainder pressed on, overwhelming the intruders and ripping their flesh from their bones. Blood and entrails were everywhere in the nightmare that followed.

I confess, I hid my face from much of what occurred. I have seen much in my days, but this—this was more than I could bear. Men were literally ripped apart, and those trans-formed women drank the blood that flowed as if it were their cheap gin. And all of the time that the slaughter went on, Bac-chus had a peculiar, unpleasant smile on his wretched face.

This was why he preferred to stay drunk—to avoid this from occurring. But now it was necessary, and he reveled in it. It was the dark side of his divinity, one that he preferred not to indulge. But now that it had come upon him, he drank it in.

Unfortunately, I did see the fate of Corvena Septimus. She had imagined that her followers were capable of dealing with any rabble, and had clearly expected this to be a one-sided battle. It was, of course—simply not the side that she had assumed would win. As she realized that her men were doomed, she turned to flee.

The Bacchae seized her, and showed her no mercy. I heard the screams, which were mercifully not over-long.

When the army passed on, there was nothing human about what they left behind.

Eventually, of course, there were no more foes to fight, and the transformed prostitutes searched for further victims. The streets had been emptied of their usual inhabitants, and the only target remaining visible to them was me. I had several moments of near terror, I can confess, but Bacchus was my protector. As the enraged women approached, he seemed to draw from them their drunken fury, and they slowly subside into weary women. They spoke not a word, but passed by, staggering from exhaustion now and not drunkenness. In a very short while, Bacchus and I were left alone as the women sought rest wherever they could find it.

The war was over.

Bacchus regarded me with a savage smile. "I did tell you that you should pray that I remained drunk," he informed me. "Now I do believe you understand. It might be best if you did not seek me out again. I shall be hard to find, in any event, as I shall get gloriously and helplessly inebriated again. And London will be safe once more."

I do not know how I made it home again, but I did, and I slept, thoroughly exhausted myself, for more than a day. And this time I have obeyed the instructions of Bacchus—I have not, up to this moment, sought him out again.

The tale, we thought, was finished. But then Cavanagh spoke up. "You said at the start that this tale of yours relates to the recent Whitechapel Killings and this so-styled Jack the Ripper. Yet I confess I do not see the connection." There were murmurs of agreement with this remark.

Carnacki gave a wan smile. "That is because there is something more that you need to know. The female lieutenant, the messenger to me from Bacchus—the one called Polly. Her full name was Mary Ann Nicols, and she was the first victim of this killer. The subsequent ones have all been major members of that army of Bacchus." He regarded us all with care. "It is clear, then, that the *Vampires* were not all wiped out, as we had imagined. Some survivor is meting out revenge on the slayers of his companions, and utilizing their deaths to create terror amongst the remainder."

"You said that this Jack the Ripper would probably never be found," I reminded him. "And that there would be no more victims."

"Indeed I did," he said, grimly. "For, just this evening, I received a message from *him*—he is sober again, and I am warned to stay far, far from Whitechapel this night... And I would advise you all to do the same."

More Doc Ardan, the return of Biggles, a brief appearance by Doctor Omega and a touch of Shangri-La, with a smidgeon of Jules Verne... But, for me, the main character is Jane. (Minus Tarzan, for once.) I've always had a thing about strong female characters, and have created several in my books. I grew up watching Emma Peel chucking the bad guys around on The Avengers *(and wrote her once). I could never understand why the girls in the stories I read were always hanging about in the background, waiting to be saved by Our Hero. Why didn't they save themselves? Well, in the Tarzan novels, Burroughs does make Jane the victim from time to time – but he also shows her as having learned many skills from Tarzan. Now, that's my kind of girl!*

The Eye of the Hawk

French Equatorial Africa, 1934

The streets of Brazzaville were difficult to navigate, even for someone as skilled as Doctor Francis Ardan. There were the inevitable street traders, offering a vast variety of fruits, vegetables and meat, and who sprawled across the pavements and into the streets. These stalls attracted crowds, who seemed blithely unaware—or simply uninterested—in motorized traffic. Added to this, there were workers and construction equipment still engaged in activities on the newly-opened Congo-Ocean Railway and its sparkling new station. Mixed in with this were cattle, pigs and the occasional sheep that were being driven, either to be fed or to be slaughtered. Steering his rented car—which appeared to have been kept, unmaintained and rarely used, in a jungle clearing for the past decade—was a lot more arduous than Doc had expected. Still, somehow he managed to make his way to the buildings of the *Institut Pasteur* eventually. The directions he'd been given had proven to

be mostly accurate. Once there, he parked next to an impecca-
bly maintained silver-colored Rolls Royce Phantom, whose
chauffeur lounged nearby, smoking a *gauloise* with an aloof
indifference to his surroundings.

Doc hurried inside the building, paused for a second to
get his bearings, and then followed the instructions he'd been
given to end in a smallish laboratory. There was a French police officer and a bored Sergeant taking their leave of the
room's other two inhabitants. The officer snapped off a crisp
salute to Doc as he passed—obviously just in case Doc was
someone whom he *should* salute—and the policemen hurried
off. Doc raised an eyebrow, and then entered the room.

The man he knew; the woman he did not.

"Doc!" Fred exclaimed, his weathered face breaking into
a relieved smile as he hurried forward to clasp Ardan's hand.
"I can't tell you how glad I am that you're here! Thank you for
coming so promptly."

"Were the police any help?" Doc asked.

"This is the French Congo," the woman said carefully.
Her accent was a mixture of Boston American and British
upper class, with a touch of something Doc couldn't identify
thrown in. "Are the police *ever* helpful here?"

Fred shrugged. "Uh, oh, this is Lady Jane Clayton," he
said, apologetically.

The name was vaguely familiar, but Doc couldn't place
it.

"Lady Clayton," he acknowledged, politely.

"Doctor Ardan," she replied.

She'd clearly been briefed by Fred, then.

"Can you tell me precisely what happened?" he asked
Fred.

"Doctor Omega has been kidnapped."

"I was hoping for a few more details," Doc said gently.

"There really isn't much more to it than that," Fred said.

He was a large man—as large as Doc, and almost as
muscular. He looked as though he wasn't overly bright, but

that was a misconception—he was actually a fine mechanical engineer and a superb chef.

"The Doctor and I came here a week or so ago" he continued. "He'd been asked to help out with some research being conducted here."

"The same research I was invited here to assist with?" Doc asked.

"I imagine," Fred replied. "Not my field, really—something to do with uranium extraction is all I know."

Doc nodded, and Fred continued:

"Well, we arrived this morning early—you know how the Doctor is when he gets his mind set on a subject, all eager and raring to go. I went to see about breakfast and ran into three men down by the kitchen. One of them had a gun and shot me." He produced a two-inch long feathered dart. "Some kind of fast-acting knockout drug. I was out like a light. It must have been about an hour later that I awoke. I immediately ran back here to check up on the Doctor, but he had vanished. I presume he was their target, and that they used the same gun on him." He shrugged. "That is all."

"Not quite," Doc murmured. "You saw no other vehicles here when you arrived?"

"None," Fred stated. "I had been given a key—we arrived before anyone else, around five a.m. That's why nobody found me while I… slept. Nobody else arrived until after I had discovered that the Doctor was gone. I'm afraid there was nobody else here to see anything. I promptly called the police, and then you."

Doc had given Fred his hotel number when he had arrived the previous evening. He had planned to confer with Doctor Omega this morning on the uranium processing; there hadn't seemed to be any great urgency in the matter, and he had been quite exhausted by his journey. Sleep had seemed to be the most important thing. But now…

"I assume that this whole business is about the uranium," Fred added.

"Never make blanket assumptions," the beautiful young woman said, rather languidly.

Doc eyed her curiously. "May I ask why you are here?"

"You may," she replied, as if giving away a favor. "I am here because I expected this to happen. I wished to confirm my theories." She gave him a dazzling smile. "Now that I have, I'll be on my way."

"If you wouldn't mind," Doc said quietly, "would you enlighten us about those theories before you leave?"

She shrugged her shapely shoulders. "Fred has been telling me about your reputation as a genius," she said, a slight hint of mockery in her voice. "Do you *really* need to be informed?"

"Perhaps not," Doc said. "But, if you would be so kind…"

She raised an eyebrow. "Why not? Doctor Omega is not the first scientist to disappear under rather mysterious circumstances. There have been two other such cases in the past week."

"Four," Doc corrected her. "Two of them have gone unreported in the press—at my request."

The eyebrow rose again. "Four? That is interesting—and significant. Thank you. When I was informed that Doctor Omega had been invited here, I was certain he would be the next victim. The previous two cases that I knew of were north of here, and both men had also been recently invited into the country. And the other two…?" she prompted.

"Also in the north," Doc confirmed. "I learned of the second of those yesterday in Casablanca—from a contact at Rick's Café." He smiled without humor. "It is said that everyone goes to Rick's. I, too, realized that Doctor Omega was likely to be the next victim. I simply didn't realize how swiftly the kidnappers would work. I hurried here yesterday, thinking I had beaten them here. Obviously, I underestimated them."

"They appear to be remarkably efficient," Lady Jane observed. "And, I must confess, a trifle puzzling."

120

"In what way?" Fred asked, annoyed. "They've kidnapped Doctor Omega, and we have to get him back!"

"From where?" she replied. "They don't appear to have left a single clue at any kidnapping site. Unless…?" She glanced at Doc.

He shook his head. "There was nothing I could find at the other two strikes. And you are quite correct—their purpose in these attacks is difficult to see."

"They're probably after the uranium," Fred growled. "That's why the Doctor was here, after all."

"But the other four scientists have nothing to do with uranium," Doc commented. "One is a nutritionist, one a marine biologist, one an astronomer and the last a physicist. And Doctor Omega isn't really noted as a specialist in radioactivity, is he? He's far more occupied with space flight, and was only here as a favor to a friend. No, none of the men so far have more than a single thing in common."

The eyebrow rose again. "And that would be?" she prompted.

"That they are the pre-eminent specialists in their particular fields," Doc replied.

Fred scowled. "Then why haven't they kidnapped—oh, Einstein, say? Or Schrödinger?"

"I am not certain," Doc admitted. "But they may have some specific purpose in mind concerning their chosen victims. They appear to be concentrating on practical scientists rather than theoreticians."

"You think that there will be other victims?" Lady Jane asked.

"I fear so," Ardan replied. "Having taking four prominent men, I can't see why they would not go on to a fifth—or sixth."

"I would agree," she said. "And I rather fear I know who the next victim will be—the man I came to this country to see. Abner Perry."

"Perry is here?" Doc asked, surprised.

"Who's Perry?" Fred asked.

"A great mechanical engineer," Lady Jane answered. "And a very good friend of my late father's—Professor Archimedes Q. Porter. I aim to protect him."

Fred eyed her with open incredulity. "I don't see how you can possibly do that," he commented.

"I'm sure you don't," she agreed.

She glanced around the room.

"Well, I don't think I can learn anything further here, gentlemen, so if you'll excuse me…"

Doc held up a hand. "One moment." He glanced at Fred. "My friend here may have been a trifle blunt, but he *does* have a point. Whoever is behind these kidnappings is well-organized and clearly powerful. I think you may have trouble in store."

She gave a delightful laugh at the thought. "Oh, I'm quite certain of that," she admitted. "Good day."

She started to move around him.

"It might make more sense if you simply told me where Dr. Perry is," Doc suggested. "I can offer him more protection than you. And if we can arrive *before* any assailants, we may be able to recover the previous victims."

Lady Jane slowly looked him over.

"Doctor Ardan," she finally said. "I will make a bargain with you—if you can keep up with me, you may accompany me. But this is a matter of some urgency, and Perry is a family friend. I will not wait for you."

Her attitude, frankly, astonished Doc. He wondered for a brief moment if she was crazy—the heat and the tropics could do that to some people. But he realized that she appeared to be in earnest.

"I should not wish to be encumbered by you," he said, frankly. "If you were there, I would be worried about protecting you."

She didn't quite roll her eyes. "How remarkably condescending of you," she said, cheerfully. "I was, frankly, thinking much the same about *you*."

Fred scowled again. "You obviously don't know who you're talking to," he snapped. "Doc is more than capable of handling himself."

"I may live most of my life here in Africa," she replied, "but we *do* get some news. I've heard of Doctor Francis Ardan and his exploits—which is the only reason I agreed he could accompany me." She gave Fred a frank stare. "*You* are not invited. You're big and strong, but you'd be clumsy in the jungle, and I don't have the time to look after you."

"Hey!" Fred looked furious. "I'm coming! It's my job to look after the Doctor."

"He does have a point," Doc stated. "And my plane is only a two-seater. Surely you can see that it would be best if you simply told me where Perry is, and allow us to go alone?"

This time she did roll her eyes. "You wouldn't be able to get to within a dozen miles of him in your plane," she said. "He's quite deep in the jungle. Frankly, I'm not sure either of you have the ability to reach him in time to do him any good."

"And yet *you* can?" Doc asked.

"Don't sound so amazed," she snapped. "I've spent a good deal of my life here in the wilds, and I have had the best possible teachers." Her face softened. "On the other hand, your plane *would* save us a great deal of time... Very well, let us both proceed *together*." She glanced at Fred. "You—stay here." From her tone, it was quite clear that she was used to giving orders—and for them to be obeyed.

"I'm not..."

"Two-seater," she said, firmly. "She pointed to Doc. "One." And then herself. "Two. End of discussion." She turned to Doc. "Come along, Doctor—my chauffeur will drive us to the airport."

"I have my own car."

"But he is used to the traffic here," she replied, gently. "Shall we dispense with the rivalry and choose the more sensible arrangements?"

Fred glanced from one of them to the other, his face twisted in agonized indecision. Doc reached out and clasped his shoulder.

"I promise that we shall do all we can to rescue the Doctor," he said, gently. "But Lady Jane is right—you must stay here."

"I should go instead of her," Fred muttered.

"You don't know how to reach Abner's cabin," she pointed out. "And you would not be able to make the trek as swiftly as I—" She glanced at Doc. "*We* can." With compassion in her eyes, she assured him: "You know that you can trust us to do our best, Fred. Please don't argue further." She turned back to Doc. "Shall we go?"

This was clearly a young woman who knew how to get her own way. She gave orders with self-assurance and suggestions as if they were velvet-gloved orders. A typical member of the English aristocracy—even if she had been born in America. Doc had a feeling that this was going to be a very sticky partnership. He was never very comfortable with women—his odd upbringing had been carried out in isolation, at the hands of strictly male scientists—and Lady Jane was clearly no mere woman. He hoped he would not be forced to leave her to fend for herself.

Fred offered no further protests, but he looked like a boy whose puppy had been stolen. Doc ignored this, as there was nothing more he could do to reassure the man. He followed Lady Jane out to her car.

The lazing chauffeur sprang to life, flicking aside his partially-smoked cigarette and holding the rear door for them. She swept in, and Doc followed.

"The airport," she ordered, and then sat back. "Swiftly."

Doc was impressed with how relaxed she appeared to be, especially considering the appalling speed of their journey. Somehow their driver managed not to hit any person, animal or structure, though he did slaughter several fruits. He drove on the road and the pavement with equal indifference, skidding around corners and whipping down the crowded streets as though they were empty. Doc was alternately impressed and appalled by his recklessness. But he managed to get the car to the airport in astonishing time, and with nothing more than fruit juices staining it.

He pulled up next to Doc's plane—not as surprising as it might have been, since it was the only non-military aircraft there. The chauffeur leapt from the barely-halted car and held the door open for Lady Jane.

Completely unaffected by their hectic trip, she stepped lightly from the car. "Thank you," she said, smiling cheerily. "I'll let you know when I need you again."

"Yes, m'lady," the man acknowledged.

As soon as Doc was out of the car, the driver leaped back inside and sped off.

"A remarkable chauffeur," Doc commented.

"He has a lot of… interesting skills," Lady Jane replied. She glanced at Doc's aircraft. "I don't believe I know this model."

"It's my own design," he replied, trying not to sound as if he was boasting. "Rather experimental, so not commercially available."

"Well, as long as it flies and lands with speed and safety, I shall be happy," she said. "Can I see your local maps?"

He pulled them from the cockpit. She studied them briefly as he started up the engine and made the pre-flight checks. When he was ready, she slipped into the seat beside him and spread the map out.

"You can follow the Congo down to here," she said, tapping the relevant spot. "There's a very rudimentary airstrip there, used by mail planes. I hope this experiment of yours doesn't need a long strip."

"No," he replied. "If airmail planes can land, we certainly can."

"Good. From that point on, we're in the jungle, I'm afraid."

"I shall manage."

He glanced at her pointedly. All he got in return was a dazzling smile—and no reassurance.

They were in the air moments later, and Doc took the craft up to a thousand feet. He could see the river heading roughly eastwards, and followed it.

"Why is Abner Perry out here?" he asked her.

The engine he had designed for this craft was quieter than any commercial model, so they could converse with ease.

"Was he lured here, as Doctor Omega was?"

"No." She chuckled softly. "Abner's an odd bird—a mechanical genius, but he's frowned upon by a lot of conventional scientists. He's a firm believer in the hollow Earth theory. I take it you've heard of that?"

"The idea that the interior of the globe is hollow and may contain another world almost as large as our own? It's not an accepted theory."

"No. Well, Abner has never been one for accepting things without proof. He believes that the crust of the Earth is thinnest below the jungle out here, and he's been experimenting with what he calls an iron mole."

"I am afraid he may well be disappointed in the results," Doc commented.

Lady Jane's lips twitched a bit, but all she said was: "He's used to disappointment. But I think you'd agree he is likely to be the next victim of these kidnappers."

"Considering the fact that they lured Doctor Omega so close to Perry, I would concur." He considered for a moment. "If there is no closer landing place to his location, then we cannot be far behind the kidnappers." He frowned slightly. "Then how did Perry get his iron mole into the jungle?"

"By river," she replied. "In pieces. He's been reassembling it for weeks now. It took several trips for him to get to this stage. The last message I got from him said he'd be ready to attempt his next experiment in about a week's time, so he's bound to be at his compound at this moment."

"Unless our opponents have reached him first," Doc observed.

He flew on steadily, as the miles of river and jungle passed below them. Eventually, Lady Jane gestured.

"The landing zone is down there," she said, pointing to what looked like impenetrable jungle. "You may want to do a fly-over first to get the lay of the land."

It was a sensible suggestion, and he took the plane lower. At about 300 feet, he finally made out a narrow area of cleared brush. He kept descending, cutting his air speed.

She had been correct—this wasn't much of a landing strip. It ran vaguely northwards from the river for several hundred yards, and ended abruptly in a wall of trees. It was literally a dirt strip, with no facilities of any kind.

"Do you think you can manage it?" There was the first hint of uncertainty in her voice.

For an answer, Doc banked and came in for a landing. Wheels touched earth a dozen feet from the river's edge, and he brought the craft to a halt about a hundred yards before the jungle reasserted its claim on the land.

"Nicely done," Lady Jane said, sincerely. "Not everyone is that good."

He could see that there were bits of aircraft on the edge of the jungle to back up her comment.

Doc was never good with being praised—especially by young women—and he tried to shrug off the pleasure he felt. He clambered from the plane, and turned to help his companion, but she leaped nimbly down before he could. He eyed her clothing critically.

"Perhaps you should simply point me in the right direction," he suggested. "You're not exactly dressed for jungle travel."

Lady Jane glanced down at her long, floral dress and high heels. "You're quite right," she agreed, cheerfully, and kicked off her shoes. When she started to unbutton the dress, Doc looked at her in alarm.

"What are you doing?" He had to fight to keep his voice level.

"Dressing for jungle travel," she replied.

"It looks more like you're *un*-dressing."

She gave a delighted laugh. "Don't look so shocked," she advised him. "I'm wearing my travel clothes under my dress."

She finished unbuttoning it and threw it back into the plane. She stood ready, cocking her head slightly. She now wore—well, barely anything. It looked mostly like a single-piece bathing suit made of antelope leather. It stretched from half-way down her breasts to considerably higher than half-way up her long, muscular thighs.

"That's *dressed*?" he enquired.

She held up a finger. "You're quite right," she agreed.

She reached into her overly large traveling bag and pulled out a knife on a belt, a bow and a quiver of arrows. "*Now* I'm dressed."

The knife was a good foot long, and the bow was a man's bow, and not a smaller woman's model. Judging from her very visible arm muscles, she was used to using this weapon.

And then, finally, he remembered where he had heard her name before. "Lady Jane," he mused. "Lady Jane *Greystoke*."

"The same," she agreed.

He managed to avoid blushing at how foolish his comments must have seemed to her.

"Isn't this more your husband's field—so to speak?"

She laughed again. "Yes, but he taught me everything I know. Not quite everything *he* knows, though."

"I don't suppose he's around?"

"No," she replied. "He's off investigating another of those endless lost cities he always manages to stumble across. We probably shan't see him for a couple of months." She gave another of those delightful grins. "He does so enjoy his work." Then she turned serious. "It doesn't look like there has been any other plane here for at least a month."

"I agree," he replied. "Which means that we may be ahead of the kidnappers."

"Or dear old Abner isn't their next target." She gestured at the trees. "If we're ahead of them now, let's stay that way, shall we?" She grinned again. "This time, it may be *you* who isn't dressed for jungle travel."

She ran lightly ahead, and he followed.

Despite popular belief, the jungle wasn't wall-to-wall trees, underbrush and thorns. Animals cleared pathways for their own needs, so there was frequently a simple path to follow. It was also cooler than the clearing, as the trees tended to intersect about twenty feet into the air, providing shade and cover. Because there was less light reaching the ground, the undergrowth was thinner and more scrub than thick bushes. There were plenty of animal tracks, but certainly no human footprints. It looked to Doc as if they were way ahead of their quarry. They should be in time to keep Perry safe.

Her bare feet didn't slow Lady Jane down at all. He understood why, of course—she and her husband had achieved almost legendary status in Africa. He was, of course, the more noted, but he had clearly chosen his mate extremely well. She showed no signs of tiring as they raced along the jungle paths. Doc was in extremely good shape, but even he was finding it hard to stay with her.

The voices of the jungle hushed as they traveled, but were loud and vocal ahead and behind them. From time to time, he caught glimpses of birds—sometimes with startlingly bright plumage—and at others small creatures drifting through the background. There were none of the larger cats, of course, as this profusion of trees was not conducive to their hunting style; they preferred the open savannah, as did the larger antelopes, zebras and other beasts. This was the home of the smaller, shyer creatures, the largest of which was likely to be that forest ghost, the okapi—and they had such good camouflage that they might even now be being observed by one that was practically invisible.

They moved swiftly through the forest. His companion didn't hesitate, somehow following a trail or memory that he couldn't see. They paused only once, by a small steam, from which they drank.

"About another fifteen minutes," she announced, "and we should reach the compound."

He nodded. "I've seen no signs of other people so far, Lady Jane."

She grinned again. "Call me Jane," she said. "Titles seem so pointless in the jungles, don't they?"

He smiled back. "Call me Doc."

She cocked her head slightly and studied him. "You don't like people getting close to you, do you?" She shrugged. "None of my business, of course—Doc." Then she was on her feet again. "Enough lazing about—come on."

And she set off again.

He followed, wondering if he should attempt to explain his motivations. In his line of work, it was important to act without being affected by emotion. Getting too close to others made one vulnerable.

Of course, *not* getting close to people made one lonely…

Now was not the time for an analysis of his motivations. There was a job that had to be done. And she was, after all, another man's wife.

They reached the compound in the time Jane had predicted. It was a small affair—three buildings and an outdoor cooking area—with several natives milling about. It was surrounded by a thorn *boma*, the entrance of which was open.

One of the men spotted the new arrivals and let out a cry. The rest immediately became alert, raising spears and shields and grouping together. Jane called out in some language he didn't recognize—there were far too many local tongues in Africa for him to have even a smattering knowledge of more than a few. One of the men called back, and Jane walked slowly forwards, her hands spread to show that she was unarmed. Doc followed suit.

The natives relaxed, lowering their weapons. Their leader continued to speak with Jane, whose face fell.

"We're too late," she informed Doc. "The kidnappers have already struck, and have taken Abner."

He felt a moment of anger, and then puzzlement. "How could they have reached here ahead of us? We saw no sign of them."

"I know."

Jane went back to talking with the spokesman. Doc couldn't help there, so he glanced around the compound. Two of the structures were clearly for resting, and that meant the third had to be where Perry had worked.

He crossed to it and entered the hut, which was of wooden posts covered with woven reeds. He saw that his guess had been correct, and that inside was an almost completed machine that had to be Perry's iron mole. It was about fifteen feet long and ten high. There was a large drill at the front, and an open door in the side. He was itching to examine it, but his curiosity would have to wait. There were open hatches all over the outside of the vehicle, showing it to be a work still in progress. Tools were scattered about, which could be a result of Perry being messy or because he'd been attacked whilst utilizing them.

There was one odd thing that he noticed. On the ground by the entrance was a pure white silken scarf. He picked it up to examine it, and recognized what it was almost immediately. Odd…

One of the natives had followed him, talking rapidly in his incomprehensible language. He gripped Doc's arm and then pointed to the roof excitedly. Doc glanced up, but saw nothing remarkable. The man pulled on Doc's arm, leading him outside, and then pointing at the sky.

Jane came over. "The head man says that the attackers came from the sky," she informed him. "There were about a dozen of them, and they walked down to the ground. They had guns, but only fired them at the ground. They captured Abner and then walked back into the sky. Then they were taken away by the eye of the hawk."

"Some kind of dirigible, then," Doc guessed.

"That's what it sounds like to me," Jane agreed. "But—how could a zeppelin have beaten us here? Your plane is much faster than any dirigible I've ever seen."

"Indeed," Doc agreed.

He could see now in the dirt the marks where rope ladders must have dragged, and several sets of shod footprints. The natives were all bare-foot.

"If this *was* an airship of some kind, it must have been a very sophisticated one—as well as very swift."

"Unless these were not the men who kidnapped Doctor Omega?" Jane suggested. "Perhaps there are *two* sets of assailants, working together?"

"It's possible," Doc agreed. "But the existence of this unknown aerial device suggests we are dealing with an uncommon foe."

"And we have no real leads," Jane said, soberly. "The zeppelin flew off to the east—but there's a lot of Africa to the east."

Doc managed a slight smile. "Even one or two of those lost kingdoms your husband enjoys so much?"

"You think that *that* is where they might have gone?"

"I don't believe they are heading anywhere in Africa," he informed her. He held up the silk scarf. "I discovered this in Perry's work hut."

She frowned slightly. "It doesn't look like anything Abner would wear. He's not what you'd call dressy."

"It isn't," Doc informed her. "I suspect it was left by one of his attackers. It's a ritual scarf, and comes from Tibet. They are used as gifts for visitors to lamaseries. Each lamasery makes their own, so they are all slightly different."

"So you can tell where that came from?" she asked, surprised.

His mouth twitched. "I do know a good deal of useful information," he admitted. "But I've never felt the need to study silk weaving in the past. However, I *do* know someone who can help us out here."

"Excellent. And where would that person be?"

"Tibet," he replied. "Which would appear to be my next port of call."

"*Ours*," Jane said, firmly. "Abner is my friend, after all. And if John is off having fun in a lost city, I think I deserve a trip to a Tibetan monastery."

He looked down at her. "You do realize that this is a trap, of course?"

"Obviously," she agreed. "They've kidnapped five previous victims and never left a clue before—it would be unrealistic to expect this to have been left by chance." Her pretty forehead furrowed slightly. "Logically, *you* are their next target, and they're politely inviting you to your own kidnapping."

"Quite." He hesitated slightly. "I am afraid that they may not have any use for you, though—so if you accompany me, you may be placing yourself in severe danger."

She laughed. "Like I said, I don't see why John should have all of the fun in the family."

Doc had to admire her calm resolve. He could see why the so-called Lord of the Jungle had picked her as his mate: she wasn't unrealistically hopeful, but determined and focused.

"I'm not sure that this could be called *fun*," he said.

"If it's not fun," she asked. "Then why do you do it?" She grinned again. "What's our next step?"

"Back to Brazzaville," he replied. "My plane isn't able to take us to Tibet—it would need to refuel too frequently—so we'll need an alternate form of transport, which I can arrange for us back in Brazzaville."

"Right," she agreed, cheerfully. "Race you back to the plane!"

Once they reached the airport in Brazzaville again, Doc made arrangements quickly to store his plane and for an alternative one that was able to travel longer distances. Jane called Fred to update him, and he joined them at the airport by the time their new flight was ready.

"This time, I go along," he said, firmly. "The Doctor will be relying on me."

"It's a larger craft," Doc agreed. "You're more than welcome."

He knew of Fred's abilities from the past, and the large man would be very helpful. Jane, not knowing Fred, was more dubious.

"What can you offer?" she asked.

Fred looked her over. "Aside from my strength and mechanical abilities? What sort of a cook are you?"

She grinned. "I can field-dress and cook an antelope as required," she said. "But I do prefer a nice restaurant."

"I'm a gourmet chef."

"Welcome aboard, partner," she replied.

Doc was the pilot again, and he had the craft in the air quickly. Fred was in the co-pilot's seat, and Jane behind them both. The airplane was a freighter, but the rest of it was empty—which would help keep the fuel consumption down.

Jane had to shout to be heard over the howl of the engines. "What's the plan?"

"Casablanca first, and then on to Alexandria. Our next ride should meet us there."

"Our next ride?"

"This crate will never be able to stand the rarified air in Tibet," Doc explained. "We need something a little better equipped. A friend of mine will meet us in Alexandria with my latest dirigible." He frowned slightly. "It will delay us getting to Tibet, but we can't meet it any closer, since it's coming from Europe. We'll need it to ascend into the mountains."

"I don't think the Doctor and the other victims are in any immediate danger," Fred said. "Nobody would go to all this trouble in kidnapping them merely to harm them."

Jane agreed. "Nobody would benefit by harming Abner, so they must be attempting to pick his brains. Doc, is there any connection between the victims?"

"Aside from their technical skills and intelligence?" he asked. "No, they all work in different fields. They're all excellent people, but at least two of them are unknown to the general public. Whoever has kidnapped these men has chosen carefully and wisely. But—to what end?" He shrugged. "I'm afraid I simply cannot see, at present."

They touched down at Casablanca to refuel, and then again at Tripoli. There was a telegram awaiting him there, and it made him smile slightly.

"The dirigible is well on the way, and will be awaiting us in Alexandria," he announced.

"That's good news."

Jane had retrieved her normal clothes earlier (Doc was rather relieved she'd covered up her rather attractive legs; he didn't need that kind of distraction), but she gestured at her dress.

"Will we have a chance to stop for a little shopping? I'm not exactly dressed for the snows. Come to that, neither are either of you."

"We'll have all of the equipment we'll need about the ship," Doc assured her. "I'm sure you'll be able to find something appropriate."

"Yes, but will it be fashionable?" she asked. Then she laughed at his worried expression. "I'm joking," she explained. "I'm sure it will be fine. And, like all women, I do love furs…"

Doc was wondering whether he'd made a mistake in allowing her to accompany him; she had a rather disconcerting habit of unnerving him. Then again, he suspected that if he'd refused to allow her to come along, she'd have found some way of making it alone… At least, this way he could keep an eye open for her safety.

He hadn't been exaggerating earlier when he'd worried about her chances—so far, nobody had been killed during the kidnappings, but the villains behind this plot wouldn't have much use for her. As likable and skillful as she was, she had absolutely no scientific training. They might simply see her as unnecessary—and if she knew where their base was, then she might move from *unnecessary* to *disposable*...

He did not need the extra worry of keeping her safe; it might interfere with resolving this issue. But, honestly, what other choice did he have? He would have to deal with the problem if it arose.

She surprised him again when she offered to spell him. It turned out that she was a licensed pilot, and did indeed know what she was doing. Being honest with himself, he was getting tired after the day's flights, and so he accepted her offer. He had the ability to fall asleep almost instantly.

Dawn was breaking on the horizon when he awoke. Fred was sleeping in the co-pilot's seat, but Jane was focused on her task. Somehow, even over the noise of the engine, she heard him stirring and glanced back.

"Alexandria in about an hour," she estimated. "Good thing, too—it'll be light when we arrive, and we're getting low on fuel." She moved aside to allow him to retake the controls. "What are the facilities like on this dirigible of yours?"

"Fairly primitive, I'm afraid," he informed her. "There's a small galley, and a couple of cabins for sleeping, but it was built for scientific exploration and not luxury."

She laughed. "I live in the jungle most of the time. I'm used to primitive, believe you me. But I do enjoy a nice luxurious bath when I can get one. Will we have the time for that?"

He briefly considered lying to her and telling her that they would, so that he could leave her behind. But he couldn't bring himself to commit such a deception. "I rather fear not."

She sighed. "Oh, well, something to anticipate, then. Rescue first, bathing later."

Alexandria was a large and bustling city beside the Mediterranean, but the airport was definitely an afterthought. It lay on the edge of the desert and on the outskirts of the ancient city itself. That was fine, as far as Doc was concerned—it made landing simpler, and meant there were less crowds about. Sunlight glittered in the distance on the spires of mosques and ancient churches, and he could see the bustling port as they approached the city. There were no other aircraft aloft, so landing was simple and swift.

As he taxied from the field, he was pleased to see that his dirigible was tied to a makeshift mast. Fred had woken up for the landing, and he grinned when he saw the airship.

"No waiting for the transfer, then," he observed.

"It *is* a bit small," Jane commented.

"It's experimental," Doc reminded her, slightly offended by her remark.

"Of course," she agreed. "I didn't mean to criticize. But it's a good job we're all friends."

Doc cut the engine as they neared the dirigible, and they jumped out. The only person in sight appeared to be fast asleep in the shade of the craft. Jane ambled across and dug the toe of her shoe into his side.

"Up, you lazy creature," she said, with a smile.

His eyes opened and he grinned up at her.

"Say—I like the local sights." He jumped to his feet and grinned at Doc. "All ready and provisioned," he said. "We can be off in half an hour."

"Good." Doc turned to Jane and Fred. "Allow me to introduce our pilot—James Bigglesworth."

"Everyone calls me Biggles," the pilot added, shaking hands.

"Are you the entire crew?" Jane asked, surprised. "I thought these things needed dozens of men."

"With Doc, yes. I fly, Doc fixes things. It works out pretty well. Doc designed this ship, so much of it is automated." He gave a broad grin. "It's a sweet little thing. Can't compare to a Sopwith Camel, of course, but she has her uses."

"It sounds intriguing," Jane confessed. "Pipe us aboard, will you?"

"With the greatest of pleasure, ma'am," he replied. "Local services are a bit primitive, so…" He gestured at the rope ladder that hung from the gondola. "Up you go."

Doc smiled secretively at Biggles' surprise at how swiftly Jane ascended. Biggles followed her with considerably less
speed and grace. Fred followed, and Doc brought up the rear.

By the time he reached the cabin and hauled in the ladder, Biggles had fired up the ship's engines, and Jane had vanished into the interior of the gondola—no doubt checking out
just how primitive the facilities were.

Fred stood to one side, trying not to get in the way as
Doc joined Biggles as they prepared the ship for flight. Below
them, two Arabs had materialized from somewhere and were
standing by the fore and aft moorings.

Fred went to the forward hatch to prepare to receive the
mooring line. Doc was about to go aft to do the same when he
saw that Jane was already there and waiting. She flashed him a
grin, and he realized he'd misjudged her again. It seemed to be
becoming a habit.

At Biggles' signal, the men below cast off the ropes, and
Fred and Jane hauled them aboard and sealed the hatches. Jane
and Fred then joined them in the cabin as Biggles throttled up
the engines and their flight began.

"Top speed's about a hundred and fifty," Biggles announced. "It's about 24 hours to our destination if we fly continually. But we'll need to make a couple of stops for fuel and
provisions, so let's say a day and a half."

Jane's eyebrows rose. "That's pretty good time."

"Doc builds well," Biggles said.

"You'll have lots of time to teach me how to pilot this."

Biggles frowned. "It's a bit hard for a girl."

She gave him an insincere smile. "*I'm* a bit hard for a
girl."

Doc took pity on him. "You may as well give in now,"
he advised. "It will save you a good deal of effort."

Biggles looked a little sheepish. Like Doc, he wasn't too
used to women. He'd basically grown up in the fledgling Roy-
al Air Force in France in World War I, and thus was a part of
an exclusive all-boys club. When most 16 year-olds were
learning how to socialize, Biggles had been soaring through

the skies after German fighters. He'd become one of England's top aces, and since then gone into the air transport business—with occasional forays into intelligence work. He'd rarely had to socialize with women, and felt rather uncomfortable around them. Doc could empathize.

Jane was, of course, quite relentless. She simply brushed aside Biggles' mild protests—she may not have been born into British nobility, but she had taken easily to the role. She simply assumed that people would do as she wished, and they very often did.

"Main airbag is 150 feet long," Biggles explained, on firmer ground when talking of things mechanical. "Helium, rather than hydrogen."

"It won't produce as much lift," Jane commented.

"No, but the risk of fire is a good deal lower. With Doc's structural improvements, that offsets the loss of lift. Four engines, all to Doc's design, and with wizard efficiency. Low running temperature, so a lot fewer breakdowns."

"It sounds wonderful," Jane said, clearly in admiration. "And 150 miles an hour steady air speed?"

"A bit higher, actually," Biggles replied. "We average 150 when you factor in the wind."

"Marvelous." Then her eyes crinkled, and Doc realized she was going to say something to prick any pomposity. "But the facilities aboard are a bit primitive, I gather?"

"As I said, it's an experimental ship," Doc said, mildly annoyed. "It's not designed for comfort—or the aristocracy."

She grinned widely. "Let me know when the mark two is available. I may want to buy one—if I can install a bathtub."

"The weight factor..." he began, before he realized she was teasing him.

"Maybe a shower?" she suggested, innocently.

"I'll consider it," he said, flatly.

"What *do* we have aboard for comfort?" she asked Biggles.

"One cabin, so we'll have to take it in turns to rest. A small galley, but plenty of food and drinking water for a day's flying. And a small w.c. Very small, sorry."

"Understandable. Right—now, what do these controls do?"

They flew on, following the Egyptian coast. Fred took a turn sleeping, and then whipped up some very tasty omelets. Doc took a short rest, leaving Biggles to field Jane's endless questions.

By the time he awoke, night had fallen. He returned to the cockpit, and took over the controls from Biggles, who was next for the small bed. Jane was a lot more silent now, watching the occasional light in the darkness below them.

"We're over Sinai now," she informed him. "Coming up on the coast." After a pause, she added, "This really is a rather nice little craft. I can see it will have a lot of uses."

"Thank you." He was uncomfortable with praise, especially when it was as sincere as hers. "I have a lot of modifications still to make."

"Improving on perfection, eh?"

"I try."

They flew on. It was barely possible to tell when they had passed over the shore and onto the sea. There was no moon, but the stars were incomparable, and the Milky Way slashed across the night sky.

"It's a bit like the jungle," Jane observed. "Only with engine noise instead of animal sounds. But the view is much the same—spectacular."

"You love Africa?" he asked.

"Very much so. My life has become so much richer since I met John."

"Do you miss him when he's away?"

"Of course I do, you idiot," she said, but good-naturedly. "But he's a wild creature, and there are times he simply has to be off on his own. He makes up for it when he returns. Besides," she grinned, "I do have some interesting adventures of my own, so I can't complain."

"Don't you miss civilization?"

She regarded him with her head cocked on one side. "I can take it or leave it. When I *want* it, John and I can head to England. The rest of the time, we vastly prefer the jungle. It's not the life for everyone, but it's the life we choose. A bit like you and yours," she added. "It's what fulfills us, isn't it?"

He found her comments perhaps a little too understandable. He tended to think of women as flighty creatures or impulse and whim, but Jane was clearly nothing of the sort. He didn't know whether this was because Jane was extra-ordinary or because he didn't have sufficient experience with the fairer sex. The latter, he suspected.

He was a lot more comfortable, though, when Biggles reappeared and Jane went to rest.

The sun arose as they neared the Indian subcontinent. They had passed over Arabia and were approaching the northern shores of India now. From here on, they would have to rise, as they approached the mountain chains that laced across the region. First, though, they would stop to refuel in Jamnagar in Gujaret Province. It would give the engines a short while to cool off, and the four of them a chance to stretch their legs.

Land was a sliver, and then a wall on the ocean. In a short while, they were passing over forests and fields, with small villages and towns far below them. They pressed on. He kept an eye on the fuel gauge, and saw that his calculations had been virtually correct. There had been a little head wind in the night, but not enough to slow their progress substantially.

They reached the airfield at Jamnagar in mid-morning. Doc had cabled ahead from Alexandria, and everything was prepared for them. He oversaw the refueling while Jane and Fred walked to the newly-built admin building. Biggles—as fastidious as ever with his craft—checked over the engines. From his expression, all was fine, though he had several long conversations with some of the Indian workers. He finally came over to where Doc was supervising the disconnections of the fuel hoses.

"The locals tell me that they have seen a huge hawk that overflew the field at daybreak," he reported. "It can't be anything other than our quarry, old chap."

"Indeed," Doc agreed, thoughtfully. "So we are only a few hours behind them, then." He eyed the horizon speculatively. "We may be able to catch up with them before we reach Tibet…"

Within the hour, they had cast off and were heading north east again, towards Rajasthan. The longest stretch would be over Uttar Pradesh, and then they would reach Napal and the Roof Of The World…

The view below was spectacular. There were small clearings around villages and the occasional town, but a good deal of the countryside was jungle. Jane eyed the view wistfully.

"Rather different from my usual haunts," she said. "But…"

"Still appealing, eh?" Fred suggested. "There's lots of talk about man-eating tigers…"

"There's lots of talk about all manner of things," Jane answered. "Including over-sized hawks. That doesn't make it true."

"Bit of a coincidence that both your native friends and the locals here describe it the same way, though," Biggles observed from the helm.

"True," she agreed. "But that doesn't mean it *is* a giant hawk—merely that it *looks* like a giant hawk." She glanced at Doc. "It has to be some sort of dirigible, correct?"

"That's one possibility," Doc agreed. "And a strong one. But if it is a dirigible, then it would have to be more advanced than this one."

Jane laughed. "And you're too modest to suggest that nobody could build a better airship than you?"

"That's not precisely what I meant," he replied, a little annoyed. "Merely that it would take a very sophisticated engineer—and none springs to mind. At least, none living…"

He refused to elaborate on this, preferring to keep his suspicions to himself until he had some evidence.

They flew on, admiring the sights below, for several hours. They passed the only major city, Lucknow, too far to the north to see it. There were trade roads winding through the hills below them, as the land began to rise toward the Himalayas. As they neared Napal, the sun sank towards the horizon.

"We will stay the night in Kathmandu," Doc announced. "We can't chance flying into the mountains in the darkness— it is far too dangerous. We'll recommence our journey first thing in the morning."

"Mmmm…" Jane said, dreamily. "Real beds and a bath…"

Fred laughed. "I thought you liked sleeping in trees and bathing in rivers?"

"Oh, I do," she laughed back. "But I do enjoy my comforts from time to time… I know a good hotel here, and I'm sure I can get us rooms for the night."

"I for one won't complain," Biggles announced. "A good night's sleep will set us up for the final leg tomorrow, chaps."

Doc concurred. He guided the airship into the bowl-shaped valley. The sprawling city lay within the bowl, with palaces, temples and vast gardens spread below them as they came into the small area selected as a rudimentary airfield. Virtually nobody flew into the area, so it saw little traffic.

Except the locals all reported seeing a giant hawk fly over a few hours earlier… Doc had been hoping—though with no great expectations—that their quarry might have paused also before heading into Tibet. It was more than likely that they had flown this route before, though, and were more comfortable than he with a night journey.

"These kidnappers seem to be going out of their way to ensure that they are observed," Biggles remarked.

"They don't want to lose us," Jane agreed.

"No," Doc added. "They clearly know these skies, but they're been careful not to be observed in the past. Their current activities can only be designed to ensure that we know where to follow them."

"Come into my parlor..." Fred commented.

"Well, I hope they've got the tea on when we arrive," Biggles said.

They rented a car and driver to take them to the hotel Jane knew. A few words with the manager and she had obtained rooms for them. "I have first dibs on the bath," she informed her companions. "Then we'll eat."

Doc could work and rest anywhere, but he had to admit that he did enjoy a touch of luxury from time to time.

The hotel was small, but very well equipped, obviously catering to upper-class visitors. The manager fawned over "Lady Greystoke", and graciously included the men in his subservient attitude. He undoubtedly thought them her retainers, but was taking no chances on possibly offending her.

Their rooms were small but extremely comfortable, and their meal was a vast improvement over the rations aboard the airship. Even Fred was impressed with the chicken and goat dishes, and wandered off to chat with their cook, undoubtedly seeking the recipes.

Despite the appeal of their beds, all of them were up early, ate a light breakfast and then hurried back to the airfield. In a very short while, they were in the air again, and continuing on the flight towards the north-east.

They were well into the mountains now. Jagged peaks pushed upwards from the plateaus below them. Kathmandu was situated at 4,600 feet above sea level, so they were flying at about 5,000 feet now. Fred had broken out the furs, and they were all dressed in the heavy outfits. Jane's was a little on the large size, and Fred's a trifle tight, but both would be able to manage. Below were mountains, rocks and snowfield. Ahead and behind were mountains, rocks and snowfields. There were occasional small villages, isolated temples and cairns of the weathered stones. But, mainly, there was raw, rugged nature.

"We're not going to find many people around here to tell us where the great hawk flew," Biggles remarked. "Are you sure we can find our way from here?"

Doc held up the scarf. "This is our map," he said. "We simply need to talk to the man who can read it." He pointed slightly to the north. "There is a small, isolated monastery ahead; the lama we seek lives there. He will be able to give us the final directions we need. We are very close now, my friends."

They flew on for about another fifteen minutes. Doc had only been here once before, but he knew that his memory was accurate. Then ahead, spread over the side of the mountain, he saw the gray stone walls of the Det-sen Monastery.

He pointed it out to his companions, and guided the dirigible in as close as he could make it before handing over the controls to Biggles.

"Close down the engines as soon as we're moored," he ordered.

Then he threw the rolled-up rope ladder from the doorway. Gripping the end of the mooring rope, he descended rapidly. He fastened it to a gatepost, and heard the engines above whine down.

He glanced around and saw that several of the monks were watching him placidly, as if the arrival of an airship was something they witnessed on a daily basis. There were a couple of novices also, who were having trouble controlling their reactions—a mixture of surprise, awe and a little fear. The only outsiders they usually saw were the occasional (very occasional!) travelers. Despite their interest, though, the novices stayed back. They had learned discipline as the first requirement of their calling.

Doc knew a smattering of Tibetan, learned from his previous visit to the monastery during his own training period, almost twenty years earlier.

"Is Sapan to be found?" he enquired.

One of the monks bowed slightly. "Master Sapan would be pleased to see his former pupil again," the man said serenely.

"I look forward to the reunion."

He glanced back and upwards as Jane descended the rope ladder quite rapidly. Fred followed her, but Biggles remained in the airship to keep an eye on things. It was probably only their training that prevented the monks from commenting on Jane. The novices had a harder time controlling their curiosity. None of them had seen a woman since they had joined the monastery, and none of them would ever have seen anyone quite like *this* woman before. Jane was tall and lithe, even in the bulky furs, quite unlike the shorter, stockier native females.

The monk who had spoken didn't even blink. "You are our guests," he said in a gentle voice. "If you will accompany me, there will be tea while I inform Master Sapan of your arrival."

"We would be honored to share tea with you," Doc replied.

The monk gestured towards two of the novices. One bowed deeply, and then moved off at an impatiently sedate pace. The other indicated a doorway, and led them through.

It was much warmer inside the building, out of the biting winds. Doc, Jane and Fred followed their guide to a reception room. Here were cushions on the floor surrounding a low wooden table. The novice gestured for them to sit, and the novice that had left earlier now returned, bearing three yellow scarves. He solemnly hung one around each of their necks, bowed and then both youngsters withdrew.

"As I mentioned, the gifting of a scarf is an important matter to the lamas," Doc explained.

Jane examined hers. "It's exquisite workmanship."

"They take great—I almost said *pride*, but that would be incorrect; perhaps *care* would be more appropriate." Doc touched his. "It is a symbol of the honor they hold visitors in."

Then one of the monks appeared, bearing a tray, on which were bowls containing rich, yellow liquid. "Please," he said. "Be welcome." He handed each of them a steaming bowl.

"Should I ask what this is?" Jane enquired. "Or are we supposed to simply drink it?"

"You should drink it," Doc replied. "It's simply tea, with butter melted in it. Yak butter. It's quite delicious, and another of their formal greetings."

Jane sipped hers and smiled politely at the monk. "You're right, it's very tasty. And quite welcome in this cold. Could you tell our host so for me?"

"There's no need," Doc informed her. "This is Padme— he speaks quite excellent English, and so already knows of your pleasure. We are old friends." He bowed his head. "It is most pleasant to see you again."

"It is also a pleasure to me, Francis," Padme answered. "I am glad that you have returned. You are following the flight of the hawk?"

"We are," Doc agreed.

"It passed over here a few hours ago," Padme said. "When your own vessel was observed, I was certain the hawk was the cause of your journey."

Doc nodded. "You were always most perceptive." He took the scarf they had found from his pocket and showed it to the monk. "This is our guide to their destination."

Padme inclined his head slightly. "Sapan will know what it means."

"Indeed." Doc finished his drink and glanced at Jane and Fred, who followed his lead in draining their bowls. "Is it possible to see him now?"

"He looks forward with much pleasure to speaking with you again, Francis. If you would all please follow me?" He glanced at Jane. "Women are not usually allowed into the heart of the lamasery," he said. "But you will be allowed as you accompany our good friend. But, please, I ask you—do not attempt to speak to any of the monks or novices. It may prove... disruptive."

Doc was expecting an outburst at this request, but Jane surprised him by smiling slightly. "I've been accused of a lot worse," she said. "Oh, sorry, shouldn't I have spoken to *you*?"

Padme merely inclined his head, and then moved to leave the room. Doc, Jane and Fred followed after him. Despite the passage of time, every step of their way was still firm in Doc's memory. The corridors were mostly bare, save for an occasional statue or prayer wheel. Rooms led off, most of them for prayer or contemplation. They saw monks from time to time, all of whom bowed slightly but otherwise ignored the visitors. Deeper into the complex they passed.

They reached the small room that served as Sapan's meeting place. The elderly monk was seated there on the floor, awaiting them as they arrived. Doc bowed respectfully, and his companions followed his lead.

"Greetings, Master Sapan."

"You are welcome here, as always," Sapan replied, indicating that they join him on the floor. "Knowing the path you have taken in your life, I imagine that there is some urgent need for this visit?"

Doc nodded and explained briefly. "So we are following the kidnappers, who left us this clue."

He passed over the prayer scarf. Sapan glanced at it.

"Clearly an invitation to step into a trap."

"Clearly."

"And yet you follow?"

"It would seem to be the simplest way to find those we seek—and the reason that they have been taken."

Sapan smiled slightly. "Your path would appear to lead you to the Shining Way monastery," he said. "This scarf is one of theirs—and one I had not expected to see again."

"Why is that?"

"Because the monastery has been closed for almost thirty years," Sapan explained. "It is high in the mountains, and the snows have made it all but inaccessible."

148

"That would be logical," Fred said, eagerly. "It makes a nice hideaway if the locals can't even reach it."

"But the great hawk can," Sapan commented. "It has flown and returned to the Shining Way three times in the past month."

"Three?" Doc was slightly surprised. "Everyone we have spoken to until now have only seen the hawk the one time."

"You should know by now, my friend, that there are ways and ways of seeing." Sapan handed back the scarf. "If those at the monastery were Tibetan—or simply Buddhist—then I would remind you that this scarf would be a safe conduct. But as they are not..."

"All bets are off," Fred muttered.

Sapan smiled slightly. "Indeed."

Doc could see that Jane was itching to speak, but he glared at her and she subsided. "Can you show us the path we must take to the Shining Way?"

"Padme will guide you," Sapan replied. He smiled again. "I imagine you will wish to be on your way."

"With your blessing."

"You have it, of course." Sapan glanced at Jane. "You are unusually silent for a woman."

Jane glared back at Doc. "I was... advised."

"Ah." He shook his head slightly. "A pity—it has been a while since I have spoken with a lady. Perhaps you would call again?"

"I should like that."

Jane bowed slightly and then gave Doc a very fake smile. As they followed Padme from the audience room, she muttered:

"Don't speak, eh?"

Doc shrugged. "Buddhist monks are not supposed to speak with women. You must have impressed Sapan somehow."

"Well, it wasn't my sparkling conversation."

Outside in the courtyard, Padme pointed to a tallish mountain in the distance. "The monastery you seek is about two-thirds of the way up the eastern side," he said. "I trust you will be careful."

"So do I," Doc agreed.

They took their leave of the monks, and rejoined Biggles in the airship.

"We have our target."

Biggles nodded, and started the motors up to full throttle.

Below them, the various novices and even some of the monks had gathered to watch them depart. It was clearly a great deal for any sort of external activity in this remote place. The air was thinner than at ground level, and it took a moment for the engines to fully fire. Two of the novices cast off the lines, which Fred and Jane reeled in, and Biggles turned the helm toward their destination.

Jane joined Doc. "You know, there's a lot of snow on that slope," she observed. "We don't all have to go in through the front door…"

"We would not be able to pause to drop anyone off," Doc replied. "This close to their lair, I am sure we are being kept under observation."

"If we were low enough, I could drop down into the snow without harm."

"That could prove very dangerous."

She shrugged. "If one didn't know what one was doing," she agreed. "I, however, do know what I'm doing."

Doc considered her suggestion. He believed her claim—while she wasn't exactly modest about her skills, neither did she overestimate them. And having a second string to his bow might prove to be very handy. On the other hand… he still couldn't quite wrap his mind around the idea of a young woman on her own being of any real use—even one as talented as Jane Clayton.

"Would it do me any good to reject the idea?" he finally asked.

She laughed. "That's a point you might want to discuss with my husband sometime," she suggested. "I'll go and get ready."

He had no idea what she had in mind, but he was clearly going to have to trust that she knew what she was doing. Biggles gave him a slightly nervous grin.

"She's a hard one to say no to."

"She does seem used to getting her own way," Doc agreed. "Do you think you could bring us fairly close to the ground at some point close by the monastery?"

Biggles judged the air flow. This high in the mountains, the winds were unpredictable.

"I can manage about thirty feet," he finally decided. "Any lower and we might find ourselves pushed down ourselves. Even though the gas bags are filled with helium and not hydrogen, a crash wouldn't do us any good." He scowled. "Do you think she can make it from that height?"

"We will have to trust her judgment," Doc replied. "While she takes risks, I don't think that they are uncalculated. She's got too good a head for that."

"Right-ho."

Biggles paid his attention to their course. Doc could see that he was unhappy, and shared that feeling. But Jane did have a point, that a second approach to the monastery would be helpful. He glanced at Fred, wondering if he might suggest that either he or Biggles join in Jane's attempt. But she had the skill for this, and they did not. Neither Fred nor Biggles were clumsy, but drooping thirty feet into a snowbank was outside their skill set.

He just hoped that she really *did* know what she was doing.

When she returned, he could discern no change in her at all. Whatever "get ready" meant, it wasn't obvious. But she didn't appear to be at all nervous. When Biggles mentioned she'd have to drop thirty feet, she simply nodded.

"Somewhere over there, I'd suggest," Biggles told her, gesturing. "That outcropping will shield us from view of the monastery for a few moments."

"That's good," she agreed.

As they approached, she grinned cheerfully at the others. "See you later."

And she simply stepped out of the cabin and dropped to the ground. When Doc looked back, she was nowhere to be seen.

"She'll make it," Fred said. "She's a heck of a woman."

"Now for our part," Doc replied, trying not to think what might happen to Jane. "With any luck, we may not need her assistance."

Their target was ahead of them now, as they flew slowly up the slope toward the rambling building. It might have been deserted years before, but it had been built to endure, and it would seem to be completely intact. Doc trained binoculars on the place, and caught some glimpses of movement, but no signs that they had even been seen. He didn't believe that this was the case for a moment.

"Doc," Biggles said, urgently. "Here's our quarry."

Moving around the slope of the mountain was the giant hawk that the witnesses had attempted to describe. It was above them, and clearly aiming to force them to commit to a landing. Doc watched it with a professional eye, and had to admire it.

It was slightly shorter than the dirigible—perhaps a hundred and twenty feet in all—but clearly constructed from some sort of metal. It did have the appearance of a hawk—a slender body and large outstretched wings—and there was some sort of windows where the eyes on a real bird would be. It moved slowly through the air, though he could see neither a gas bag nor engines that held it up or powered it. Whatever they were facing was sophisticated to the extreme. Whatever science powered it, it was one with which he was completely unfamiliar.

And now there was motion clearly visible at the monastery. The large gates had been thrown open, and a force of men was moving about. Several of them held rifles, though fairly casually, and none were aimed at the approaching airship. Yet. The hawk slipped through the sky until it was directly above the dirigible, and then it dropped a dozen feet.

The message was perfectly clear, and Doc nodded at Biggles to follow the order to land.

As they dropped, several people moved out, hands raised, and Fred dropped the mooring ropes to them. The workers gripped the ropes and fastened them to the uprights beside the main gates. These had probably been built to hold yaks, but they would suffice to keep the airship moored safely.

Biggles, with a sigh, shut down the engines. Fred threw out the rope ladder, and they clambered down to join the people below.

Some of them were obviously locals, but there were mostly Europeans in the small crowd. Four men with rifles moved forward. They held their weapons at the ready, but didn't actually point them at Doc and the others.

"Where's the girl?" their leader asked.

"We dropped her off," Biggles said—with reasonable honesty. "You didn't think we'd bring a woman into this, did you?"

The man scowled, and then shrugged.

"Right, follow me. The boss wants to see you, and he doesn't like to be kept waiting."

Either he'd accepted Biggles' story, or he simply didn't care. Doc thought this an interesting attitude.

The people who had gathered to see them arrive now began to disperse again. Doc noticed that two of the armed men stayed by the mooring ropes, clearly to ensure Doc and his friends didn't make a break for it. He glanced at the people in the small crowd. None of them seemed to be hostile, and a couple were even grinning. None of the kidnapped scientists were visible, though.

"It's obviously quite an operation, Doc," Fred muttered softly.

"Indeed," Doc agreed.

What puzzled him slightly was that none of these men—not even the ones with rifles—looked like criminals of any

153

kind. Doc had, over the course of his career, discovered that most criminals had a feral look about themselves, as if they were constantly picturing what they could steal from other people. Most of the faces in this crowd looked like ones you could find in the streets of any town in Europe or America. Most were clearly workers, some with their bearings suggesting that they were overseers. It was quite puzzling.

They entered the monastery, which looked pretty much like Det-sen—a sprawling, grey stone complex built into the side of the mountain. There were no prayer wheels or statues here, though—it was mostly bare surfaces, with a few mats on the floors. There were other people in the buildings, including a number of women. Again, a few were obviously locals, but most of them were not. The people they passed had only the vaguest interest in the newcomers, and were clearly occupied in their own affairs—whatever they might happen to be.

Again, it was more puzzling than enlightening. Their armed guides didn't seem to be particularly alert, and didn't point their weapons anywhere near Doc, Fred and Biggles. Doc could have taken them out in seconds, had he wished to. This was the oddest captivity he'd ever been in. He was looking forward to discovering the answers to all of his questions, as they were clearly being taken to somebody in charge.

"What do you make of this, Doc?" Fred asked under his breath.

"I'm not sure yet," Doc admitted. "But I imagine we're on our way to the answers."

He was rather surprised that they weren't ordered to be silent. A very strange captivity indeed.

They had climbed a couple of hundred feet in the passageways by now, and they were ushered into a room.

"You'll be met shortly," their guide informed them, and left the three of them alone.

Doc glanced around. The room had several large pillows scattered about, and a table with an urn of steaming tea and several delicate china cups. It was some twenty feet square, and the far wall was a large window looking out onto the

154

slopes below. Doc could see their airship and the still-hovering hawk down there. There were drapes hanging from ceiling to floor in several places about the remaining three walls.

"Doc," Biggles called.

When he had Doc's attention, he opened the door into the corridor.

"No locks, no guards…" he said. "What kind of prisoners are we?"

Doc shook his head. It was puzzling—and more than a little disturbing.

Fred snorted. "We're half-way up a mountain, there are no other buildings around and they have the dirigible. We don't have exactly very far to go, do we?"

"You are quite missing the point," a fresh voice broke in from the far side of the room.

Doc turned—there had been a door hidden behind one of the wall hangings. Holding back the drapes as he entered into the room was a quite imposing figure. He was tall and muscular, and appeared to be in his early fifties. His neat, dark beard was speckled with grey, as were the edges of his temples. He looked to be very fit, and had penetrating, hooded eyes. There was something of the hawk about this man.

"You are our captor, I take it?" Doc asked.

"My dear Doctor—no. I am your liberator."

"You'll forgive me if I find that… difficult to accept?"

The man laughed. "Of course," he agreed, readily. "But—do come and sit. It's so much more civilized to discuss matters over a pot of tea, don't you find?"

He lowered himself, cross-legged, onto one of the cushions and started to pour tea for them all from the urn.

"Introductions first," he said, handing the tea around. "You are Doctor Francis Ardan—I have long admired your work, my friend. And you are James Bigglesworth, but I do hope you allow me to call you Biggles."

He handed over a cup of tea. Biggles glanced at Doc, who had settled onto one of the cushions, and then followed suit. Finally, the man smiled at the suspicious Fred.

"And you are Fred. I'm afraid I don't know your last name."

Not many people did, as Fred never informed anyone of it.

"And you would be...?" Doc prompted.

"I am Robur."

Doc raised an eyebrow. "I find that difficult to accept. Robur died in 1903. If he had somehow survived, and you were he, then you would be about eighty years-old."

"That was my father," Robur replied. "He did indeed perish in the wreckage of his *Terror*."

"I see."

Things were starting to make sense to Doc now. Robur had once been the most brilliant of inventors, initially creating an unprecedented airship—the *Albatross*—powered by electricity, and capable of staying aloft almost indefinitely. After this was destroyed, he had created the *Terror*, a super-vessel that travelled on land, sea and in the air at amazing speeds. Neither vessel had been duplicated, even to this day. But Robur's brilliance had been matched by bouts of insanity, and he had taken the *Terror* to its destruction in one such fit, challenging the powers of nature—and losing.

"And that hawk-ship down below?"

"My modification of his original concepts," the younger Robur explained. "My father was a brilliant inventor, but his mind was more than a trifle unstable. Possessed by his plans to remake this world, he had abandoned my mother and I in one of his fits. When he regained his senses for a while, he contacted us, and left directions for us to meet with him again. Sadly, his illness recurred, and he perished before we could be reunited. But we were able to make our way to his hidden workshops, which were filled with half-developed wonders. I am—in some ways—my father's son, and I was able to complete some of his visions. Including the *Hawk* below, yes." He smiled. "I look forward to showing you how it operates; I am certain you will find it most fascinating."

"This is an odd way to treat your prisoners," Biggles commented.

"Prisoners?" Robur shook his head. "My dear sir, you are mistaken—you are not prisoners." He gestured to the door. "That is not locked, and no one will stop you if you choose to leave. Have I or any of my men threatened you, or offered any kind of compulsion to you at all? No, you are invited guests who followed my little challenge—quite neatly, I might add."

"And what about Doctor Omega and Abner Perry?" Fred demanded. "They were certainly not offered any choice about accompanying you."

Robur looked a trifle embarrassed. "Ah, well, there you have me," he confessed. "I am being driven by the needs of time, and didn't have the luxury of explaining to them why they were required. But they will be offered the same choice that I give to you."

"And that is?" Doc asked.

"Hear my plans and then decide whether or not to join me in my crusade."

Doc didn't need to consider the offer for a moment—it was clear that Robur wished them willingly to join him in whatever his scheme was, and that the man preferred persuasion over imprisonment.

"Very well," he agreed. "We will listen. Feel free to explain."

Robur hesitated. "If you're agreeable, I should prefer to do so over dinner in a few hours. Your missing friends will be present, and I can explain to you all at the same time, and then you can confer together."

Doc nodded. "That seems reasonable," he agreed.

Robur stood up and extended his hand to shake Doc's. "Until dinner, then," he said. "Incidentally, I understand that Lady Greystoke is no longer with your party?"

"No."

He shook his head. "A pity. Our men do outnumber our women by a considerable margin, and she would have been a useful as well as attractive addition to our numbers."

Biggles smiled slightly. "She is a married lady," he said. "And appears to take her marital vows quite seriously. Perhaps she wouldn't have been quite as useful as you imagined."

"We do not subscribe to conventional morality in our refuge," Robur replied. "She might have found the attention… appealing."

He nodded and then left the room.

"She might not."

It was Jane's voice, from behind the window drapes. She jumped lithely to the floor, grinning.

"If you ask me, his father wasn't the only batty one in the family."

Doc was relieved to see that she was obviously well, but he kept his delight private. "I'm reserving judgment on that matter until I have further information."

Jane poured herself a cup of tea. "It's rather cool outside." She hugged the cup comfortingly. "Not the place, really, for a jungle girl." She grinned again. "It's good to see you chaps again."

"Likewise," Biggles said. "Did you hear all of that, then?"

"Most of it. It took me a while to climb the outside walls. I'm not used to doing everything wearing furs." She opened her coat. "Mind you, it's quite warm in this place, so I might be able to discard it for the time being. So, what are your plans, Doc?"

"Dinner," he said, firmly. "Robur junior has promised that Doctor Omega and Abner Perry will be present, so that will save us from having to seek them out. Besides, I confess a desire to hear what our non-captor has in mind."

"He sounds as nutty as a fruitcake to me, Doc," Biggles admitted. "His plans may not make a lot of sense."

"Well, we'll find out later," Doc said.

"Meanwhile," Jane added, "I'll stay hidden—just in case—and back up whatever play you may need to make." She frowned slightly. "Me—after attention! Perish the thought. As if anyone here could match John..." She glanced up. "Ah, no insult implied, chaps."

"And none taken," Doc assured her.

In fact, he was rather relieved that she was so obviously devoted to her husband. If she had taken a shine to any of the three of them, it could have been a serious problem...

As there was nothing they could do for the moment, they all rested and waited. Doc considered testing the limits to Robur's promises by exploring the monastery, but decided against it. It seemed to be more fruitful simply to wait and see if Robur would provide the revelations that he had promised.

It was some three hours later that there was a gentle rapping on the door. Jane bolted behind the drapes, and Fred opened the door. There was a young woman there, dressed in local clothing, although she was clearly an American by her accent.

"Time for chow," she announced.

Doc, Fred and Biggles followed her as she led them back through the way they had come before turning off into a corridor that led to a fairly sizeable hall. Doc guessed that it had been the monks' dining hall when this had still been a monastery. Now it served a similar function, though with a mixed group. As Robur had mentioned, the men outnumbered the women quite substantially.

It was clear that they were from many different countries. There was a preponderance of Westerners, but there were also a fair number of Asians and a lesser number of Africans. All appeared to be of equal status, though, with those seated and those waiting on the tables being similarly of mixed races. There was a strong scent of stew and the delightful scent of freshly baked bread, which proved to be the main courses.

Doc and his friends were led to a large table that was headed by Robur.

"Fred!"

Doctor Omega leaped to his feet, grinning, and clasped his friend's hand.

"And Doc Ardan! A pleasure to see you both. Indeed, a pleasure! And do introduce me to your young friend."

While Fred introduced Biggles, Doc saw that there was another elderly scientist beside Doctor Omega, and recognized him as Abner Perry.

Doc greeted the old man, who seemed somewhat bemused by what was happening. The other missing scientists were nowhere to be seen, however, which worried Doc somewhat.

Beside their host was a stocky, muscular man in his late thirties. Like Robur, he was neatly bearded, and had deep-set eyes. Other than that, there was no resemblance between the two men.

Robur gestured to him.

"Permit me to introduce Sergei Zattan—my invaluable right-hand man."

Doc nodded, and Sergei nodded back.

"Now, sit and eat—yak stew, a local specialty. Our cooks prepare it remarkably well, I assure you."

Doc followed the invitation and discovered that Robur was correct—the food was delicious. He hadn't realized how hungry he had been until he started to eat. The bread was fresh and doughy, absolutely splendid. To drink he was offered spring water or yak milk, which was thick and buttery.

"You did promise us an explanation," he finally reminded their host.

"Indeed I did," Robur agreed, laughing. "Look about you, my friend—do you find this scene convivial?"

"It appears most egalitarian," Doc answered.

Robur nodded. "Nice and no-committal. To be expected. Yes, everyone here is equal."

"But some are more equal than others?" Biggles asked.

"We are not communists," Robur replied. "Yes, some of us have positions of authority, but that is because we have specific skills in certain fields, and not because we are inherently any better than our fellow men." He waved his hand. "What you see here is a model of what we wish the world to become."

"A utopian society?" Biggles inquired. "It has been tried before, you know—and found lacking."

"I understand and accept your skepticism, my friend," Robur said, equably. "But—you are all realists. Take a look around this room—is it not something to be desired in the world at large? Here the color of a man's skin is not as important as the content of his heart, and what is in his mind is the most important thing of all."

"You both make good points," Doc said. "But I would prefer to learn why you have been kidnapping scientific minds."

"I am coming to that," their host/captor answered. "I am sure you all have looked at the societies you live in with equal attention. And I am certain that you must see that we are heading into another war—one that will be more terrible, more lethal and more destructive than the so-called Great War of 1914 to 1918."

"There are good people seeking to prevent another such devastation from occurring," Doctor Omega pointed out.

"And what sort of a chance do they stand?" Robur enquired. "Germany is rebuilding its armed forces, and it is inching towards totalitarianism. As my friend Sergei here can tell you, Russia, too, is preparing to expand its borders through warfare. Britain is occupied with increasing the size of its armed forces, and America is constructing a fleet to be loosed in the Pacific Ocean. Japan occupies Korea and Manchuria. Need I go on? It doesn't take a soothsayer to realize that the world is heading for war. Yes, I grant you that there are men of goodwill and peace—but they are out-matched by those who favor war. I tell you, a greater conflagration is on the horizon."

"Perhaps so," Doc agreed, uneasily. "But—even if we grant you the possibility of another war—what has this to do with kidnappings?"

"Because the next war will be one that will involve the entire planet. Greedy men in charge of so many countries wish for fresh territories, resources and power. They will band together to attack those they feel are weaker and susceptible to conquest. And these men at war are developing more numerous and devastating weapons. As a result, the next war will wipe out many millions, and lay waste to huge sectors of the world. I can even foresee that there is the possibility of weapons of almost infinite force being utilized. Several of the great minds I have gathered say that it may one day be possible to harness the very energies that bind atoms and molecules together in forces of such destruction as to terrify even the bravest of men."

"The power of the atom?" Doc nodded. "I have heard speculation on that concept from a man called Jimgrim..."

"You're a well-educated man, Ardan," Robur said. "No doubt you have heard that such atomic fires could ignite the very atmosphere about our planet, and burn this planet to a cinder?"

"Of course—but that is merely supposition."

"Are you willing to gamble the future of the human race on the belief that is may *not* happen?" Robur shook his head. "No, I say that we have to act as though this were the inevitable outcome of such a destructive force. So that the human race might not perish from this universe of ours, we *have* to take the threat seriously."

Doc paused. "If we do, then we have to admit that the human race would be burned from the face of this planet."

Robur's face was filled with ecstasy. "Precisely! *From the face of this planet*! But not necessarily from the *depths* of this planet."

"What do you mean?"

Robur flung his arms wide. "Why do you imagine I chose *this* place for my life's work?" he asked. "The ancients

162

called this place *The Roof of the World* because almost every human being on this planet lives at lower altitudes." He gestured around again. "I propose to dig a refuge for the chosen few out of the solid rock of these ancient mountains—to burrow down and seal ourselves within. Then, when the atomic conflagration strikes, it will burn over the surface of the world, but leave us untouched in the depths."

He turned to Abner Perry.

"You see why we need you, then? With your Iron Mole, you can do the burrowing for us, open up the inside of the mountain for us."

He turned to Doctor Omega.

"And your invention of the amazing substance stellite will also prove to be invaluable. Its ability to shield us from space and time will enable us to accumulate the light and energy we will need to stay buried until such time as the Earth above us has recovered, and we—or our children—may emerge and reclaim the surface of our world once more."

Doc stared at the man. "It is an audacious plan," he admitted. "But one that may be completely unnecessary."

"It *may*," Robur admitted. "But would you gamble with the future—the very existence—of the human race on that word *may*?" He shook his head. "I am not willing to take such a chance. Neither are my friends assembled here. We will be the stock from which the human race may be rebuilt. And you are all invited to join us in this venture. You are a scientist and engineer almost without peer, and would be of great assistance to us. And your two friends are courageous and would be most welcome. So, I beg you all—agree to work with us in order to save the human race from its premature extinction. What do you all have to say, then?"

Abner Perry coughed into his hand. "I—ah, well—I'm afraid that I have to say no. It's not that I don't think your aims are admirable," he added hastily. "It's simply that I have urgent business elsewhere that I cannot ignore."

Robur stared at him in surprise. "More important than saving the human race? What could possibly be more important?"

Perry shook his head. "That I cannot tell you," he replied. "But—believe me—even if this super-weapon you describe does somehow annihilate the surface of our world—it will not destroy the human race. And that is all that I can tell you."

Robur was clearly shaken by this, but he turned, pleading, to Doctor Omega. "You, at least, will join us in this endeavor, surely?"

"My dear fellow," the Doctor answered, "you really have no idea of the dangers that are posed by attempting to harness the power of stellite. One small slip, one slight miscalculation, and your band of survivors could easily be wiped out. I have abandoned using the material myself because of the frightful danger it poses. No, my friend, you must look elsewhere for your power source."

His face a mask of worry and confusion, Robur turned to Doc. "And what of you and your friends?"

"What you propose is admirable," Doc said slowly. "But it is not my way to retreat and hide from an upcoming battle. War is inevitable, you say? I fear that you may well be correct in your analysis of the world situation. But I cannot bring myself to believe that the optimal solution is to build a retreat *from* the world, but to attempt to *save* that world. I must face the situation as it is, and do my best to ameliorate it."

Biggles nodded. "My loyalty is to England," he said. "If she's in danger, then I have to stand ready to help out."

"But this cause is far greater than mere nationalism," Robur protested. "It is for all of humanity."

"It seems to me," Fred said, "that the best way to help the whole of humanity is to help whatever small portion of it we can. Like Biggles here, my loyalty is to my native France first."

Robur looked from one to the other in despair, and then finally shook his head in bewilderment. "I had expected better of you all," he confessed. "I thought that you would be able to see the strength of my vision, and its utter necessity. But if you cannot… Then you are free to leave. I shall have to attempt a different solution."

"No!" Sergei cried, springing to his feet. "Robur, these men are absolutely necessary to our plans. We cannot save humanity without them. They cannot be simply allowed to desert us." His eyes narrowed. "Besides, what is to prevent them from telling everyone of our plans? The governments of their petty, insular countries would never allow our project to go forward—they would see it as a revolution against their corrupt and warlike regimes."

"My friend, we cannot compel them to remain." Robur shook his head. "If we did that, we would be no better than those foul governments."

"Robur, this is about *survival*!" Sergei exclaimed. "We cannot back down from this."

Their host shook his head again. "No, my friend, we will not employ brutality and slavery to achieve our goals. What you suggest goes against everything that we believe in. Men must be free to make their own decisions—even when we disagree with their conclusions."

"This is not a polite debating society," Sergei snapped. "We are facing the extinction of mankind, and that I will not allow. Nothing—not even your high ideals—will matter if the human race is wiped out. After we survive, we can discuss what the fresh world will be like. But we *must* survive."

"Everyone must be free to follow the dictates of their consciences," Robur insisted. "It may be that these men may come to see the errors of their ways before the inevitable end. They may then return to aid us."

"*May?*" Sergei shook his head. "Oh, no, Robur—we cannot stake the very future of humanity on such a small, powerless word. For the sake of survival, we must impose out will."

"I will not allow it," Robur replied, angrily.

"Then you, too, must be compelled."

Sergei Zattan drew a revolver from his pocket, and pointed it at Robur. More than two dozen men sprang to their feet also, each of them holding pistols or rifles. Doc realized that the Russian had planned ahead for this moment.

"What is the meaning of this?" Robur exclaimed in shock. "Put those guns down immediately."

"We are no longer following your path," Sergei replied. "For the sake of humanity, we do what we must."

"The mark of all tyrants at any time in history," Doctor Omega stated. "When you allow your goals to outstrip your morality, you simply replace one evil with another."

"Be silent," Sergei ordered. "You are hereby conscripted into the army of the future. You are to work to ensure the survival of the human race."

"You may be able to compel us to remain using those weapons," Perry said. "But you cannot force us to work for you. What will you do—shoot us? But you *need* us."

Sergei shook his head. "We do not need *all* of you. If you do not agree to work for us, we are quite prepared to kill the superfluous amongst you."

"Sergei, come to your senses!" Robur pleaded. "This is no way to ensure the future we envisioned."

"It is the *only* way," Sergei answered coldly. "And you had better come to see that, Robur, for you have placed yourself amongst the disposable."

"You would turn against me, after all our time together?"

"You have left me no choice," Sergei answered. "To preserve our plan, this is the only way forward."

He turned back to face Doc and the others again.

"Will you join us willingly, or shall I be forced to compel you all?"

Doc considered the possibility of jumping the man, but he knew that it would be pointless. Even if he could take Sergei out, the other armed men wouldn't simply stand by.

"You are making a grave error," he stated. "Robur is correct—you cannot build a good society on bad foundations."

Sergei sighed. "Then you force me to use compulsion," he stated.

He turned his revolver towards Biggles. "You are the least valuable to us, I think…"

He raised the weapon to fire.

And gasped slightly. There was suddenly an arrow buried deep into his breast. He looked down at it in bewilderment, as his life-blood pumped from his split heart, and then he crashed down, dead.

The suddenness of this had shocked his companions for an instant. Another started to aim his pistol, and went down with a second arrow directly through his heart.

Doc glanced at Biggles and Fred, and the three of them went into action. The main body of the men and women in the room had been sitting, confused and undecided by what had been occurring, but they now understood that their lives were in danger. Most panicked, crashing to their feet and heading for the nearest exits. The men with guns were ignored, and even battered aside by the fleeing people. Doc and his companions waded into them, punching and disarming the men. Some of the gunmen, seeing the bodies of Sergei and the other man, threw down their weapons and fled with the general throng.

Out of the corner of his eye, Doc caught a glimpse of Jane, dressed in her hunting gear, her bow in hand and an arrow nocked and ready to fire should it be needed. But the gunmen were demoralized and leaderless. More went down to well-placed blows, and the final few simply threw aside their guns and raised their hands in surrender.

It was all over in a few short minutes. Doc, Fred and Biggles collected the discarded weapons and tossed them into a pile on one of the tables beside a still-steaming pot of stew. Jane slipped the arrow back into its quiver and the bow over her shoulder as she joined them.

"Thank you for your assistance," Doc said.

"I'll say!" Biggles agreed, enthusiastically. "But aren't you cold, dressed like that?"

"Just watching you lads fight warmed my heart," she replied, grinning. "Though I shall have to find my furs soon, I think."

"Jane!" Abner Perry said, happily. "It is so good to see you again."

He gave her a huge hug, and she laughed.

"Try not to crush me," she suggested.

"I think you're far too tough for an old man like me to injure."

Biggles tapped Doc's arm, and pointed to where Robur was still seated, looking confused and dejected.

"What are we going to do with him?" he asked.

"Do?" Doc shook his head. "Nothing. He is not really a villain, is he?"

"No, but he's had a rude awakening."

"Yes, quite." Doc went over to the would-be savior of the world. "What will you do now?" he asked, gently.

"Do?" Robur shook his head. "What is there *to* do?" He gestured at the fallen. "Men I thought believed in my plans attempted to overthrow and perhaps even kill me. My plans are in ruins. I am a fool and a knave."

"You, young man," Doctor Omega put in, "are an idealist—and you've run head-first into reality." He chuckled. "But that doesn't mean that your vision is entirely mistaken, you know. The vast majority of your people appear to support your ideals, you know. They will be back."

"You may need to rethink and recalculate a little," Doc added, "but I am sure that you will think of a different way ahead. And there will be those who will be just as inspired by your vision. I am truly sorry that we don't share it—but, as you said, it may be that you will be proven ultimately correct, and that we are wrong."

"You think so?" Robur looked hopeful.

"I do," Doc said. "Stay here and work for your vision. It may prove to be essential to this world. Meanwhile, my companions and I will go out into the world again to fight for what we believe in." He held out his hand. "Goodbye—friend."

"And the best of British luck," Biggles added.

Robur reached out and grasped the offered hand. "Will you be able to reach civilization again?"

"I think we can, even with a few extra passengers." He raised his voice slightly. "Come along, friends—we'd better get started back."

Jane laughed. "I'd better get my furs again," she said. "You know, I can't tell you how much I am looking forward to getting back to the jungle again."

She smiled at Robur. "No offense, but you can keep your snows and hawk's nest; I'm going after the sun."

Once again, Jean-Marc inspired this story, this time by sending me a copy of Etienne de Lamothe-Langon's The Virgin Vampire *(1825) (available from Black Coat Press), the novel that Alinska appeared in. I was intrigued by this tale of love, betrayal and revenge. And, of course, this led to my penning this tale.*

Blood Calls for Blood

The Suffolk Downs, England, 1827

Sarah hesitated by the cottage door, considering her actions for the final time. She was, at the last moment, suddenly desperately afraid of doing something foolish. It wasn't her desire for revenge that bothered her, but the horrible thought that she might have been misinformed—or even deliberately lied to—and that the old woman wasn't what Sarah had been led to believe. To come this far, only to be made a fool of—*that* would be too much.

The cottage itself wasn't much—old, even by local standards, with the thatch clearly in need of repair in places. The whitewash on the walls and the paint on the wood were chipped, but the garden was very tidy. There were rows and patches of herbs and flowers, most of which she didn't know. There was a row of fruit trees over to one side, and a spread of vegetables growing. It looked like the cottage of any old woman who was conscientious but lacking in money.

It didn't look like the cottage of a witch woman.

Then again, what *would* the cottage of a witch woman look like? Sarah was in front of the door, but still she hesitated. If she could only be *sure...*

"Come in, m'dearie," a strong voice called to her. Sarah started, but she saw that a window beside the door was slightly ajar, which explained the volume of the voice. And the old

170

woman had undoubtedly seen her coming up the pathway. Well, now that the woman knew she was here, she might as well enter.

Inside the cottage was similar to the garden—in need of a lick of paint, a little work, but basically clean and orderly. There were stems and flowers of plants hanging drying from the rafters, and old glass jars containing powders and foodstuffs scattered across shelves that had long since departed from their horizontal origins. It was a trifle dark indoors, despite a small fire burning in the hearth, but she could plainly make out that there was just the single main room that was for living, cooking and storage, and then on the far side a single door led to a small bedroom. It wasn't much, but it was clearly sufficient for the old woman who sat in a large chair beside a table. She was engaged in shelling a large pile of peas.

The woman indicated a second chair at the table. "Sit yourself down, m'girl," she said, kindly. "It's lovely to have a visitor. Don't mind me, don't mind me." She went on shelling the peas.

Feeling somewhat foolish, Sarah nervously sat on the edge of the seat. It wobbled slightly, but then stabilized. *How to begin? Should she just come right out and ask the old lady if she was a witch? But that might get her laughed at—or even a justifiably angry retort. After all, an old lady living alone wasn't necessarily anything other than an old lady living alone...*

There was a slight movement in the shadows beside the fire. Sarah glanced at it, and saw that it was a black cat that yawned, stretched and then settled back to sleep. But even owning a black cat didn't *really* mean anything—did it?

Plunging ahead, she said: "People tell me—"

"Oh, I'm sure people tell you a lot of things," the old woman said, mildly. "Primarily how beautiful you are, I imagine."

That burned where it hurt, of course. "Yes," Sarah agreed, gritting her teeth. "They have said that."

171

"Ah!" The old woman's eyes were twinkling in the dim firelight. "One man in particular, no doubt? One *faithless* man."

She seemed to be able to see into Sarah's soul, and that gave her the courage—and anger—to plunge on. "People tell me that you have... abilities."

"Oh, I'm sure they don't," the woman contradicted her, gently. "I'm sure they tell you that I'm an old witch." She smiled. "Let us be blunt, m'dearie—that *is* why you came to see me, and not because you've taken pity on an old lady's loneliness." Sarah started to protest, but the woman waved it away. "Oh, I'm used to that, m'girl. I know what I know, and there's no use fretting over what can't be changed. Let's get back to you, shall we? You're here for revenge."

Sarah was startled. "How can you know that?"

"I'm a witch, m'dearie, remember?" The old woman laughed. "But it's simpler than my using supernatural powers. People come to me for three things. First—" she ticked it off on a gnarled finger, "for money." She eyed Sarah up and down. "And from the look of your lovely dress and those expensive rings on your fingers, that's not something you're in want of. Second—"—another finger—"for love. Again, as I've already said, you're uncommon beautiful, so you've no doubt more men flittering around you than flies around horse shit. So that leaves third—revenge."

"You're right," Sarah agreed, quietly.

"I know I'm right, m'dearie—I can always tell in these matters. So, it must be someone rich and powerful." She smiled again. "If it weren't, you could get one of your legion of admirers to help you out, no doubt. The fact you've come to me says that this person is too powerful for you to handle in your own fashion. I'm sure I know who it is already, but I'll ask you to name the name yourself, if you wouldn't mind obliging an old lady."

Sarah knew she was being outmaneuvered, something she wasn't used to, but she had little choice left her now. "Lord Arden."

The old woman chuckled. "And who else would it be?" she asked. "Lord Arden." She suddenly stared at Sarah over the bowl of peas, a cold, hard glance that chilled her through. "You don't imagine you're the first girl to come to me asking for help to hurt him, do you? There's been quite a parade of them, you know. He's got quite an eye for the pretty ones—though I will admit as how you're prettier than most. But revenge costs you, you know, and not everyone can pay."

"I can pay any price you name," Sarah said. She pulled a garnet ring off her finger. "This is worth—"

"Oh, I know what that's worth, m'dearie, I know it right well. Down to the penny, if truth be told." She shook her head. "But that's just *money*—it's not *payment*." She held up a hand to stave off Sarah's protest. "Oh, I'm not saying I wouldn't be grateful for a few coppers, m'girlie." She eyed the ring as it lay in Sarah's hand. "But what would I do with that?"

"You could sell it," Sarah suggested. "It would enable you to live better than this."

The woman laughed. "But I *like* this," she said, mildly. "And can you imagine what they'd say if I took that to some jeweler's shop, hey? Call me a thief, like as not, and try to throw me into jail."

"Then I'll give you money." Sarah reached for her purse, but the old woman waved that away.

"Leave me a handful of coins when you go," she said, "and I promise I'll be happy. But that's still not *payment*."

"Then what is it that you want?" Sarah cried, frustrated.

"Blood calls for blood," the old lady said simply.

"Blood?" Sarah smiled faintly. "I'd gladly give all that I have. My life is worthless, meaningless now. I would cheerfully give my life to end his."

"That is more like it," a fresh voice said—a cold, hard voice with a faintly foreign tinge to it. Sarah whirled around in her seat and saw a third person was now in the room, standing beside the fire. She had evidently scared away the cat, which was nowhere to be seen. Sarah stared at the woman, who was the most beautiful creature she had ever seen. Men called *her* beautiful, and they knew they spoke the truth—but, compared to this woman, she was a pale imposter. The stranger was tall and lithe, her form exquisite, her face a wonder. She looked a trifle pale in the wan firelight, but other than that was quite magnificent.

"Who—who are you?" she asked.

"I am Alinska," the woman replied, simply. Then she glared at the old witch. "I had hoped to be at rest, but that, it would seem, has been denied me."

The old woman smiled gently. "You have a task assigned to you," she said, as if reminding the foreign woman of something she should have known along. "You have not yet been given leave to rest from it."

Alinska sighed, and shook her head. Then she turned to Sarah and raised her left hand—which alone was clad in a long, dark glove. "Revenge is a bitter taskmaster," she said. "I serve a cold, hard God of vengeance, and that is who you call to. Be very certain you are willing to pay His price. Blood calls for blood."

Sarah steeled herself. "I am willing to pay whatever price is required of me," she said firmly. "Up to and including my life."

Alinska sighed again. "Very well; the payment is acceptable. You have a contract with my implacable God, and I am his agent on this transient world. I will do whatever it is you require of me. Tell me, then, what it is that you wish."

"I seek rightful vengeance on Lord Arden," Sarah said, forcefully.

Alinska inclined her head slightly. "Perhaps you had better tell me your tale," she suggested. "I need to understand this desire of yours, and to be certain that it falls within the duties assigned to me."

Sarah gathered her thoughts, forcing her hatred down for a while. "It began with Caroline—my best friend growing up. Our families were close, and she and I were closer. I had no siblings, but she was a sister—and better than a sister—to me. No two people could have been closer." She glanced at the old woman. "You called me beautiful, and that is true enough, but I am pale beside Caroline. *She* was truly resplendent, and with a heart that was generous and loving. We swore oaths of eternal friendship as children and were inseparable then and until her marriage.

"I am not poor by any means, but Caroline inherited great wealth when she turned eighteen. She went on the Grand Tour of Europe—I was to have accompanied her, but at the final moment I came down with an illness that laid me abed for several months. Caroline wished to delay the trip, but couldn't, and so she took along another of our friends. I, at least, could write, and Caroline kept me up to date with what was happening to her in numerous letters that we exchanged.

"It was in Venice that she first mentioned Lord Arden, and then, after that, references to him came thick and fast. He accompanied the party to Austria, and by the time Caroline returned to England, the pair were engaged.

"You must understand that he feigns concern and compassion with great skill. At the first, I did not suspect his true nature. When I first met him, I saw only how handsome he was, how caring toward my friend, and how passionately he appeared to be in love with her. When they wed, I rejoiced that Caroline had found such happiness. For a while, all appeared to be perfect. Then Caroline had a child, a daughter, and it all collapsed. My friend suffered through childbirth—her body was too weak, it seemed—and before I could realize it, she was upon her deathbed.

"I was devastated, but Caroline was stronger than I. She extracted from me an oath that I would care for her daughter—also named Caroline—and be as a mother toward her. I gladly agreed to this, and it is a promise I have never regretted making. Caroline the younger is like a true daughter to me, and I feel that we could not be closer were I her true mother. Lord Arden happily gave his consent to this arrangement—at the time I thought he wished the best for his child, but I was later to discover that he covets only a son to inherit his name, estate and fortune, and that he was glad that someone else should take over the care and raising of a daughter he had no affection for.

"Still, as Caroline resided with her father, it meant that I was thrown into his company a great deal. He showed me great attention, made many flattering remarks and eventually confessed to me that he loved me. I—weak and foolish fool that I am—believed everything. I *wished* to believe, for I had fallen in love with him. As I said, he is a handsome man, and feigns affection and concern with ease.

"And so it was that I made my fatal mistake. My dear friend Caroline had been dead but eighteen months, and he said that he wished to marry me, but that sufficient time had not elapsed since his wife's death for propriety's sake. He swore, over and again, that he intended to wed me, and I allowed myself to be seduced by him."

Alinska held up a hand. "You say he swore he would marry you? I must be clear on this point."

"Better than swore," Sarah assured her. "His house has a small chapel attached to it, and he took me into it. Before the altar of God, he made a solemn vow he would marry me."

"Ah." Alinska cocked her head to one side, as if she were hearing a voice that was meant for her alone. "It is as you say," she agreed. "In which case, I am granted leave—no, in which case I am compelled—to wreak vengeance on your behalf. But, please, continue your tale."

"I *wanted* to believe him," Sarah continued. "I was weak, and gave in."

"Many of our sex do the same," Alinska said, coldly. "You are not the first, and I am certain you will not be the last to allow false words to persuade you to an action you now regret."

"Perhaps not, but that does not excuse me." Sarah gathered her thoughts. "I went to his bed, gladly at that time. I thought myself the happiest of women, and that I possessed the kindest and gentlest of men. But then…" Sarah shook as she continued. "I discovered him with a woman I supposed my friend, in an intimate moment. Furious, betrayed, I confronted him.

"He merely laughed at me. When I spoke of our engagement, he denied it. He actually told me that it had been nothing more than a ploy to seduce me and that he had no intentions of marrying me—that he was, in fact, engaged to wed yet another woman. He told me that he would have barred me from his house if it were not for the fact that his daughter required the services of a guardian." Sarah lowered her head. "I suspect I went a little crazy then. I began to see him as he truly was—a vain and selfish man, caring only for his own needs and pleasures. The wedding to Caroline had brought him her fortune, and the new marriage he intends will more than double it. Though I have money, it is of much less degree, and he never intended to marry me. He merely wished to pleasure himself."

He has treated you abominably," Alinska agreed. "And he has taken lightly a vow that should have been sacred. I am empowered—nay, *compelled*—to serve justice on all oath-breakers. He has now become my prey."

Sarah smiled for the first time. "What will you do?"

"I shall act as I see fit," the foreign woman replied. "You are still allowed at his home?"

"I look after little Caroline," Sarah said. "She is all that I have left that I care for in this world. He wishes to have nothing to do with her, and is glad to leave her in my care."

"Then go about your life as you have in the past," Alinska said, firmly. "Fulfill your sworn duties to the child. I shall work upon Lord Arden in my own way. I shall be calling upon him shortly. When I do, you must act as if we are strangers to one another. You do not know me, and I shall not know you. Do not be surprised at anything that happens from now on, no matter how strange or dire it may seem to you. Once you have stepped upon the path to vengeance, you must see the journey through to the bitter end—and the end is always bitter. Remember, I have warned you—blood calls for blood. Payment will be required of you, too."

"I am ready," Sarah promised. "I will suffer what I must, only that he suffers first and greatly."

"So be it," Alinska said. "And so it begins..."

Lord Arden stiffened as he entered his morning room and saw that Sarah was already there. "God's blood, woman," he growled, "what are you doing here, you steaming great pile of misery?"

"I am here out of duty," the woman replied, in her inevitable prim manner. "I am here for your daughter—she needs *someone* to care for her."

Arden considered the coffee, but decided he needed something stronger to enable him to deal with this bitch so early in the day. He poured himself a brandy, looked at her again and made it a double. "Then care for her and leave me in peace, you harpy," he snapped.

She looked almost amused. "Is your conscience troubling you, my lord?"

"*You* are troubling me," he informed her. "You always do. Why can't you wed and set about irritating another man?"

"You know the answer to that well enough," she replied coldly. "You deflowered me and made me unacceptable to any other man."

"Nonsense," he said. "You're still a fairly attractive package—I'm sure there must be dozens of men stupid enough to look no further and take you for that alone—without even considering your money."

"And on the wedding night they would discover I am a ruined woman," Sarah said. "I would be shamed all over again."

"For God's sake, you stupid cow, you could simply lie to them and tell them you're a widow! That would explain your... condition. I'd be more than happy to back up your story. It would be worth a little lie to be rid of you at last."

As usual, she fell back on her petty morality. "Lies again—well, I'd expect no less from you. As if I'd take your word for anything after what it cost me the last time."

"The *last time* cost you only your imaginary virtue and, as I recall, gave you considerable pleasure at the time." She had, in fact, been quite voracious between the sheets. If he didn't know what a great bore she was, he might have been tempted to try and repeat the pleasure.

"A few moments of pleasure, which I pay with by years of regret and torment."

"By your own choice, woman," he growled. "If you chose, you could enjoy yourself at any time, instead of flagellating yourself over sins committed before an imaginary God."

"You'd *have* to believe Him imaginary, considering the way you take His name in vain. As you did when you vowed before His holy altar to wed me."

He smiled at her, pleased with that particular trick. It had worked on more than just her. "The pursuit of pleasure is what is most important in this life," he replied. "Any stratagem to achieve that end is moral as far as I am concerned. You women need your petty reassurances to gratify your trembling morality, but in the end you enjoy the carnal as much as any man."

"But there is always payment to be made," Sarah answered.

"And always fresh pursuits," he countered. "Which reminds me—I have a visitor coming this morning. I would prefer it if you weren't around when she arrives."

"Another poor victim of your seductions?" she asked, coldly.

"Perhaps—who can say? But in this case it is a new neighbor, one I've not met before. She is, I believe, a Hungarian, and she has rented Broughton Hall." Not a cheap lodging! "It implies she has money, and my valet reports she is far from unattractive. So I do not need you about dispensing your stinking dollops of misery. If you must be with my daughter, take her out into the grounds or something."

"You might see more of her—your daughter, I mean," Sarah suggested.

"I have no interest in her," Arden answered, honestly. "I have nothing against her—I clothe and pay for her, and, no doubt, one day I shall have to find a husband for her. Beyond that, what do you expect of me?"

"Of *you*?" Sarah gave a brittle laugh. "I expect precisely what I get—selfishness and a lack of any true feeling. Would it kill you to *love* the child? She is the image of your departed wife."

"Who, as you so correctly phrase it, is *departed*. Would that her child was, too." Struck by a thought, he said: "How would you like an incentive? You have some affection for the girl—how about I find you some foolish Lord or other peer to wed, and I'll even give you the girl, tell the fool she's your child. That way we should both be happy, and I'd be rid of my two encumbrances at once."

"Is that how you see your own child? As an encumbrance?" Again, that accusatory face of hers!

"What else?" He had finished the brandy and considered a second. Reluctantly, he decided against it—he wanted to be crisp and alert when his visitor arrived. "I am so tired of you." He waved his hand. "Go, take Caroline and stay out of my sight—preferably for the rest of our lives."

Sarah turned sharply and for once did as she was bid. Arden watched as she took the child and her nurse into the grounds, and was glad that she would not be about when the Hungarian woman called. He finished his breakfast and then went to his library to await the woman's arrival.

He had been vaguely interested when he had heard of the new arrival, but far more so when told she was a striking beauty who lived alone. He had sent over an invitation, which had been accepted with gratifying speed. Now he sat, waiting and speculating. What would she be like? Would she be worthy of his time and attention?

Eventually, there came a rap at the library door, and the butler entered to announce the Lady Alinska. Arden rose swiftly to his feet as the lady herself entered. He couldn't help a slight gasp and a widening of his eyes. Rarely—if ever—had he seen such a beauty as this! She was tall for a woman, and dark-haired, with perfectly formed features and a slender, elegant body clad in a long black dress that accentuated her stunning form. She wore a single long black glove on her left hand, and a rope of pearls about her neck.

"My lady," he purred. "I had heard that you were beautiful, but the reports do not do you justice."

"My lord," she said, in a voice with barely a hint of an accent. "I had heard you were a flatterer—the reports barely do you justice."

He laughed. "It is not difficult to flatter such a one as you—you quite take my breath away."

"Do I?" She gave him a sharp glance. "We shall see."

"I hope we shall see a great deal of one another," he said, easily.

"Oh, be assured of that," she replied. "I am quite certain that we shall."

She had a strange look in her delightful eyes. But what a pleasure it would be to explore the body of this one! She seemed a trifle cold in her manner, but that was no doubt due to her being a stranger in this country and unused to its ways. He was certain he would be able to light a fire in her heart that would well repay his time…

Time passed, and little seemed to happen. Sarah sat on the great lawn, watching little Caroline play, and waiting for Alinska to call upon Lord Arden—yet again. It had been almost a month since her supposed angel of retribution had arrived, and Arden was still alive—and, unfortunately, happier than normal. He was being almost civil toward Sarah and had even given some slight attentions to his daughter. Sarah recognized the symptoms—he was anticipating another seduction.

And Alinska seemed to be going along with it! Not only had she done nothing to repay Arden, she seemed to be almost mesmerized by the man. Was it possible that she had allowed herself to be swayed by his superficial charm?

Caroline coughed and little and then started to cry. She was not yet two years old, but had started talking. Still, she could not express herself well, and was clearly frustrated by this failure. Sarah enquired of her health, but it was the elderly nurse who replied.

"She has a slight summer cold," the woman replied. "It is nothing much, but it makes it difficult for her to sleep. She has nightmares and cannot get enough rest. That makes her miserable and inclined to wail."

"My poor girl," Sarah said, sympathetically. She stroked the child's hair until Caroline calmed down. "Perhaps we should take her inside? The air may not be doing her good."

"The doctor said the fresh air would help to clear her lungs, ma'am," the nurse contradicted her.

"Then perhaps she should stay out," Sarah agreed. She had just caught sight of Alinska's carriage approaching the house. "Excuse me for a few minutes—I have something to say to Lord Arden's visitor." She hurried to intercept Alinska as she alighted from the carriage.

The Hungarian turned to look at her with that same dispassionate glance she always gave. "You wished to speak?"

"Yes." She drew Alinska out of the hearing of the servants. "What is happening?" she demanded, softly. "You have been here a month, and he is happier than I have ever seen him."

"Of course." Alinska gave her a bleak look. "The higher he rises, the more he expects, then the longer and harder his fall. Everything progresses well."

"Are you sure you are not allowing your heart to soften toward him?" Sarah demanded. "He is handsome, and can be very glib. Are you certain you are not falling in love with him?"

"If you knew my heart," Alinska answered coldly, "then there would be no need to query me. It is no longer mine to do with as I will, so there is no question of it being given to another man. Believe me, I am doing what I agreed when we first met." She abruptly looked across the lawn to where Caroline sat with her nurse. "You look to your duties, and leave me to mine. The child appears to be less than completely healthy."

"It is nothing but a summer cold and a lack of sleep," Sarah snapped. "It will soon pass."

"People may die of summer colds," the other woman answered. "You had best take good care of her."

"Do not speak to me of my duty!" Sarah exclaimed. "I know my duty!"

"And I know and will fulfill mine," Alinska replied. "Let us both be about our tasks then, shall we?" She turned her back on Sarah and marched toward the door of the house.

Sarah stared after her, a flame of fury burning inside her. Perhaps she had made a grave mistake in involving Alinska in her vengeance. Despite her assurances, Sarah was not convinced that the stranger was fully committed to her task. And it was a constant pain that Arden was looking so happy! She wanted him dead, not in love!

She heard Caroline cough again, and whirled about to go to her charge.

Lord Arden stared at his guest with mixed emotions. He had never met anyone as entrancing or exotic as the Lady Alinska—nor anyone so cold and withdrawn. He had hinted passion over the past few weeks, and she had always reacted in a casual fashion. She was clearly drawn to him, for she had been to the house almost every day, and yet she had shown no warmth in her manner toward him. But neither did she appear to be repelled. It was very hard for him to read her. Normally he was adroit at discovering what a woman wanted and to use it to get her to his bed. Some wished trinkets, some merely vows of eternal love, others merely an excuse to shed their clothing, but none of those appeared to be of interest to this beauty. What was the key that would unlock her passion?

They drank tea and spoke of the vague things both had done. He had no idea what he asked, and even less of what she replied. All the time they spoke, he studied her, trying to pry out her secrets. Why, for example, did she always wear one single black glove? He had asked her once, and she had simply replied that she had her reason, which he might one day understand. But he understood *nothing* about her. It was as if she were not a human woman at all, so impossible was it to divine her secrets.

"Enough!" he cried suddenly, surprising even himself with the force of that one word.

Alinska raised a perfect eyebrow. "You wish me to cease talking?" she enquired mildly.

"I wish you to say *something* with meaning to it," he told her. "Not this endless prattle that we constantly exchange."

For once there was a rare smile upon her lips. "I have been told that you English are very reserved," she said. "I had thought that was why we talked so long about so little."

"My reserve has gone," Arden said. He rose to his feet and crossed to where she sat. "I am tired of saying nothing when I have so much to say. I am in love with you."

"Was that so difficult to speak?" Alinska asked him.

"I do not wish to hear more nonsense from your lips," he told her. "I wish to kiss them, and for them to kiss me."

Again, she gave a slight smile. "Ah! Now we are indeed speaking words that have weight. But are you sure that you know what it is that you wish?"

"I am a man!" Arden informed her. "You are the most beautiful woman I have ever met. Of course I know what I want—I want *you*!"

"Ah. And those are the words I have been waiting for," Alinska replied.

"You feel the same way that I do, Alinska?" he asked her, feeling that he had finally unearthed the key that would unlock her passions.

"I feel as though we have reached a point where our paths have finally converged," she answered him. "Where we are walking together at last to the consummation of our relationship."

He was right! She *did* want him! They were both thinking along the same exact lines. He grasped her hand—the ungloved one—and kissed it passionately. "You are cold," he said, surprised, given that the day was warm.

"I am always cold," Alinska said. "I am afraid I shall never be warm again."

"I shall warm you!" he promised. He drew her to her feet. "Come with me, Alinska, and we shall warm each other. We shall feast on our mutual pleasures." He could scarcely believe how easy this was finally proving to be! She allowed herself to be eased to her feet and he kept a grip on her chilly hand as he led her to his bedchamber. She saw his bed and to his delight she neither resisted nor cried out; she must want what was to happen as much as he did. "I want your kisses," he told her. "I want to worship your body. Come to me, my Alinska." He touched his lips to hers, and was again surprised at how cold she was. "Can you not bring yourself to kiss me?" he asked her.

"You shall feel my kisses," she promised him. "And you shall see my body and worship it if you wish. Shall we begin here?" She held up her left hand and started to peel back the black glove. He smiled and watched as she began to strip.

And then he was suddenly more chilled than she.

Under the glove there was no flesh—only bone. As Alinska tugged the glove completely off her hand, he gasped in shock. There was no hand—only bone. Yet it was bone that somehow clung together and moved at her will, with neither muscle nor sinew to move the digits. She reached out with it, as though to caress his cheek. He stumbled back in shock, his fires extinguished.

"What is this?" he asked her, his voice weak with shock and fear.

"*This* is what I am, my dear man," she informed him. She moved in, and he stumbled backward, crashing into the post of the bed and then clutching at it for support. "Do you wish to see more of me?" She was mocking him now, but she gestured at her chest, near the heart. Blood was seeping out of the cleavage there. "This is the wound that killed me," she informed him. "Would you like a closer look?"

"Killed?" He was stunned, unable to think coherently. "But you... you..."

"I... I..." she mocked him again.

He was shaking—he couldn't help it. What she was saying made no sense, none at all. She was there before him, real, solid, breathing...

Bleeding...

"Ah, but you haven't tasted my kisses yet," she said, smiling. For the first time, she appeared to have true warmth in those beautiful, cold, dead eyes. "And you did so want my kisses, didn't you?" She opened her mouth, and moved forward.

He screamed.

Once.

Sarah sat out in the lazy warmth of the sun. The nurse had taken Caroline in to rest, as the child had been suddenly very tired. It was common at her age—bouts of mad energy followed by deep sleep. Sarah had elected to stay outside a while, half-dozing in the sunlight.

Then she was aware that she was no longer alone. She blinked and struggled back to full awareness, and saw that it was Alinska standing before her, tall and grim and still. "I am sorry," Sarah said. "I was dozing. The sun..."

"You should be very pleased," Alinska informed her. "It is over."

Over... Sarah stood up, abruptly, staring intently at the other woman. "He is dead?"

"He is dead." Alinska licked her lips quickly. "He died in his bed, which seemed to be appropriate. He will be discovered shortly."

Sarah felt dizzy with relief. It was *over*! She had her vengeance—Arden had paid for his lies and sins. Elation flooded her, and she gripped the arm of the Hungarian woman. "Thank you, Alinska."

"Enjoy your happiness while you may," the other woman said. "There is still the price to be talked of."

Sarah didn't care; she had lived only to see her false lover punished. If she had to die too, then so be it. Her life had ceased to have any meaning since Arden had cast her aside. "I am ready," she said, simply.

"No," Alinska contradicted her. "You are not."

Sarah frowned. "I assure you, I am ready to pay the price," she vowed. "I will be true to our agreement."

"Indeed you shall," Alinska replied. "But you are not the price."

Confused, Sarah shook her head. "But I promised you my life in payment for his. You mean that I do not need to pay?"

"I mean that you are incorrect—you did *not* promise me your life. You promised me anything you had, up to your life."

"Oh." Sarah didn't quite understand this, but if she did not have to die… Well, then that would be an unexpected blessing! "I do not wish to sound ungracious," she admitted. "But is there a reason you do not require my life?"

"Because it is worthless," Alinska said. "When we first met, you told me that your life was worthless. You cannot pay for anything with something that is worthless."

"Oh." She didn't know quite why, but she was certain that Alinska meant this as some sort of insult. "Then—what *is* the payment to be?"

"The payment has been taken," Alinska said. "The only thing of value that you had."

At that second, a scream came from the direction of the house, startling Sarah. "They have found his body."

"Not *his* body," Alinska said, sadly. "Not quite yet."

Sarah stared at her dumbly. Alinska for once seemed to have some genuine emotion. "Then…?" And a sudden chill stabbed at her heart. "No…"

"The payment had to be something of value," Alinska said. "I am sorry. You should have been more careful in the bargain you struck."

Sarah, her heart shaken and broken, fell at her feet in a dead faint.

Alinska wished she had the freedom to feel true sorrow, but her grim, implacable God would not allow her that. She could only feel a small satisfaction for the job she had done.

She had reunited mother and daughter in death.

I'd better admit that I have a terrible sense of humor, and that the strangest things appeal to me. In this case, I'd been reading about Benjamin Franklin's experiments with electricity (he was a foremost authority on the subject in his day), and I wondered what might have happened if his experiments had been taken a bit too far... The title is merely an example of my horrible taste in puns.

Franklinstein

Philadelphia, September 1776

"Surely, Mr. Franklin, as a man of science there must be something that you can do to aid our cause?" suggested Thomas Jefferson. He waved a handful of papers in the direction of his colleague. "General Washington's reports do not offer us much hope."

"General Washington's reports *never* offer us much hope," John Hancock grumbled. "The man is an inveterate pessimist. Nevertheless, there is truth in his assessment of the situation." He, too, twisted in his chair to look toward Franklin. "And you are one of the best-read and most advanced thinker in the Colonies—as you are fond of reminding us yourself on the chance that we might forget it."

Franklin smiled and waved his spectacles vaguely in the direction of both men. "I do have a few thoughts on the matter," he admitted.

"You have more than a few thoughts on *every* matter," John Dickinson observed. "And you are rarely as reluctant as this to share them with us."

Franklin blinked mildly. "I am reluctant merely because the thoughts I have are perhaps a little... unorthodox. I would not wish to upset any of you."

"Dammit, man," Jefferson growled, "these papers—if they are to be believed—say that we are losing our struggle with the British Crown. Nothing you can say would be as upsetting as this."

Franklin nodded. "You point is well taken, Thomas. Very well, then. It seems to me that the main problem we face at this time is that we simply lack the troops to send up against those damned Hessians the Crown employs. We need more fighters and they are proving to be in short supply."

"Mostly because we cannot pay them," Hancock said. "Men may risk their lives for ideals, but it helps their morale if their families can eat while they are off fighting."

"And, too often, when the men go off, they are killed in the fighting," Franklin stated. "Which tends to negate their usefulness as troops." He stared around the small, smoky room at his fellow rebels. "But I do have a suggestion that might remedy the problem."

"I hope it involves raising money," Hancock muttered.

"No, John—it involves raising the dead."

This comment brought all eyes and attention to Franklin. Finally, after a pause, Dickinson scowled. "I trust you are not considering adding necromancy to your numerous skills," he said.

"Not necromancy as such," Franklin replied. He fumbled with relighting his pipe, which had gone out while he was talking. "Are you aware of my inquiries into the nature of electricity?"

"I did hear something of you flying a damned kite in a thunderstorm," Dickinson answered. "Or some such nonsense. Damned foolish idea, if you ask me."

"Then it is a good thing that I did *not* ask you," Franklin snapped, clearly rather annoyed. "It was an experiment into the nature of lightning and I was able to show that it is a form of electricity. Whilst I was in Europe these past few years, I had the chance to speak with some of the foremost of scientific minds on the continent. One of these is Alessandro Volta, who resides in Italy. He is the improver of a device known as the electrophorus and we are in constant communication through the medium of the mails." He smiled. "For whose efficient workings I myself must take some credit." He waved his hand. "Another man of science I met and am corresponding with is a certain Baron Frankenstein. He has been working on the theory that the bodies of animals and people are powered by electricity."

"Come now, man!" Jefferson exclaimed. "You cannot seriously believe that the human body is powered by lightning!"

"Not lightning as such, no, of course not," Franklin agreed. "But a milder form of the same energies. After all, we've all felt the shock of static electricity, have we not? And where would such electrical shocks come from if there were not electricity flowing within our forms? It's all quite logical, you know. Anyway, Frankenstein's thoughts are that the main cause of death is that the electricity that powers us stops in its course. His idea is that life might possibly be returned to a corpse if there is an infusion of fresh electricity from an outside source."

Hancock frowned. "What are you getting at, Ben?"

"Simply this: perhaps I can aid our cause in this war by revitalizing our fallen. With the aid of my electrical experiments, perhaps it will be possible to resurrect the dead and have them live once again to fight on."

Dickinson stared at him in horror. "You are proposing to storm the gates of Heaven and snatch the souls of the departed from the hand of God?" he asked.

"I would not couch my idea is such belligerent terms," Franklin said mildly. "I would, at best, be merely borrowing back the dead for a while. And in a good cause, surely? If God is on our side—as we all so fervently believe—then I am certain He'd have little objection to my attempts. And if I am wrong, surely He—whose power is far greater than mine—will cling onto those souls with greater strength than I can muster to wrest them from him. At any rate, gentlemen, that is my proposal." He glanced at his pocket watch. "I can spare a half an hour to hear any comments you may have on the matter."

Franklin stared at the dead man on the table in his laboratory. It wasn't the first corpse he'd attended, nor, sadly, was it likely to be the last. A young farm-hand named Jacob Miller, shot in the chest and died but the previous day—as good a candidate for his resurrection scheme as could be found. "Well, Christopher," he said, with as much cheer as he could muster, "are you ready to commence our great attempt?"

"As ready as I'll ever be, Ben," his companion agreed. Dr. Christopher Rowley was an old acquaintance, and the pair of them had often shared a fine brandy and finer book. Franklin could think of no better assistant on this project.

"I confess a little uncertainty as to how to proceed," Franklin admitted. "Being new to this reanimation business, as it were."

"Well," Rowley said, thoughtfully, "the plan is, I believe, to restore this young… man to full working order—vitality to his limbs, thoughts to his mind, purpose to his life?"

"That is it."

"Well, then, as a practical suggestion, I propose we sew closed his wound," Rowley decided. "If we succeed in getting his blood pumping again, it would otherwise make quite a mess on the table and floor."

"An apposite point," Franklin agreed. "And as you are the medical man of us, I suggest that is your task. I shall meanwhile ready my apparatus." He gestured at the immense electrophorus he had constructed over the past few days. There was the rumble of thunder from outside, presaging the approaching storm he needed to implement his plan. Rowley nodded and set to work with thread and needle, sparing the occasional glance to see what Franklin's preparations might be.

"There are already maggots in the wound," Rowley complained. "They eat at dead flesh, you know. I suppose I'd better remove them?"

"Whatever you can," Franklin agreed, carelessly. "They eat only dead flesh, so if we succeed in restoring life, any that you miss should cease their feasting forthwith." Satisfied with the electrophorus, he turned his attentions to the rods that were attached to a hoist.

"What are those things, Ben?" Rowley asked, curiously.

"My own invention," Franklin said—with what he felt was justifiable pride. "Lightning rods. I discovered that lightning is merely an atmospheric form of electricity, and is attracted my metal. My initial idea with my rods was that they should attract lightning and funnel it safely into the ground, preventing strikes on houses that might cause fires. I then realized that I could adapt them to attract the great amount of electricity I should need to restart a deceased body. You see, it is the vital spark of life—electricity!—that is currently missing from that poor corpse. By replacing the lost electricity with fresh we should then be able to restore animation to the lifeless shell of the man."

"Admirable in theory," Rowley agreed. "But in practice?"

"That we shall soon discover," Franklin replied. "Are you finished with your repairs?"

"I am."

"Good. Then stand away from the table, Christopher." Franklin laid his hands on the chains that would raise the hoist. "Well, my friend—now it commences." He began hauling up his mass of lightning rods to the roof of his laboratory. The framework connected to the rods was joined to the massive electrophorus though a thick wire that should carry any lightning captured by his device directly into the body of Jacob Miller. Once the rods were raised, he fastened the ends of the chain. "And now," he said, "we wait."

Waiting was always the hardest part for Franklin; he was impatient to be off doing—*something*. There was a war to be won, Congress to be rallied, experiments to conduct, books to read… So to be forced to simply wait was like purgatory for him. Somehow, though, he managed it. Eventually there was a great flash of light above the laboratory and an immediate clap of titanic thunder.

The rod arrangement above their heads lit up as the lightning struck and was drawn down to the electrophorus. The great machine howled with the strain of the effort and then discharged its full force into the corpse. Sparks and lights played about the form and Franklin held his breath, wondering, agonizing.

Would this work?

The light faded as the power dissipated. Franklin and Rowley stared intently at the dead body, willing it to move in even a small way. But there was nothing—nothing!

"Well, Ben," Rowley said, sadly, "I am afraid the experiment is a failure."

Ben shook his head. "So it would seem. In this round, at least, the Almighty has kept his secrets to himself. Perhaps if I —" He broke off and cocked his head. "Did you hear something?"

They both looked at the form of Jacob Miller. Was the mouth slightly open now? Did that finger twitch? Excitedly, afraid he was imaging things, Ben moved forward.

The corpse groaned.

Franklin laughed, delighted. "It worked! It worked, Christopher! We have succeeded after all in reclaiming the dead!"

The eyes of the man opened and after a moment managed to focus upon Franklin's beaming face. There was an odd depth to them, as if they were staring not over the space of a short foot but across a chasm of a million miles. The man's jaw moved, though no sound came out. He tried again.

"What... have... you... done?" The voice was hollow, echoing, distant and pained.

"Done?" Franklin laughed. "Why, my dear sir, I have done the impossible—I have called you back to life again. You are become the first of a new breed of man! Your name will be immortal!" A thought struck him. "Actually, you may indeed *be* immortal. Can a man once dead and resurrected die again? It's an interesting thought, Christopher, is it not?"

Miller seemed to be immune to Franklin's excitement. "Why?" he asked.

"Why?" Franklin was puzzled. "What do you mean *why*?"

"Why bring me back from Heaven?" the man asked.

"Oh, *that*! Because we have further need for you on this good earth, my man. We still need soldiers to fight for our righteous cause. You will be the first of our resuscitated brigade! We need you out there, helping to win our war!" He gestured broadly.

The man's hand abruptly shot up and fastened about Franklin's throat. "Whatever you do, man," he growled, "do *not* bring me back again!" He released the scientist, who staggered back, rubbing at his sore throat.

"As you wish," he agreed. "As you wish. One time only. Absolutely." Then his genial nature returned and he beamed once more at Rowley. "My dear fellow, we have succeeded! Now even the dead will fight for Independence!"

A few days later, Franklin was back with Adams, Jefferson and Dickinson, reporting on his experiments. "Thanks to the terrible weather we've been having, I now have been able to bring back a dozen men, all of whom have gone on to fight bravely for us," he concluded.

"Perhaps a little *too* bravely," Dickinson objected. "The last report I had said that seven of them had attacked so ferociously their bodies have been shot almost to pieces. Certainly there is little chance that you could resurrect them again."

Franklin rubbed his throat, a trifle nervously. "No. But I have to say that we seem to have no shortage of possible future candidates."

"Sadly, that is true," Jefferson admitted. "The British are still advancing. Your resurrection troops are aiding our cause—the Hessians have heard of them and seem to be quite terrified of facing them, so there is a little extra help on our side there. And, thankfully, there are still great American patriots to inspire us." He removed a letter from his pocket. "For example, just yesterday in New York the Redcoats hung a school teacher as a spy. One Nathan Hale, poor man. But he had the wit, even at the end, to make a great patriotic cry." He read from the letter: "I only regret that I have but one life to give for my country."

Franklin beamed. "Maybe I can help there?" he suggested.

Being English, I've always loved the folk mythology of our country, from Robin Hood (who hailed from my home town of Nottingham) to King Arthur and the Knights of the Round Table. Robin was a hero for the poor, and Arthur a model for the rich. I liked the idea of writing an Arthurian tale set before the days of Camelot, and showing one of the minor knights, Bedevere, and that led to this tale. In the Middle Ages and earlier, woods were not places to go to commune with Nature—they were terrifying places to avoid as much as possible. Who knew what might lurk in there?

To Protect and Serve

Maybe this wasn't such a great idea after all, Bedwyr thought, eyeing the thick forest entanglement ahead of him. He shifted his grip on his father's sword, wishing he'd thought to bring along the scabbard as well. He was starting to understand how badly he'd planned this little "quest" of his. Last night, his vow in the chapel to God not to come home until he'd had an adventure had seemed brilliant.

Of course, last night he'd been intoxicated in more than one way, and probably anything would have seemed brilliant to him. He'd just turned sixteen, and his father, Pedrawd, had thrown a big feast for him. Bedwyr had overindulged on the thick Grecian wine his father liked, and his head had swum. Then there had been that rather fetching maid, Mawr, who had shown him pleasures he'd heard joked about but never experienced. That had been as heady as the wine, and a lot more pleasurable. Having bedded his first wench and been drunk for the first time, he had believed that he was ready to take on the responsibilities of a knight. True, he hadn't yet been dubbed, but that was a minor point when you were drunk. It was the *thought* that counted, the intent, the desire. So he had stumbled to the family chapel, and made that vow. Then he'd collapsed, and slept off the effects of the wine.

Well, most of them, at least. His head felt as if it was wrapped inside a woollen blanket and some blacksmith was pounding on the inside, trying to break out. Other than that, he was perfectly fine.

Except for the fear, of course.

If there was one lesson his father had drummed into his thick skull it was never to go into the deep forest. *Nobody* went into the forests—and came back again. His father and grandfather—the Bedwyr he had himself been named for— had explained that the Isle of Albion had once been home to creatures and monsters born at the dawn of time. When Christianity had come to the country and the light of the True Cross had shone upon the fairest isle, then the spawn of darkness had retreated into the depths of the forests. In the deep woods deeper evil dwelled.

Hence the reason for Bedwyr's oath the previous night in the chapel. He had vowed to slay evil to repay God for the goodness he had been granted. When he was drunk, that had seemed like a very fair and honest payment. Now that he was sober—and a little hung-over—it was starting to look like youthful stupidity. But—another thing Bedwyr's father had driven home to him—a knight always keeps his word, no matter how inconvenient it later becomes. "A man who backs out on his given word," Pedrawd has growled, "will back out on anything."

Bedwyr would not back out. No matter how much he wished to.

But the forest looked evil. A normal forest would start as a small cluster of light bushes, a copse of trees, a smattering of ferns, before getting to the oaks and ashes or tall sycamores. There would be proud chestnuts, or bowed willows. Bedwyr, even though he was the son of a noble, was also a son of the fields, and he knew his trees.

He couldn't name a single one of the gnarled, warped growths he was looking at now, though. It didn't look like a forest as much as a defensive barrier set up about the hollow beyond—a living wall, all but marked *keep out*. He knew that if he was sensible he would heed that warning. But, then, there was his vow...

Swallowing hard, he moved forward again, pushing his way past the first of the twisted branches, and so on into the forest. Here the shadows intensified, sucking the light and warmth from the air. He shuddered, and not only from the fear crawling, spider-like, up his spine.

"Who are you?"

He whirled around, bringing the sword up in a clumsy attempt at defense, before he realized it wasn't called for. The person who had spoken so jarringly was a woman—perhaps only a girl—who looked at him from around the bole of an ancient tree. All he could see of her was her pale hands, her paler face and her silky yellow hair. Her eyes were large and black, and boring into him.

"I'm Bedwyr," he told her. "Knight."

"Bedevere?" she asked, pronouncing his name in the Saxon fashion. They could never get the timbre of the old names correct, but he was used to it. "You look a bit young to be a knight."

He was on a holy quest, and knew that he was bound to tell the truth. "Well, I'm not, yet, quite," he said stumblingly. "But I hope to be one soon."

"Then you'd best turn around and go back to the open fields, *knight-to-be*," she said, and there was distinct mockery in her voice. "This is no place for a boy."

"I'm not a boy," he growled stubbornly. "I'm a man. I'm sixteen."

"Not by much, I'll wager," she said. But she seemed less timid now, and came out from her hiding place. She was small, but well-shaped. Her clothing was poor and old, but she wore the dress as if it was of finest silk of the orient. Bedwyr had never seen silk, of course, but the traders sometimes spoke of it with awe in their voices.

"By a day," he admitted, being committed to being honest with her.

"Well, if you'd like to be sixteen and two days, the way is the way you came in."

"I'm on a quest," he informed her. "I've vowed to God not to return until I have slain something evil, an abomination in His sight."

"Have you indeed?" She was mocking him again. "And what makes you so certain that *it* won't kill *you*?"

"I'm on a *holy* quest. If I'm righteous, then God will protect me."

The girl/woman shook her head. "Somebody should protect you," she observed. "In this wood dwells a *thing*."

Bedwyr felt a prickle of fear and exhilaration. He'd been right to hunt here! "What sort of a thing?" he asked.

"I don't know. What sorts of things are there?"

"All sorts," he said. He knew about this from the traveling singers and harpists. "There are dragons and their kin. There are the wolves and their folk. There are the goblins and the fair folk. There are the banshees, and spirits and —"

"Things that go bump in the night," she said, tossing her head and laughing. "Oh, I've little doubt such creatures exist and roam about, but they're not what lives near here. This is a creature of pure evil. A man-eater."

"How come it didn't eat you?" he asked her, a little piqued by her belittling of him.

She pushed out her bosom a little more. "Do I look like a *man* to you?" she laughed. "Or are you still too young to know the difference between a man and a woman?"

Bedwyr recalled the delights he had touched and tasted the previous night, and reddened. "I know the difference!"

And so does this *thing*," the woman replied. "It takes only men." She looked him over again. "And, despite your youth, there are clearly the makings of a man about you, Bedevere. If I can see them, so then can it. Don't provoke it by going further into its range. It may be that it has eaten last night and isn't hungry enough to come after you yet. But if you tread its pathways and challenge it, it could hardly allow you to live, now could it?"

Bedwyr burned with her mockery. "I have taken an oath to slay evil," he repeated. "And a creature that kills men simply because they are men is clearly evil."

"Or more human than you are," she said lightly. "Nothing kills man as easily and frequently as another man."

There was some truth to that, of course, but she seemed to be speaking only to confuse him. "Do you seek to defend this monster?" he asked, puzzled.

"No, you idiot, I'm trying to defend *you*."

This didn't make a lot of sense to him. "I'm a knight," he tried again to explain. "Or shall be soon. It is my task to protect and defend you, not yours to protect me."

"Perhaps," she suggested, "you should seek first to find out what I wish to be defended *from*? This creature is of no threat to me."

Bedwyr blinked. He wished his head was a little clearer, because this strange girl was confusing him. "But you are a beautiful girl—woman," he said, quickly, lest he should offend her. "And someday you will want to take a husband. This *thing* will clearly seek to prevent it by slaying your would-be spouse. So by slaying it, I am serving you."

"Amazing," the girl muttered. "You men can find an excuse for killing *anything* if you really want to." She shook her head. "I can see that I'm not getting through to you. All right—if you *must* get yourself killed, on your own head be it. Just for the record, you're not doing this for me, you're doing it for yourself." She gestured behind her. "Follow this path, and you'll find it. Or, rather, *it* will most assuredly find you." She pointed back the way he had come. "Or go that way, save your life and I promise never to speak of this to anyone again, so you needn't be afraid you'll be labeled a coward."

She really knew how to hurt him, this girl! "I am *not* a coward!" he snapped, reddening again. "And I am a man who keeps his oaths."

"Well, I'm sure both will comfort you in your grave," she replied, shrugging. "I did my best. On your own head be the results of your foolish pride."

He shrugged, and moved on. She moved aside to let him pass, and he thought he saw a momentary look of real concern in her eyes. Then she hardened her expression and half-turned away. "Idiot," she muttered. Then she lunged out and planted a kiss on his cheek. "You're worse than the others," she said. "At least they deserved their fate. You're simply too stupid not to realize that nobility is an empty shell to hide within."

"If a man believes in nothing larger and better than himself," Bedwyr replied, "then he is truly hollow, for he has no support in times of crisis." He wasn't going to stand here debating with the woman, for he knew that his courage would drain away if he did. While the after-effects of his drunkenness and his oath still numbed him a little, he pressed onward, not looking back.

The woods, already dark and depressing, managed to draw even more gloom about them. He pushed aside branches that seemed to reach for him like wooden fingers, all the time listening and scanning the area carefully. In the deep shadows, it was hard to see anything, and he could hear nothing. No birds moving, let alone singing; no animals scurrying or burrowing, or hunting for food. Not even any insects. Perhaps within this forest, nothing but the trees were alive.

So, where was this *thing* of which the girl had spoken? He saw no signs of any life at all. Even the trees didn't seem to have fresh leaves on them. It was as if something had sucked the vitality out of this twisted mass of growths. He stepped carefully, though, looking and listening. He had an odd feeling, as though there was indeed something out there in the shadows, unseen and unheard, and yet moving closer to him. His senses could not confirm his fears, but that did not make them any less certain.

There was something here, something ancient, something evil.

He wanted to take the girl's advice, to turn and run, to leave this forest and never return. It wasn't yet too late. The thing out there was moving closer, but he still had time to escape. True, he had taken an oath, but would God hold him to such a naive vow? Wasn't it the equivalent of suicide, and wasn't suicide a sin? To avoid death here would not be dishonorable, but sensible. He could turn and flee.

No! Bedwyr caught his runaway thoughts, and tried to rein them in. That was his fears speaking! Justifying cowardice and breaking a vow were not the actions of a true knight. He had no option now but to press on and to confront this ageless evil. If it slew him, then it would prove that he was not fit to become a knight, and if he were not to be a knight, then he was better off dead. Tightening his grip upon the sword and his nerves, he pressed on.

Besides, what would Mawr think of him if he turned and ran? Even if the girl he'd met had been telling the truth, and would never speak of his cowardice to anyone, *he* would still know. Last night, Mawr, laughing with pleasure, had shown him some of what it meant to be a man. He still hoped she would show him more. But how could he allow her to treat him like a man if he was nothing but a coward? He could not run.

Mawr! He couldn't help thinking of her again, picturing her in his mind. He hadn't known what to expect, not exactly, when she had slipped out of her clothing. He'd been delighted with what she had offered, and she had gently led him to pleasures he'd never known. He really wanted to return to those explorations. But he never would, if he didn't turn back now. The monster would stalk him and slay him. His flesh would be eaten, his bones cracked and the marrow drained. He would be dead, and would never again know such pleasures as Mawr had shown him...

The darkness of the forest was creeping into his soul. He jerked his attention back from within to without. If he didn't focus his thoughts, he would be simple prey for any creature that came along, even a hedgehog, let alone a monster.

Fighting to retain control of his thoughts and not to give them over to his fears, he realized that he had stopped moving. He had to keep going. He managed to stumble forward a step —

His mind returned to a vision of Mawr's delicate skin and memory of her scents and tastes, and he licked his lips. When he returned, he prayed that she would be interested in sharing more of her secrets and pleasures with him. Of course, actually, she couldn't refuse. She worked for his father, didn't she? So she could simply be ordered to do as he wished. If she didn't, she would be punished.

Maybe, Bedwyr realized, stunned by the thought, maybe that was why she had come to him in the first place. Maybe she hadn't shared herself willingly, but out of fear of being punished if she refused the wishes of the lord's eldest son? As he thought about it, he began to see that this was indeed how it had been. She hadn't been giving of herself freely, but out of compulsion. She had been *forced* to serve his needs, and he had taken advantage of her weakness and powerlessness. There was nobody that she could complain to that he had raped her.

And there was nothing to stop him from doing it to her again.

Women had neither rights nor recourse if they disliked how they were treated. Men held the power, power of the sword and of wealth. Women were dependent upon men in all things. And, as a result, they could not deny him anything he wanted of them. It wasn't just Mawr who he could force to show him their secrets, and to share his bed: it was any woman he chose. He would soon be lord in his own right, and then their lives would be his to deal with as he desired. That was, of course, how it should be: the weak were helpless captives of the strong. Women were weak, and men strong. They had to do as they were told, when they were told.

No! Again, Bedwyr rebelled against the thoughts that were flooding his mind. He was ashamed and disgusted by these concepts. True, women were weak and reliant on men, but that didn't mean that they should be taken advantage of!

They were to be protected by a true knight. After all, Christ, who was true God, had emptied himself of his power and majesty and deigned to be born on Earth, mortal son of a weak woman. If God himself had such an exalted view of women, how could a knight have less?

But Bedwyr knew in his heart that he wanted Mawr again, and that he would do anything to get between her legs once more. She would have to do as she was told, and to submit to his will. After all, she had done so once, hadn't she? Out of fear of punishment, she had shared her body's secrets with him. Even now, she was probably back home, sobbing and ashamed of what he had forced upon her. Bedwyr felt the strength draining from him as he realized what it was that he had inflicted upon the poor child he had so savagely abused. He fell to his knees, sobs jerked from his tight throat, his grip on the sword loosening. He could feel the darkness within his own soul reaching out to choke him. This forest was the rightful place for such a person as he was—the gloom and blackness of the trees echoed the darkness and despair of his own evil soul.

It felt as though the branches were closing in about him, making a cage of his body. He didn't care. He had looked into his own heart, and seen nothing there but selfishness and hollow pride. A knight? He couldn't even make a decent serf! He had forced himself upon an innocent girl, ruined her life, perhaps left her with child, scandalizing her family and friends. She would be forced to bear a bastard child, or else to commit the sin of suicide to assuage her shame. And it was all his doing. He didn't deserve to live...

Mawr! How could he have done this to her? How he had enjoyed her laughter, and now he was about to still that bubbling merriment forever...

Laughter? Dimly, Bedwyr focused on that remembered sound. Mawr had laughed, tinkling sounds of pleasure as she had guided his clumsy, untrained fingers about her delightful body. Laughter... That had not been faked. Mawr had not been terrified, pleasing him out of fear. He concentrated harder, recalling how it had truly been. *She* had come to him, flirting, laughing, teasing. *She* had taken him from the feast, and led him to his room. *She* had slipped her hands into his clothing, touching, tantalizing and then delivering her whispered promises.

She had not been forced, or raped. She had acted willingly, delightedly. The sound of her laughter again filled his mind, and Bedwyr blinked and awoke.

Tendrils of woody growth were trailed about him, slipping and sliding in a black mockery of an embrace. With all of his strength, he raised his father's sword. Crying out wordlessly, he spun about, and slashed with the blade, cutting through the woody fingers, and deep into the trunk of the tree that was embracing him, and draining his life. The judder of the blow shocked his arms, but the scream of pain that ran through his brain pained him more. He dragged the sword free, and struck again and again. The mental howls grew softer and softer with each blow, as chips of wood flew under the force of his attack.

The tree-thing tried to escape, but it moved terribly slowly on its roots, dragging across the ground. Bedwyr would not allow it to retreat. He finally understood. *This* was the man-eater of which the girl had spoken. Somehow it sensed the fears and weaknesses of its prey, and projected them outward. Stunned by inner contemplation, the prey would stand still, allowing the slow-moving tree-thing to creep up on him and envelop him in its branches/arms. Then it somehow drained the life of its victims and awaited fresh prey.

But Bedwyr had awakened, seeing the illusion for what it was. True, like all men he was a sinner, but he was not the one that the tree-thing had tried to paint him. The truth had broken through the illusion and the truth had set him free.

He hacked and slashed at the monster, severing branches and limbs, gouging into the trunk. The waves of mental attack upon the darknesses in his souls slowly faded, and finally the tree shuddered a last time and collapsed. Bedwyr realized that it was finished, dead at last. He stood, panting, leaning on the hilt of the sword. It was dripping sap, and he couldn't restrain a bubble of laughter. He had expected to blood his father's sword, and instead had wielded it like a woodsman's ax! Well, either way, he had kept his vow: he had confronted and slain evil.

Staggering a little, but immensely lighter in his soul, he started back the way he had come. The monster had used his own doubts and fears to attack him, but there certainly had been some truth in the visions. Bedwyr resolved that he would be more careful in his dealings with women from now on. It was the task of a knight, he knew, to protect and serve a lady, and not to take advantage of her.

On the other hand, if she *offered*, freely and willingly....

Bedwyr grinned at the thought. He really hoped that Mawr would offer.

Or maybe that bewitching young lady he had met on the way into the woods...

My good friend Kara Dennison asked me to contribute a story to her collection Unearthed *to raise money for archaeology. The theme was "things dug up." Other people thought artifacts and treasure; I thought bodies... I suspect that says a lot about me.*

Long Time Dead

"Barnaby," Harry Pryor said, plaintively. "I'm scared."

His companion glared at him before his expression softened. "Harry—what are you scared *of?*"

Harry gestured all around him. "This." They were standing on the pathway in a graveyard at two in the morning. The vagrant moon drifted in and out of the lazily moving clouds overhead, causing creeping shadows all around the pair. Every time a shadow seemed to slither past him, Harry jumped.

Barnaby rolled his eyes and sighed. "Harry, you couldn't ask for a more peaceful place. There is literally not a single living person in here, barring the pair of us."

"It's not the living that scares me."

"Well, it should be. The dead are harmless. You know what they're doing, Harry? They're *rotting*. Nothing else. They're just in their boxes, under six feet of earth, decaying away to nothing."

"But I've heard stories—"

"We've all heard *stories*," Barnaby replied. "And that is literally all they are, my son—stories. Harry, this is 1878—the age of science. Ghosties and ghoulies and long-legged beasties are old wives' tales. When you're dead, you're dead. That's it. Nothing more, nothing less. So, stop worrying, and come on. We've got work to do."

"I wish I hadn't agreed to this, Barnaby. I really do."

"But you *did*, old son, and I need your help. And you need the money. Your family has to eat, doesn't it?"

"Well, yes," Harry admitted. He had six siblings, and his dad was crippled. They'd starve without the money Harry brought in. "But, well, you know…"

Barnaby sighed again. "I thought we'd been through all of this," he said, obviously mustering all of his patience. "All we're doing is helping science."

"We're digging up dead bodies, Barnaby."

"Right we are, so come on." He studied the slip of paper he held again. "This way."

"But—people's *bodies*," Harry objected.

"Well, they've no use for them anymore, have they? And the doctor does. By dissecting them, he's learning how our bodies work, and advancing science. He's learning ways to keep other people alive. So we're doing the community a service, aren't we?"

"Well, yes," Harry agreed, not at all convinced. "But the families of the dead think those bodies are resting in peace— and they're not, are they, Barnaby?"

Barnaby gave a heaving sigh. "Look, my lad—think of it this way. Those bodies are *helping* science. They'll *save* lives in the long run. These flaming relatives of which you speak are therefore standing in the way of science, aren't they? Try looking at it that we're saving them from their own selfishness."

That make a *kind* of sense, Harry had to admit, but it didn't settle his qualms. "But the family thinks the person is in his or her grave."

"And that's what's important, isn't it?" Barnaby asked. "That they *think* it. As far as they'll ever know, that's *exactly* where it is. So, they're happy to think that. And the doctor is happy because he can now save more lives. And we're happy because we're being paid handsomely for this little job. So, it hurts nobody and benefits everybody, my boy. It makes everyone involved happy, so buck up and let's get on with it."

"But it's still *illegal*," Harry protested.

"Then stop dilly-dallying and let's get on with it before we're caught." Seeing his companion's worried expression, he added: "Look, according to the law, it's illegal to steal a loaf of bread to feed your starving family. But it's *not* illegal to let children starve to death. Clearly, then, the law isn't always right, is it?"

"No, of course it isn't," Harry had to admit.

"Then why are you worrying about breaking laws that shouldn't be laws in order to feed your starving family?"

Harry nodded. "You're right, as always, Barnaby."

Barnaby put a comforting arm about his shoulder. "I know I am, lad. Now, let's be on with it. We're only a short time alive, but a long time dead. Let's make the best use of what time we have, eh?"

Following the note he'd made of today's internment, Barnaby led the way. Barnaby worked by day for a funeral director as a professional mourner. By day, he buried the bodies; by night he dug them up again. This one, though, was to be even simpler—it hadn't been buried, but placed in a mausoleum. That meant there was no strenuous digging to do, just breaking into the crypt and removing the body from the coffin.

Harry had helped him before, but each time it had been harder and harder for him to steel himself to do it. Tonight... He shuddered as more long shadows scuttled past his peripheral vision. Tonight felt *bad*. It wasn't that he believed in ghosts—well, not exactly, despite the stories he'd heard. But he wasn't entirely convinced that Barnaby's view of the world was right. Barnaby was a big believer in Science, and a very vocal disbeliever in any kind of religion. *Up-and-up fraud,* he called them all. But Harry had been raised C of E, and he couldn't quite put that upbringing out of his mind. When Barnaby argued that the stinking state of society was proof that there was no God—because any self-respecting deity would have blasted all those corrupt politicians and the stinking, selfish rich to Hell and back—Harry tended to think that this was taking logic a bit too far. In the back of his mind, he was pretty certain he'd be going to Hell himself for helping to steal bodies.

But—as Barnaby continually pointed out—Harry was doing it for purely unselfish reasons, to feed his family, and how could God (if He did exist!) object to such brotherly devotion? Harry had a suspicion there was a flaw in that reasoning somewhere, but he knew that he wasn't educated enough to spot it. Just educated enough to feel uncomfortable about it.

And, because he couldn't rule out God or Hell from his thinking, he was scared of what his desecrating graves might result in... *That* was really what frightened him. Well, that and these creeping shadows that might serve as cover for, well, almost anything. Ghosts, maybe. Or worse. He wasn't sure what *worse* covered, but his imagination was continually trying to offer up suggestions...

There was a sudden flurry of movement in the nearby bushes, and he almost had a heart attack.

"It's just a bleeding owl," Barnaby growled. Now it had been identified, Harry could see that was exactly what it was. The graveyard was home to many rats and mice, so the local owls had plenty of prey. A few more tiny deaths to add to the total in this cemetery...

Harry tried to calm down, but his heart was racing. All he could do was to try and remind himself that his family would be able to eat tomorrow... He glanced nervously around, seeing vague shapes of grave stones looming in the gloom. *If he lived till the morning...*

He couldn't recall where they'd been before in this place, digging up the graves of the freshly-dead. Actually, he didn't *want* to recall, he wanted to forget. At least there was no back-breaking work involved in this one. But he could still remember the faces of some of the others he'd unearthed, looking as if they were just sleeping, but feeling like— pardon the expression—dead weights when they had to be lifted. And he had to do the carrying, because Barnaby was the one who covered up their tracks behind them.

They came to a line of large, dark shapes in the night. There were seven crypts in a row here. He couldn't read the names in the darkness, but, then, he wasn't that good a reader

211

to begin with. Neither, he suspected, was Barnaby, despite his companion's claims to the contrary. At any rate, Barnaby had terrible handwriting, and he was peering hard at it, trying to make it out. He had a dark lantern, but he never liked to light it if there was a possibility of it being seen.

"Third one in," Barnaby said firmly. He counted as they walked along, and stopped at the third mausoleum. "This is it," he announced. He had no option now, and so he lit the dark lantern, narrowing the beam to little more than a slit. He held the light up to the chain that sealed the door. "Piece of cake," he announced. "Here, hang onto this." He handed the lantern over, and pulled his rucksack around on his shoulder. He took out a pair of bolt cutters. "Shine the light on the lock," he ordered. Harry did so, and Barnaby cut through one of the chain links, replaced the bolt cutters and then unthreaded the chain from the door handles. He slipped it into his bag, and then gripped the large handle. "Keep an eye open," he said.

Harry did so. They'd never run into anyone else in this graveyard before, but that didn't mean you could assume there might not be a first time. Harry had heard instances of the coppers setting ambushes for Resurrectionists from time to time, and he'd not be able to do his family any good if he was caught and sent to the Colonies. Or, worse, hanged.

There was a grinding noise as Barnaby pried open the door. It sounded horribly loud to Harry, and his eyes flickered about the darkness, looking for any sign that somebody else might have heard. Half a hundred shadows seemed to stir, but none of them resolved into a policeman, thankfully.

"Right, lad, come along." Barnaby had the door half-open, and he held out his hand for the lantern, which Harry passed quickly over. Barnaby opened the shutter a little more, casting a slightly brighter beam into the crypt. He jerked his head for Harry to follow him into the tomb. With more than a shudder of fear, Harry followed along.

The room inside was about ten feet on a side. There was a stained glass window high up in the back, and a picture of an angel and some indistinguishable words on it. Weak moonlight managed to penetrate it a trifle. There were half a dozen filled shelves and several empty ones. The latest coffin was placed on a pedestal in the center of the room. It wouldn't be placed on its destined shelf until the bronze plaque identifying the occupant had been made.

There were flowers scattered around the coffin, but they were all withered and dead.

"Are you *sure* this is the right crypt?" he asked Barnaby in a whisper.

"Third one, just like I wrote down," the other man answered. "Of course it is. There's the coffin to prove it."

"Those flowers don't look fresh to me," Harry objected.

"You wouldn't look fresh if you'd been in here a day," Barnaby replied. "You'd be surprised how fast they can wither in here, in the darkness. Stop being silly, and let's get on with it." He fished in his rucksack again and this time pulled out two crowbars. He handed one over the Harry, who took it in a shaking hand. "Buck up!" Barnaby said, sharply. "We'll be done here soon."

Harry couldn't help feeling that they'd be buried here soon… He knew he was being foolish—he'd helped Barnaby before, and nothing had happened—but here and now, for whatever reason, he felt completely shaken.

Even in the darkness, Barnaby must have seen him shaking. "What's wrong with you?" he growled. "Haven't you ever been in a butcher's shop before? Your Sunday roast isn't going to come to life and gore you to death—and these dead bodies aren't going to do anything, either. When you're dead, that's it—there's only a body left behind, nothing else. And you're a long time dead. You don't go anywhere, you just stay still and rot. Now, be a man and help me with this damned coffin."

It was easy for Barnaby to say—he wasn't afraid of anything much, and he had no imagination at all. He didn't jump when the shadows crept, or there was some whispery noise in the darkness. But it wasn't like that for Harry—his heart was pounding, and even in the cold gloom of the crypt, he was sweating. But he needed the money for his family, so he tried to bury his fears deeper than these corpses and stepped forward to help with the coffin lid. With trembling hands, he worked at getting the point of the crowbar under the edge of the rim. It proved to be difficult, and not simply because his hands were shaking.

"Bloody hell," Barnaby muttered, clearly suffering the same problem. "They really nailed the lid down on this one, Harry me lad." He gave a chuckle. "Maybe they were afraid he'd pop out for a walk, eh?" After a few moments, though, he managed to get started, and, with a cracking sound, the lid moved slightly. Harry was able to shove his crowbar in now, and together they worked at getting the coffin open.

It wasn't easy. Most lids were held down by a dozen or so four inch nails—this one had more than two dozen nails that had to be six inches or more. "Somebody took their job seriously," Barnaby muttered. "Don't they have any consideration for us poor hard-working Resurrectionists?"

"Maybe that's why it's closed so tightly?" Harry suggested.

"Could be. And if I ever find whoever did this job, I'll lay about him with this crowbar." There was a final loud crack that echoed about the crypt, and the lid was free. Barnaby collected both tools and replaced them in his rucksack. Then he moved to the head of the coffin and gestured for Harry to take the foot.

Again, Harry hesitated. He felt a tremor of fear shake his entire body, and every instinct he had screamed out that this was a bad idea. But what else could he do? Barnaby wouldn't let him flee now, and he'd get no money if he did. But he could barely stop the trembling in his limbs as he reached out to grip the lid.

"Off with it," Barnaby ordered, clearly not at all bothered. Harry tensed, pushed down his terrors, and lifted. The heavy lid moved off and they slid it down to the floor. Harry straightened up again, and saw the grin on Barnaby's face as they both looked at the body in the coffin.

"Perfect," Barnaby said. "See, Harry? I told you this was the right crypt. This little beauty has only just been buried today."

The corpse *did* look remarkably fresh. It was of a man in the prime of his youth—no more than thirty, clearly. Handsome and refined, with dark hair and a pallid complexion. He looked to be muscular. There was no sign at all of whatever had killed him—but, then, any decent undertaker would hide that.

The thing was, he didn't look *dead*. More like he was sleeping... Harry had heard tales of people being buried alive, and wondered if that was somehow what had happened here. Perhaps some mistake by an over-eager doctor? None of the other corpses he'd handled had ever looked—well, so *alive* before.

"Stop staring and help me with it," Barnaby complained. He reached down to grab the body by the shoulders—

The corpse's eyes opened, and even Barnaby jumped. Harry fell back, shaking.

The body moved quickly. It grabbed Barnaby with two powerful hands and dragged him forwards. Barnaby gave an inarticulate cry, but couldn't fight that strength in those arms.

The dead man snarled, and then bit Barnaby's throat, hard. There was a sudden stench of blood.

Harry couldn't help himself. Terrified, he backed away from the coffin, until his back slammed into the vault wall behind him. Part of his mind knew he should be trying to help Barnaby, but he couldn't overcome his numbing fear and force himself forwards. Another part of his mind told him that Barnaby was beyond help.

Most of his mind simply shrieked in fear. Harry didn't know whether the screaming was internal or external, and honestly didn't care.

Barnaby struggled to pull free, but he was held by inflexible hands. His eyes bulged, his body spasmed—and the thing in the coffin continued to suckle at his blood-stained throat. Barnaby's struggles slowed, and then died, and his expression of disbelief and terror remained etched on a face that was now paler than the moonlight. A moment later, the dead man pushed him away, and Barnaby collapsed into a heap on the floor of the crypt.

The corpse removed a handkerchief from its pocket and wiped away the blood from around its mouth fastidiously. He was sitting up in the coffin, and then he looked directly at Harry. With a slight smile, he bent his knees and then sprang easily out of the coffin and onto the floor.

Harry was frozen, unable to move, barely able to think. He was staring his death in the face, he knew, and there was nothing at all that he could do. He was too terrified even to try and save his own life.

The creature—surely he was no man of any kind?—moved slowly, hypnotically forward. He licked his lips that had suddenly grown to be red and living, and he reached out a hand that was now warm. He stroked Harry's face almost tenderly.

"What am I going to do with you, my boy?" he asked, quite gently. The contrast between this and his previously savage attack on Barnaby was even more unnerving to Harry.

"Please—don't kill me," Harry managed to squeak.

The vampire—now the correct name popped into Harry's brain—laughed gently. "I've drunk my fill for the evening," he said. "One person's life-blood is quite sufficient. And I am a predator, not a murderer—there is no need to kill you."

"Then… you'll let me go?" Harry asked, almost eagerly.

"If I do, you'll tell people about me. That would be… unfortunate."

"I wouldn't say a word!" Harry burbled. "Honest I wouldn't! Besides, who'd ever believe me?"

"Granted, not many would," the vampire admitted. "But the people who sealed me inside my coffin would, and they would come after me again." He shook his head. "No, I am safe only as long as they think me still entombed. So, I cannot allow you to talk."

Harry felt the fear gripping him by the throat again. "But you said you wouldn't kill me!" he protested. "That there was no need!"

"True. And I am a man of my word." He suddenly put an arm around Harry. "My, you're shaking! Are you cold? It's been a while since I felt warmth or chill, so I'm really not sure if it's a raw night or not."

"No, no," Harry said quickly. "It's a pleasant night." He glanced at Barnaby's corpse. "I mean…"

The vampire followed his gaze. "Ah! I see. You're *frightened*. Well, that's a perfectly sensible response, my boy, in the circumstances. You'd have to be an idiot not to be scared, and you're clearly no idiot." Then he laughed, and snapped his fingers. "I have it! I am going to be in need of a servant, my lad—how would you like the job?"

Harry stared at him in shock. "A servant? Me?"

"A servant. You."

Not killed and drained, then, was Harry's first thought. He nodded, eagerly. "Yes, yes, fine—a servant."

"Splendid." The vampire patted him on the shoulder. "Well, we had better get to work then, hadn't we?" He glanced around the crypt. "Well, the first thing to do, I think, is to move to somewhere considerably less gloomy. I'm sure my old family home still awaits me. But we'd better tidy up before we go. It wouldn't do to leave this tomb is such a mess, now, would it? Quite disrespectful to the family in here—and it might alert my foes that I'm free again."

Harry's fears were starting to dissipate now. After all, if he had a vampire on his side, what else did he have to worry about? There was nothing worse in the night. He pointed down at Barnaby's body. "Should we put him in the coffin, then?"

"Dear me, no, my lad. Don't you know *anything* at all about vampires? We have to sleep in our own coffins during the day, so we'll have to take that with us." He smiled again. "Since you and… that… were obviously body-snatching, I assume you have a cart around here somewhere?"

"In the street," Harry admitted.

"That will be most helpful." The vampire glanced around the crypt, and he smiled again. "Ah! Cousin Ada! Perfect." He chuckled to himself. "She always swore she'd never be caught dead in bed with a man… Help me pull her coffin out."

As they slid it from its alcove, Harry suddenly remembered one thing he *had* heard about vampires. "Hang on a minute." He gestured at Barnaby's body. "You drained all of his blood, right?"

"Indeed. Quite delicious." They had the coffin on the floor, and the vampire simply tore the lid off it. Inside was the desiccated remnants of a female corpse in a faded dress. "Ah, Ada—looking better than usual, I see."

"But… if you drained all of his blood… isn't that going to make *him* a vampire, too?"

"Indeed it is, my boy." He bent and lifted Barnaby's corpse up without any obvious effort. "Tomorrow night, he'll awaken as a creature of the night, yes." He dropped the body on top of the woman's corpse, and then artfully arranged Barnaby's arms in an embrace. "Doesn't that look charming? Do you have a hammer?"

"Barnaby has one in his bag."

"So he does." The vampire extracted it, and then used it to hammer the coffin lid firmly back into place. "Now, we'll replace this, and nobody will know we've been here, will they?"

"But—won't he arise and come back as a vampire?"

"Yes and no, dear boy," the other replied. "You see, there won't be any room in that alcove for him to be able to lift the lid of the coffin. He'll awaken, but he won't be able to get out. I certainly don't need any competition for victims, and he won't be any brighter as a vampire than he was as a human. He'd be bound to create attention, and then the people who imprisoned me would know I'm out and come looking for me again. And we can't have that, can we?

"I heard what he was saying when he opened my coffin, and I'm sure he'll discover he was exactly right.

"He will be a long time dead…"

218

I seem to be drawn to "theme" anthologies. In this case, it was for horror stories set in New York. My heroine, Melissa, was engaged in an activity I'm very familiar with: shopping at The Strand bookstore in New York (one of the largest in the world) and then catching the subway uptown from Union Square. It's a journey I've taken myself a large number of times. Fortunately, never like this one.

Now Departing...

Death came, inevitably, at the most inconvenient moment.

Melissa was standing—slouching, more accurately - on the uptown platform of the N, Q and R train at Union Square, reading her book. In her backpack were two new purchases from the Strand, one of her favorite shops to explore in the city. "Seven miles of books" made the place irresistible to her, and she visited it at least twice a week without fail. Then, afterwards, the first train up to Herald Square and on to her favorite pub, Brendan's, on 35th. She had her routine well planned, and she enjoyed the predictability of the pleasure it brought her.

And then—this.

She had cultivated a style that kept most people from intruding on her personal space. She wore clothes in layers—leggings and leg warmers, sweater and heavy jacket, scarf and shapeless hat over her somewhat stringy hair. Large glasses—"men never make passes at girls who wear glasses" her mother would say at frequent intervals (though whether as warning or out of approval Melissa never had been able to figure out) and the inevitable book. Even on the subways, nobody much looked at her.

Except now.

Melissa was annoyed, at first. She could manage to screen out almost anyone around her, but this man was... different. It wasn't simply that he was staring at her. It wasn't even that he was incredibly good-looking, though he was. Movie-star attractive, and dressed almost entirely in black (which was a cliché, when she considered it)—leather shoes, socks, suit and shirt. Only his tie was different—so white it virtually dazzled. It wasn't even that nobody else was even looking at him, though there were certainly several women, and more than one or two men, who were bound to have found him sexy. It was mostly that she *knew* he was Death.

Once he knew he had her attention, Death smiled at her. His teeth, naturally, were white and perfect. There was even a little sparkle to his eyes. "Hello, Melissa," he said, pleasantly.

"What do you want?" she growled, eyeing her page in the book.

"Come now—you *know* what I want. I want *you*."

"I'm busy. Come back later. In about a century."

"I'm sorry." And he did sound sincere. "I'm afraid I can't. I'll be elsewhere then. It has to be here and now."

"I'm not ready," she said, crossly. She was surprised that she wasn't afraid, but there was something kind of likeable about Death. He seemed almost like a friend. A very inconvenient friend you really didn't want to run into.

"Nobody is these days," Death said, sadly. "Not like the Middle Ages—ah, those were good days. Warriors prepared to die with their weapons in their hands, blood everywhere..." He sighed. "Or maidens willing to collapse from consumption at a heartbeat's notice. People were glad to see me then."

"Well, they didn't have a lot to live for, did they?" Melissa pointed out. "Not like today." She indicated her book. "I've only got three chapters to go. I want to see how it turns out."

"The butler did it," he informed her.

"There *isn't* a butler in the story, and it's not a murder mystery."

"Well, I can't be expected to know everything," he said. "I tend to keep busy, you know. Lots of deaths to arrange."

"Then go and arrange somebody else's and leave me in peace," Melissa snapped.

"Sorry, I can't do that," he said. "It's against the rules." He examined his immaculately manicured fingernails. "You're next on the schedule, so here I am."

Not for the first time, Melissa wished she'd taken those self-defense lessons her Mom had suggested, over and over again. "And what will you do if I refuse to go?"

"Nothing."

She was caught by surprise. "Nothing? Nothing at all?"

He spread his hands. "Nothing at all. I'll just wait until you agree to go. Then we go."

"You're going to have a long wait," Melissa told him. "I have lots of plans. Finish this book, for one. Then there's a couple more in my backpack. A drink and a meal at Brendan's... And that's just for lunchtime today. After that..." Her voice trailed off as she saw his pitying look. "What?"

"I told you, I'll do nothing if you don't go with me. I should have added that *you'll* do nothing, too. Look about you."

She lowered the book she'd been employing as a kind of shield (though what good it would have done against Death she couldn't say) and glanced about the platform at her fellow travelers. There were about thirty of them, the usual suspects. A gaggle of Asian girls, a couple of family groups, the inevitable shoppers, various people with those annoying roll-along suitcases that always seemed to clip you in the legs, the obligatory homeless man, a few conspicuous tourists with their German-language guide books...

All of them frozen in place, like a still from a movie.

"What have you done to them?" Melissa asked, startled.

"To them? Nothing. I'm not here for them, remember." Death examined his fingernails again. "I've simply stopped your personal time. From this moment until you go with me, it's simply *now* for you." He shrugged. "I have millions of deaths to arrange every moment, from the lowliest bacterium to Heads of State. It would be impossible if I couldn't stop time. Trust me, these days *everybody* wants to talk and talk before they go with me. I really long for the good old days and the *today is a good day to die* attitudes. Still, at least this way I do get to know my charges before we go. I guess all changes have their pros and cons."

"But why *me*?" Melissa asked. She was aware she was starting to sound whiney, and Mother had always told her that this was an unattractive feature in anyone. "What have I done?"

"This isn't a case of having *done* anything," Death said, as patiently as he could. "It's simply your time. Death comes for everyone, you know." He smiled, and she could detect the hint of a skull in that smile. "I'm greedy."

"But who decides it's my time?"

"Not me. That's an Executive decision, and I'm strictly field work. I have my list and I go visit everyone I'm told to."

"Well, who tells you?" she asked.

"Sorry, sweetie—those are the sorts of questions you get answered *after* Death, not before. You'll just have to wait."

"Then there *is* something after Death?" she asked, hopefully. "I've never really been sure about that."

He shrugged. "Does it matter what I say? You have no way of knowing if what I tell you will be the truth. I mean, if I say there isn't, then you're going to want to stand here jawing forever, and that's going to get really dull for me. And if I say there is, how can you be sure I'm not just saying that to hurry you along?" He glanced at his expensive-looking pocket watch. The hands were not moving, and he clicked the cover shut and put it back into his suit's pocket. "You just have to face the fact that I'm Death, and that you have to come with me sooner or later. It's just a matter of setting your mind to it and doing it."

"But I don't want to go," Melissa protested. "I'm happy as I am. I want to stay."

"Happy?" Death rolled his eyes. "You're wrapped up tighter than a nun to avoid getting to actually *know* anyone. You hide from the world behind your books. And your only lasting relationship is with the battery-operated toy in your night-stand."

Melissa's face burned. "Let's leave my night-stand out of this. And I *like* all of the things you mentioned. We can't all be raging extroverts, you know."

"There's so much more to life, you know."

"No, I *don't* know—and, apparently, I'll never have the chance to find out, will I?"

"That's true," he agreed. "Well, there's so much more to Death, then."

"You're just saying that so I'll go with you." Melissa glared at him. He smiled back.

"That's always a possibility," he agreed. He held up a finger. "Hold onto that thought for a moment, will you?"

She followed his gaze, now riveted on a rather scraggly rat that was foraging along the edge of the rail. "Hey," she complained. "I thought you said time was stopped for everything but me. What about him?"

"He can move for the same reason you can move," Death replied. "Because his moment is *now*."

Melisa jumped and squealed in shock as he suddenly became fluid motion. From appearing to be a tall, handsome man he somehow slipped into the form of a cat—an immense leonine shape. She took in a flash of sharp teeth the size of her fingers and long, vicious claws as he leaped from the platform onto the tracks. Another swift motion and he had snatched up the rat in those teeth and snapped down. The rat shrieked once. The cat turned and jumped agilely back onto the platform. Melissa saw that it had an all-black coat with a single white stripe down the chest before she wondered if the jaws were intended for her next.

Instead, Death smoothly slipped back into the form of the charming man again, the stripe now a tie against his black suit. He used his left hand to push the tail of the rat into his mouth and crunched down hard before swallowing. "Now, where were we?"

"Well, *you* were eating a rat," she managed to say.

"Yes, sorry for the distraction, but as I said, departures have to happen on schedule, and I'm so much better at sticking to schedules than the MTA." He looked at her in concern. "I'm sorry, did that disturb you?"

"Oh, no—people change into giant cats and gobble up rats in front of me every day."

He sighed. "I'm sorry, I do seem to have upset you. But when it's time, it's time, and there's really very little I can do about it."

Melissa swallowed. "Is that… is that what will happen to me?"

"What?" Death seemed confused for a moment, and then understood. "Oh, no, my dear—have no fear. I shalln't chow down on you. To everything there is an end—in the case of rats, it's as a snack. With you it will be much nicer, I promise. All you have to do is to kiss me."

"What?" Melissa stared at him. "Kiss you?"

"Yes. I know you're rather out of practice, but, trust me, it'll come back to you." He smiled at her. There was a bit of rat fur caught between his teeth and she shuddered.

"Kiss *that* mouth?" she said. "After what's just gone into it? No, thank you."

"It's what you have to do," he said, gently. "The kiss of Death, and all that…" Then he smiled charmingly again, this time the fur having vanished. "But if you prefer, it doesn't have to be *this* mouth…" He waved at his lips which had suddenly become rather fuller and feminine. Melissa blinked as she realized that Death had changed again, this time into a very female form. She wore a tight black sheath dress, very low-cut, high-heeled shoes, and her hair was long, thick and dark. About her neck was a string of pure white peals that hung over her ample and prominent breasts.

She was *hot*… Despite herself, Melissa found the thought of kissing her quite a turn-on… before she remembered that this was still Death. "That's... quite a change," she murmured.

"You like it?" Death cocked her head on one side and grinned at her seductively. "I do get a lot of response out of this form. And I can tell it appeals to you more than *he* did..."

"But it's obviously not real," Melissa objected. "I mean, the way you zip between bodies like that..."

She shrugged, which made her breasts move enticingly. "What difference does it make? You already knew I wasn't human, anyway. This form is as real—or unreal—as any other I can assume. And I assure you, it's quite anatomically correct." She grinned. "Play your cards right, and you may get to find out."

Melissa had to force her mind to focus. "No! You're still Death! And if I kiss you, I die."

"Yes, you've grasped the essential point." Death grinned again. "Want to grasp a couple more points?" She wiggled her chest.

"Stop that!" Melissa begged. "Bribery isn't going to work. I'm not going to do it."

Death pouted. "Oh, come on—you know you're going to have to, sooner or later. I don't mind you having some fun doing it, but this offer won't last forever. This moment lasts just as long as you hold out—ten seconds or ten thousand years. Nothing will change until you give in."

"I've got my books," Melissa said. "I can keep busy."

"How many times can you read those three books before you go crazy?" Death asked her. "It doesn't matter how good they are, you'll get sick of them in time."

Melissa knew that Death was right—she was just putting off the inevitable. But what other option did she have? She really didn't want to die, having not yet seen very much of life. It just wasn't *fair*! But fairness, it seemed, didn't have a thing to do with it. And if she *did* have to go, maybe having a little fun doing it. It would, after all, be her last chance.

She must have been taking too long to make up her mind. Death started to get pouty again, and scowled. "Maybe you need another sort of incentive?" she asked. "Excuse me while I change into something more... helpful." Melissa was just starting to wonder what Death would look like in a sheer negligee when Death changed.

Melissa screamed, and backed away. She remembered the admonition to avoid the edge of the platform just in time. She backed into one of the posts, clutching at it as if that helped her clutch onto sanity.

Death was now a woman-sized insect, an immense preying mantis. Her antennae twitched, the over-large mandibles clacked open and shut, dripping saliva, and her long, thin forelegs reached out toward Melissa... Panic welled up inside her as this nightmare form advanced slowly toward her and then lunged. Melissa screamed, but the attack wasn't at her. Instead, the mandibles shot forward and latched onto a cockroach the size of Melissa's palm. The jaws crunched down, and with a cracking sound the cockroach died. Death munched on it, and then slipped from the mantis back into the beautiful woman, licking her lips.

"Death's a bitch," she murmured. "And my patience is wearing a little thin. You can embrace me one way or the other, sweetie, but embrace me you will."

Melissa was shaking, and on the verge of retching. "I don't like my options."

"Tough." Death examined her nails, which were long, pointed and painted a lustrous black. "Death is sweet, or Death is a bitch—that's it. Your choice, but you'd better pick fast." She grinned, nastily. "You won't like the default choice, believe me."

She was beaten; Melissa knew it. While Death was seductive she could probably withstand it. After all, she'd had plenty of practice at saying no. Now she was starting to wish she hadn't been quite so prudish. She'd been saving herself, as her mother had always advocated—but now there was nothing to save herself for. Now, if she had to go, would it be so bad to die in a brief moment of passion? She looked at the gorgeous woman again, but shook her head.

"I can't do it with you," she said. "Can I have him back?"

"Him?" Death looked surprised. "Do you really prefer him to me? I could have sworn I'd read you right…"

"And you probably have," Melissa admitted. "If I was going to have sex, I'd most likely prefer playing with you. But since I'm not, and it's just a kiss… Honestly, I'd rather kiss rat-eating lips than cockroach-chomping ones." She shuddered. "And that mantis is kind of stuck in my memory."

"He's still the mantis also," Death said.

"Maybe. I know it's not logical. But you said it's my choice, and I've made it." She screwed up all of her courage. "I'll kiss *him*. Then you can get on with your wholesale slaughter."

"It's just a job," Death said. Then she gave another seductive shudder, jiggling all the interesting bits that Melissa would have loved to explore, and Death was male again. "You've made the right choice, my dear," he assured her.

Melissa hoped he was right—but it wasn't really a choice, after all. It was simply inevitable. "Let's get on with it," she said. She moved forward, trying to suppress the memories of the cat swallowing the rat as she focused on his lips. She leaned in and kissed him.

He was surprisingly gentle, kissing her back with what appeared to be true passion on his part. Melissa felt tingling in her pants, and was amazed at her reaction. She kissed him again, this time longer and with more feeling. This was starting to become quite arousing…

"Come with me," he whispered gently in her ear. Melissa forced herself to look away as he indicated the edge of the platform. Right on cue a train drew in. It wasn't a Q, though—this was sleek and black, and there was no sign of a driver. It was a single car, swift and silent until the doors sighed open. The interior was all black, with white highlights. There were seats that actually looked comfortable. And was that a *bed* toward the back? It was difficult to tell, as it was black in the blackness. Death took her hand and stepped into the car. "Come," he repeated.

Amazed, Melissa went.

"And then what happened, ma'am?" Transit Officer Rick Gomez looked at the shaken old lady. It helped, sometimes, to sound detached.

The woman took a deep breath. "She just... stepped off the platform, right into the path of the train," she said. "Calm as anything, as if she was just crossing the street. Then..." she shuddered.

Rick could imagine. He'd seen the results of a handful of jumpers in his time. They tended to involve lots of blood and unpleasant cracking and squishing noises. The platform had shut down after the young girl had stepped in front of the Q train, and recovery and clean-up had begun. The old lady had been the only one who'd admitted to seeing the girl's final moments, so when everyone else had been hurried from the platform, she had stayed. Rick carefully didn't look over her shoulder, where the crew were picking up what was left of the suicide. At least she hadn't been pushed, as sometimes happened.

"Thank you, ma'am." He had the woman's contact information and preliminary statement. If the authorities needed more, they could contain her. "I think you can go now," he said, gently. "Will you be all right?"

"All right?" The old lady blinked. "Not for a while, young man. But I'll manage." Rick led her to the stairs, and watched as she climbed them. She'd be taken to a bus to complete her trip.

There was a small crowd of gawkers up there, of course. Whenever there was a death, people *had* to gather, it seemed. In the bunch he saw a gorgeous young woman, dressed entirely in black, with a string of pearls so white they almost glowed. She smiled at him and mouthed the words: "See you soon." There was something vaguely familiar about her, though he surely would have remembered seeing someone so stunning before. He hoped she was right, and he *would* see her soon.

She was hot...

Okay, my warped sense of humor at work again. I've not seen a huge amount of anime, but my favorite is Dirty Pair. That involves two amazingly beautiful girls who are trouble consultants in the future. They solve all of their cases, but somehow always seem to cause an incredible amount of destruction in their wake. So I wondered what would have happened had they been born in the 16th century instead...

Pink Samurai

"It's not our fault!"

The Samurai Master took a deep breath, closed his eyes for a moment to contemplate either harmony or murder and then favored the two women with a glare that could wither trees or melt snow. Neither Azami nor Hoshi seemed to pay it the slightest mind. Instead, both appeared to be on the verge of tears.

"Then whose fault is it?" he asked, with as much patience as he could muster. "It was, after all, your dragon which ate the Shogun's third favorite shih-tzu, given to him personally by the Emperor of China."

Hoshi - smaller, darker and quieter of the two cousins - gave Tatsu a pat on his scaly head. The small dragon, barely four feet tall, almost purred at the touch. It did nothing for the Master's blood pressure. "It's not Tatsu's fault either," she protested. "That wretched dog provoked him. And you know what a wretch it was. It was always pooping on your dojjen floor."

"That's right," Azami agreed swiftly, with what she clearly hoped was an ingratiating smile. "Why, just two days ago, you stepped right in it and went sliding…"

"I know very well what I did," snapped the Master, while he still had a little dignity left. The other Samurai in the room were managing to retain their impassive faces, but there was

230

no guaranteeing how long that would last. Sooner or later, one of them would burst, either with laughter or anger. And, either way, the harmony of his dojjen would be ruined. Yet again.

"That is still no excuse for your dragon to eat the wretched dog," he added.

Hoshi pouted. "Well, you won't let us feed him fresh meat, and a growing dragon can't live entirely on rice."

"Growing?" asked the Master, alarmed. "Growing how fast?"

Azami shrugged. "A lot slower than normal on his rice diet. If we can just keep him away from dogs..." Her voice trailed off under the Master's withering glare.

"Because you are the Shogun's nieces," he said, his voice astonishingly composed, "your punishment will be minor... this time. You will go out to the Cherry Temple, and cleanse it."

Fire burnt in Azami's eyes. "We are Samurai, not cleaning women," she replied.

"I didn't say clean it, I said cleanse it," the Master informed her. "According to the priests, it is being haunted by several mamono. Two priests have already been beheaded by these demons."

"Well, that sounds like our kind of thing," Hoshi replied, clapping her hands enthusiastically. "I haven't seen a good haunting in months." Eagerly, she turned to her cousin. "Come on, Azami, let's go right away! You, too, Tatsu." She gave the Master a suspicious glare. "You'd better stick close to us for a while... just for safety's sake." She gave a semi-respectful bow to the Master, and then skipped out of the room, Azami and the dragon more sedately in tow.

When the door closed behind them, the Master let his breath out in a long sigh. Despite his training, it was extremely hard to retain his composure with the two women around. "It's the Seventeenth Century," he muttered under his breath, quoting the instructions the Shogun had given him months earlier. "Get with the times. Women are no longer merely wives, daughters and pillow-talkers. They are becoming more liberated. It's time for a couple of female Samurai. Hah!" He turned to see several of his students staring at him. Their expressions varied from pity to disgust; he liked none of them. To the unfortunate student who happened to be standing the closest, he barked: "Why do you have that disgusting look on your face?"

The student cringed, but answered in a voice that almost managed to be steady: "Honorable master, I do not understand why you put up with those two... girls. They do not respect you or our traditions, and they are... unharmonious."

"Besides," added his less-restrained neighbor, "they are all wrong."

"Wrong?" asked the Master, with a gentleness that would have terrified anyone who really knew him. "In what way?"

"Their armor, honored master, for one thing," the hapless student answered. "A Samurai paints his armor with the most ferocious faces to intimidate his foes and scare away the demons. They have their armor painted pink! And with happy faces on their helmets! It is an abomination and should not be allowed!"

"Really?" asked the Master, almost tenderly. "What is an abomination and should not be allowed," he barked in the student's left ear, "is a student who presumes to know better than his Master! For such temerity, you shall run around the Holy City fourteen times. Starting now!"

The student paled as he realized his dreadful error. Then he bowed, and immediately sprinted from the dojjen. The Samurai Master smiled to himself, and then composed his face as he turned to face his remaining students. "Are there any more who think themselves wiser than I?"

Absolutely silence, without even the intake of breath.

"Good. Perhaps you are not beyond education even yet." The Master dismissed them, and then considered what he had done. Azami and Hoshi were likely to be the death of him yet...

"I can't take it any more, Hoshi!" howled Azami, throwing her hands in the air, and her head back. "If I have to act like a cheerful bimbo another minute, I'm going to crack up."

"Azami," Hoshi said gently, "I know it's tough. But you did want to be a Samurai. Now you have to go through with it."

"It's not being a Samurai I object to," Azami growled. "It's this oh-so-cutesy act you insist we do. I'm ready to heave up my breakfast. And the day before's. Why can't we simply act like the warriors we are?"

Patting her cousin on the arm, Hoshi shook her head. "We tried that, and it didn't work. The male students were all offended that we were better than them. They were constantly challenging us to duels to prove they were the best." She sighed. "I don't know about you, but after being forced to kill three of them, I had had quite enough. You know these men are utterly convinced of their own superiority. A competent female Samurai offends their dignity. So it's better that they think we're a couple of cheerful bimbos who got the job because we're the Shogun's nieces. Or would you rather go back to having to kill them to prove you're better than they are?"

Azami growled, and pounded her fists in the air. "No, I don't want to kill any more of them - at least, not yet. But I may, if this keeps up. I can't stand what they're saying and thinking about us. We're constantly being made fools of by the Master. Another punishment. And just because Tatsu ate that stupid dog. I was about ready to eat him myself." She grinned nastily. "Shih-tzu sushi!"

Hoshi giggled at the thought. She could almost believe that Azami would have done it, too. "But we are not being punished," she said, more soberly. "I do not think we fool the Master at all. You will kindly note that we were the ones who were given this dangerous assignment, not one of the boys. By calling it punishment, the Master staved off their resentment."

That hadn't occurred to Azami, obviously. She considered the point. "You think he sees through us?"

233

"I'd be willing to bet on it," Hoshi answered. "And I think, deep down, he approves. So we have to continue to be cute and dumb for everyone's sake." She bent down to scratch Tatsu under the chin. "Anyway, look at the good we've been able to do. If the Master had sent two of the males to slay this dragon, Tatsu would be dead by now. And we wouldn't be able to enjoy his cute little face, or scratch his tummy. Our silly act saved his life. The boys only think about glory, blood-shed and trophy heads for their walls. We have the more important virtues to consider." She smiled at her cousin. "So, what do you say?"

Azami managed a wide grin, and looked particularly cute and silly. "I say, let's go see how cute these mamono are!"

When they arrived at the Shinto temple, they were dressed in full armor. As always, passers-by had given them some very odd looks. Their somewhat idiosyncratic pink armor did take a little getting used to, Hoshi knew, but the element of surprise it gave them never hurt in a fight. She stared through the slits in her smiley mask at the torii at the entrance to the Shinto shrine. Normally such a welcome gate would be in the form of two uprights with one or two crossbars over it. This one was warped and twisted, with extra pieces of wood added, to make it into an idiogram. It was a good job nobody could see her blushing under her helmet.

Azami sounded irked. "I'm not very good with script," she complained. What is that torii spelling?"

"You don't want to know," Hoshi assured her. "And it's anatomically impossible, anyway. I think this is the work of the mamono, changing the welcome gate."

"I'd say you were right," agreed Azami, gesturing at the headless corpse of a monk beside one of the uprights. "That's downright unwelcoming."

Turning to Tatsu, who was already licking his lips at the sight, Hoshi said sternly: "Stay here until I call you. And no snacking!" Tatsu tried to give her his what, innocent little me? look, but even he could see she wasn't fooled for an instant.

Hoshi wasn't joking. It was one thing to munch on a disliked dog; if he tried sampling a dead monk, that would be too much for the Samurai Master to forgive.

Azami shrugged, withdrew her katana, and walked slowly past the corpse. Hoshi did likewise, noting that there didn't seem to be any blood. Either the monk had been killed elsewhere and moved here as a warning, or else something had drunk the blood. Either was possible for a demon.

The path ahead was lined with cherry trees, which must be why the shrine had received its name. It was actually quite beautiful and restful, if you didn't pay attention to the two large, translucent demons that were attempting to drop-kick the severed head of the monk over another torii. Naturally, Hoshi paid very careful attention to the demons indeed. Both were about eight feet tall, with hideous faces that only a mother could love. And demons didn't procreate. The temple itself was beyond them, and Hoshi could just make out several pallid heads peeking through slats in the shutters. That had to be where the rest of the monks were hiding out. The one who had been killed had probably tried to banish the demons. Nobody else seemed in a hurry to retry that experiment.

Boy, are they ugly," Azami muttered. "The one on the left reminds me of my last date, in fact."

"You had a date?" asked Hoshi. "And didn't find a boy for me, too?"

"You're grown up. Find your own dates." Azami stepped forward, and raised her voice. "All right, listen up. I'm in a bad mood right now and would just love to kick some mamono butt. So either leave right now, or face my wrath."

"Um, Azami," Hoshi said urgently, "that's not really a very good move."

"Shut up," growled Azami. "I want to beat the crap out of something. It'll make me feel better."

"I doubt it," Hoshi muttered, knowing it was too late to stop events now.

The two demons had whirled around to face the Samurai when they had heard Azami's challenge. Their faces scowled, making them look even worse. That amazed Hoshi, who would have bet such a transformation was impossible. Then the first mamono caught sight of what faced them and his face furrowed in puzzlement.

"What have we here?" he howled, gesturing at Azami. "Can this really be a Samurai?"

"It must be a joke, brother," the second demon answered, fangs exposed by his dreadful grin. "No self-respecting Samurai wears pink."

"You want respect," Azami yelled back, "then come here and feel my steel." She raised her katana threateningly.

The first demon paused, frowning. "That's a woman!" he exclaimed. "They sent a woman after us. And I was so looking forward to eating the brains of a Samurai."

"They did it to annoy us," his fellow answered. "They know that this one doesn't have any brains to eat. Or she wouldn't be here."

"That does it," fumed Azami, striding forward. "Hoshi may prevent me from slicing and dicing our fellow students, but it's open season on mamono. Come on, suckers. Make my day."

The demons laughed, and then came toward her. Hoshi winced, knowing what was bound to happen. Azami gave her battle cry and leaped forward, whirling her katana in a deadly pattern.

The sword went right through the demon. Azami paused, surprised. She was even more surprised when the hand she'd failed to sever whirled back and slapped her hard enough to send her tumbling several feet.

Hoshi ran forward and helped her cousin to her feet again. "I wish you'd listen to me sometimes," she hissed. "Mamono aren't truly material. You can't harm them like that."

"Why doesn't the rule work both ways?" complained Azami. "It's not fair!"

Hoshi shrugged. "It just is. That's one of the rules of demons."

"So we can't defeat them?" asked Azami, aghast. "This is a suicide mission? I knew it - the Master hates us!"

The first demon grinned, exposing long, sharp, curved fangs. "That second pink thing has a brain," he growled. "Dinner time!" He stomped forward, flattening a lovely cherry tree as he did so.

"There's another magical rule," Hoshi told her companion. "You can make a demon solid if it meets another magical creature. So..." She whirled around and yelled: "Tatsu!"

The dragon had been waiting for the call. His wings were very rudimentary, unable to carry his long, sinuous body very far. And his legs were somewhat ridiculously short. But when working together, both sets of appendages meant that Tatsu could move with very respectable speed. He half-flew, half-skittered to the two Samurai.

The attacking demon tried to draw up short, but his earlier eagerness worked against him. He managed to stop barely four feet from Hoshi and six from Tatsu. Hoshi whirled her katana and struck.

The demon's head lifted neatly from its body, spun twice in the air and then flopped to the ground, rolling slightly. Tatsu licked his lips and pounced. After all, there were certainly not any rules against devouring demons...

"Payback time!" howled Azami happily. She launched herself at the second demon, who tried to turn and flee. Now he was solid, he had suddenly lost all interest in a fight. Azami had no intention of allowing him to get away. Or to die too quickly. "Take that!" she screamed, lopping off one of his claws. Tatsu followed her eagerly, snapping up each little piece she hacked off the demon. Both of them were having a whole lot of fun.

Hoshi decided that they didn't need her help. Trying to dodge all the portions of demon anatomy that showered around her, she headed for the temple, sheathing her sword. She rapped on the wooden door-frame and smiled at the bewildered face of the monk who timorously opened the door a crack.

"I think your problems are just about over," Hoshi informed him. She checked back over her shoulder, just in time to hear Azami yell: "Timber!" as she hacked off the demon's left leg. Since she had already hacked off its right, the poor demon couldn't hop away from her any more. Seeing the end of her amusement in sight, Azami sighed and finally sliced off the mamono's head. Tatsu chomped it up, and then belched a small blue flame.

"Yes," Hoshi said cheerfully. "We're just mopping up." Tatsu was wandering about the yard, gulping up the last of the demon body parts and licking up stray drops of sizzling mamono blood. "No need to thank us. We're just doing our job." She bowed respectfully at his ashen face and then went to join her cousin. "Now do you feel better?" she asked.

"Lots," admitted Azami, satisfaction in her voice. "I'm feeling almost bimbo-like again. I can face those idiots back at the dojjen with a smile now."

"Good." Hoshi turned and called Tatsu to heel. He trotted over, licking his lips and long, curly whiskers. He'd enjoyed himself and managed to get in a good snack, too. Hoshi frowned. "Does Tatsu look a little bigger to you?"

Azami studied the dragon. "Yes. I think demon flesh must agree with him. He might be too big to fit back in the dojjen door. I don't think the Master's going to be too happy."

"We've slain the demons and cleansed the temple," Hoshi pointed out as they walked back through the torii. "He can't complain too much. Besides, if he does say anything..." She paused, and they chorused happily together:

"It's not our fault!"

This is the exception in this collection: it's never been printed before. It has, however, been recorded. I was asked by Chris Pederson to write a Doctor Omega *story for him to help raise money for the Galapagos Conservancy, only this time with the Doctor traveling to parallel worlds instead of in time and space. I was happy to do so, and immensely surprised when instead of printing it, he had an audio version made up, read by the talented John Guilor. Anyway, now here it is in print form at last.*

Doctor Omega and the Silent Planet

"That's... odd."

"Odd?" Denis Borel's head shot up from where he had been studying the instruments on the closest panel. He appeared to be alarmed by this simple pronouncement. "I don't like it when you say things like that, Doctor. What's wrong?"

Doctor Omega was staring in quite the opposite direction to his young friend. His calm gaze was fixed on the view outside of the Omega Tuner. The walls were—as the Doctor preferred—currently transparent, so the world they had arrived on was visible to them. "Wrong?" The Doctor blinked. "I don't know that anything is exactly *wrong*—just... unexpected."

Borel looked worried. "Considering the fact we're hop-scotching about parallel worlds and each is vastly different from the last," he said, "hearing you say *odd* and *unexpected* worries me."

"My dear boy, you should calm down," Doctor Omega advised. "Stress can be quite deadly, you know."

"Visiting these parallel Earths of yours can be quite deadly, too," Borel said darkly. "Maybe we should just skip this one and go on to the next?"

"What? Where's your scientific curiosity, my boy?" the Doctor asked.

"That died at birth," Borel replied. He scanned the view, clearly happy to be safely inside the Omega Tuner. "I don't see anything wrong."

The scientist sighed. "I repeat, I didn't say that anything was *wrong*; it is merely… odd."

Borel gestured at the bleak landscape surrounding their strange craft. "Rocks, sand, dust and sky," he said. "In what way is that odd?"

"Because that is *all* that there is," the Doctor said. He rummaged in a locker and pulled out what looked like the bag of a country physician. "Why don't we take a little look and see, hmm?" He threw the lever that opened the external door and strode outside. Borel waivered in indecision a moment and then hurried after him. Once they were both outside, the Doctor closed the door, and the Tuner looked like almost any rock in the area. He tapped Borel on the chest lightly. "Better make a mental note where the Tuner is, eh?" he suggested. "Wouldn't want you to try climbing inside another rock." He chuckled at his own joke as he ambled off.

"It's the one with footprints leading from it!" Borel called. "Even I know that!" But he did stop and confirm his observation before setting off after the Doctor.

Doctor Omega pottered around in an apparently haphazard manner, peeking and peering, stopping from time to time to mutter over a rock or a small gully. Borel looked around, trying to take in the larger picture. The Tuner appeared to have materialized on a relatively flat plain leading down to a small river. Jumbles of rocks were everywhere, and dust and sand swirled lightly about their feet as a slight breeze blew. There was nothing else to see, and he rapidly became bored. The Doctor, on the other hand, seemed to be most intrigued. He stopped by one patch of rocks and opened his bag. Inside were several scientific instruments that Borel couldn't recall having seen before. Whatever they measured, the Doctor seemed to be satisfied with their readings. Murmuring happily to himself, he scuttled off to take further readings elsewhere. Finally, he ended at the river and spent several minutes looking at it before scooping up a cupful and subjecting it to analysis.

He straightened up, snapped his bag closed and brushed off his hands. "Well, my young friend," he asked, "what do you make of all of this?"

Borel shook his head. "I make nothing of this," he replied. "We've landed in a desert somewhere, that's all."

"A desert?" The traveler shook his head. "No, no, no, no." He gestured toward the bubbling waters. "Not a desert, not with that river." He smiled. "I believe you enjoy a little fishing—what would you make of this spot?"

Borel glanced around. "No shade," he said. No grass to sit on." He peered down at the river. "And I don't see any fish."

"Aha!" The Doctor's eyes twinkled. "*Now* perhaps you're starting to comprehend."

"Comprehend *what*?" Borel asked, exasperated. "I don't understand what you're getting at."

"Dear me, and I did so think you were starting to use that brain of yours at last. What a pity, what a pity."

"There's no call to insult me," Borel growled. "Just explain what bee you've got in your bonnet now, will you?"

"Aha!" The Doctor's face was split by a wide grin. "Perhaps your subconscious is more alert than your conscious! A bee, indeed! Have you seen any bees? Any insects of any kind, in fact?"

"No," Borel admitted. "Generally, I'm happy when I am not bothered by them. Most are quite annoying."

"No, my friend—they are quite essential to the chain of life." He waved his hand airily. "And there are none. There are no fish. There are no birds. There are no animals. There is not even a blade of grass."

"Well, we're in a desert."

"You can be quite the blockhead sometimes," the Doctor snapped. "Even in a desert, there is life. In every environment, there is life. In every world we have visited, there has been life. But here—there is no life." He paused to let that sink in. "None."

Borel considered for a moment. "Then perhaps we have reached a world where life never evolved?" he suggested.

"Now you're using that brain of yours!" the traveler said happily. "Not very well, admittedly, but you are using it." He shook his head. "No, this is not a world where life never evolved. That's what is so puzzling about it."

"How can you be certain?"

The Doctor sighed. "Look around you, man!" he exclaimed. "Look at these so-called rocks of yours. They are made of concrete—and they're laid out in reasonably straight lines. We are not standing in a desert, but the wreckage of a city."

"A city?" Borel peered around more closely. Now that the Doctor had mentioned it, he could see that there were patterns of sorts in the arrangements of the rocks. The walls had crumbled and collapsed, which had served to disguise their regular nature. "But... what happened to all of the people? And the rest of the life?"

"*Now* you're getting to the point that intrigues me!" Doctor Omega said, rubbing his hands in satisfaction. "From the tests I've taken, I would say that this city was standing perhaps a thousand years ago."

"Then are we standing in some modern Babylon?" Borel asked. "Have the people moved on to some fresh site for some reason, and left this ruined estate?"

"The people *might* have done so," the Doctor agreed. "But the animals would not—nor would the birds and fishes. No, we must seek a more dire explanation for their lack, also."

"Do you have any ideas what might have happened?"

"Ideas?" The Doctor shrugged. "Plenty of *ideas*—but what we need is *proof...*" He started to wander off again.

"Uummm..." Borel said, suspiciously. "You did say that this city has been dead a thousand years?"

"At the very least, my boy," the traveler replied. "Why?"

"Well, I was just wondering…" He looked around, nervously. "You don't suppose whatever caused all of this might still be lingering around, do you?"

Doctor Omega came to a sudden halt. "I hadn't really thought about it," he admitted.

"Perhaps you *should* think about it?" Borel suggested.

"Yes, perhaps I should—perhaps I should." He started off again, looking around the ruins. This didn't exactly inspire confidence. He seemed lost once again in his thoughts.

Borel cast a longing glance back at the Tuner. He wondered for a moment what the chances were of getting his companion back into it and off to somewhere less disturbing, but then he knew he had no hope of getting Doctor Omega to abandon a mystery before he'd taken a stab at solving it. Curiosity was his weak point. All he could hope was that the solution to this mystery wouldn't get them both killed. Perhaps if he were to look for clues himself, they might be able to leave this desolate, silent planet a trifle faster. Of course since he had no idea what might have caused all of this, he didn't really have any idea what a clue might look like… The pair of them wandered about the ruins for the better part of an hour before Borel literally stumbled across something.

He caught himself before he fell into the small pit. It was only about four feet deep, so he'd hardly have hurt himself greatly, but he might have twisted an ankle. He frowned, wondering who would dig a pit like this in the middle of a deserted street. Then he saw that there was an identical pit about six feet away, and another one at right angles to both of these about ten feet in the other direction. Glancing up and down the street, he saw that there were, in fact, a whole row of these pits, quite regular in pattern. He called the Doctor's attention to them and his companion hurried over.

"Ah!" he said in satisfaction. "Things are starting to become a little clearer."

"For you, perhaps, but not for me," Borel complained. "Who dug these pits? And why?"

"Nobody dug them," the Doctor answered. "They are not pits. A better word for them might be *footprints*—except they were not made by feet."

"I am sure you believe you are explaining matters," Borel growled. "Let me assure you, though, that you are not."

"I am sorry, my boy—I sometimes forget how slow you are when it comes to piecing facts together. Well, no matter, no matter." He patted Borel condescendingly on the arm. "These prints were made by some mechanical contrivance walking down this street. I'd say from the size of these strides that it must be about eight feet wide and perhaps twenty long. It has... five—well, legs, for want of a better word. These legs end in circular pads, and it is these pads, sinking into the ground, that have made these *pits* of yours."

"But the pits are four feet deep. It must weigh..."

"A considerable amount, yes," the Doctor agreed.

"But why would anyone build a mechanical device with five feet?" Borel asked, confused.

"They wouldn't," the scientist answered. "It is slightly unbalanced as it walks, so I assume it was originally constructed with six legs. One has become inoperable and the mechanism walks slightly akilter now."

"The edges of these pits are quite sharp," Borel said. "They cannot have been made very long ago, else wind and rain would have eroded them."

"Capital, my boy, capital!" the Doctor enthused. "Yes, I'd say that they can't be more than a week old."

"Then whatever made them is possibly still about."

"Yes," the Doctor agreed. "It's quite exciting, isn't it?"

"That is hardly the word I should have chosen," Borel confessed. "*Worrying* would be a better option."

"And why so?"

"Because there is neither animal nor plant life," Borel pointed out. "And yet there are mechanisms stalking these ruins. The two can hardly be unconnected."

"A reasonable assumption."

"We are also in these ruins," Borel concluded. "And we are alive. I should prefer to remain that way. I do not think it unreasonable to assume that the presence of this mechanism and the lack of life are linked. In fact, I would say it is fairly logical to assume that this mechanism is seeking out any possible life-forms, with the expressed intention of exterminating it."

Doctor Omega clapped his hands together in delight. "An excellent train of thought," he agreed.

"Then perhaps we should speed our way back to..." Borel's voice trailed off as he heard a faint sound. "Doctor, listen!"

The noise was growing louder. He couldn't quite place it, but it sounded like the beat of the Tuner as it was in operation. The Doctor grabbed his arm and jerked him into the shade of a large piece of the ruined walls. "Stay down," he hissed.

Further down the wrecked street, movement finally became visible. Borel crouched low beside his companion and they stared from their point of concealment at the emerging shape. It was low and compact, like some vast, metallic beetle, perhaps ten feet in length. It was supported on four tracks, and carried what looked like a rack of ammunition on its armored back. There were the barrels of several guns issuing from the various sides of the mechanism, and it looked vaguely like the tanks he had seen on one world they had visited. Somehow, though, it looked more inhuman, and he had the distinct impression that there was no human agency guiding this device. There was some form of sensor that looked like a head, twisting and turning at the front of the machine. As it drew slowly closer, Borel could see that there were numerous places where the mechanism had been damaged and then patched—without much care taken to ensure that the patches were seamless.

Borel scarcely dared breathe as the tank-thing trundled past them without detecting them and passed on up the rubble-strewn street. The tracks helped it to maneuver over the wreckage, and in moments it was gone.

"That was quite unnerving," the Doctor admitted, quietly.

"And disturbing in another way, Doctor," Borel said. "That mechanism had tracks to move on, and so it could not have left the pits we saw earlier. That means there are at least two devices actively hunting targets in this ruin."

"Indeed it does," the scientist agreed. "And I think this would be a very opportune time to remove ourselves from this barren world. Quietly now, come along."

They began to carefully pick their way back toward the Tuner, Borel keeping a wary eye on the area of the ruins where the device had vanished in case it should backtrack for any reason. The ammunition carrier on the machine's back had been half-empty, but he didn't think it would need much ammunition to dispose of two humanoids...

And then the Doctor stopped dead in front of him, and he slammed right into his companion. He was about to protest when he saw the reason for the sudden halt.

A second mechanism had swung into the street ahead of them. And this one had clearly seen them.

Borel could see that this had to be the one which had made the earlier tracks. It was a large crab-like machine, six-legged and with several arm-like protuberances at the front of it. Two of these were clearly claws, and two more terminated in small cannon. Eye-stalks that must contain sensors waved about and zeroed in on the two of them. Pistons fired up and the cannon were raised to fire.

The Doctor thrust Borel sideways, into the shadow of a half-standing wall as gunfire exploded about them. Shrapnel whined about their heads, but they managed to get to shelter somehow unscathed. Terrified, Borel could hear the mechanical legs moving, pistons thumping, as the killer machine closed in on them. Needless to say, neither he nor Doctor Omega carried any weapons—not that Borel could imagine anything short of a bomb having any effect on their hunter. Now they had been spotted, he was certain that this machine would not stop until it had annihilated both of them. There was nothing he could think of that might stop it and save their lives. And, for once, he doubted that the Doctor had a plan to cover this emergency... A glance at his companion's ashen face convinced him of this belief.

Slowly, the stalking mechanism drew closer. Borel could smell the machine oil now, and a slight scent of burning rubber. The noise the device produced was increasing, and he could barely hear the pounding of his terrified heart. He had bare seconds left to live, and he wondered if the stories were true and that he would see his life flash before his eyes as he died.

Instead, he heard the sound a second engine. For a second he couldn't place it, and then he realized that it was coming from the direction where the earlier machine had vanished. Borel almost laughed insanely—as if one killer mechanism wasn't sufficient to destroy them both utterly, now there were *two* of them teaming up to destroy them! The irony seemed somehow deliciously silly to his frightened mind.

The beetle-machine opened fire, and there were more bullets and shells flying. Borel screamed, and then was astonished to realize that he was still alive and thus able to scream... He raised his head slightly, confused and relieved.

The second machine had indeed opened fire—but not at the two living figures. It had aimed at the crab-thing instead. The crab reacted by re-aiming its weapons at the new arrival. It, too, ignored Borel and the Doctor and targeted its companion mechanism. The two devices, firing wildly, approached one another. Borel and the Doctor, seizing their chance, started to move away in the shadow of the walls.

Beetle and crab clashed, running into one another and firing their weapons. Two of the crab's arms closed upon the guns of the beetle, gripping and tearing, attempting to rip the weapons from their housing. As Borel watched in shocked fascination, though, hatchways opened in the surface of the beetle and flexible arms emerged to grapple with the crab. One of these arms had a chainsaw attachment that started noisily up and started to slice into one of the pincers.

"What is happening?" Borel asked his companion, hopelessly confused.

"It is what I feared," the Doctor explained. "This world has been destroyed by war. Both sides sought to wipe the other out. They each built mechanisms designed and programmed to annihilate all life they encountered. With grim mechanical efficiency, they achieved their goals—and then the two different sides of the machines turned on one another, continuing the foolish war even further. They have no other purpose in life than to destroy, and to keep on destroying. This world has been ravaged by war, with no end in sight, though there is nothing to be gained by its continuance."

"At least we can escape while they carry on their futile struggle," Borel pointed out.

"Yes," the Doctor agreed. "Let us take advantage of their foolish programming." He led the way out of the combat zone. As they hurried away, Borel was relieving to hear the clash diminishing behind them. It didn't matter which one won the struggle, he and the Doctor would become targets as soon as combat was over. What was important now was to regain the Tuner and to escape from this insane world. With no longer any need for silence or caution, they both ran as fast as they could back through the wrecked cityscape and toward the fake boulder that held their means of escape.

And then there was silence behind them. The Doctor glanced back. "The combat has a winner," he said, puffing.

"And we'll be the losers in a few moments!" Borel exclaimed.

And then they could see the Tuner. As they scrambled through the dusty streets, they could hear the sound of an engine behind them. The victor was on their track, and it was a race to the finish—possibly literally the finish. The Doctor managed to trigger the door mechanism and they stumbled inside the Tuner barely in time. As the door closed behind them, the craft was rocked by an explosion. Through the transparent walls, Borel could see that the crab-thing was firing at the Tuner. He knew the craft was armored, but how much of this could it take?

Fortunately the Doctor reached the controls and hung on grimly with one hand as he then adjusted the settings. The world about them faded away, and the shuddering ceased as the Tuner settled into its dimensional voyage.

Borel collapsed onto the floor. He was even grateful he could feel the aches and pains in his body, as these proved that he had managed to survive. He managed to grin up at the Doctor. "What do you think will happen on that world?" he asked. "Will it remain lifeless forever?"

"No, my boy, I don't think so." The Doctor settled himself on the floor beside Borel. "Sooner or later those killer machines will destroy one another, or run out of weapons to fight with, or simply freeze up through lack of maintenance. And then…"

"And then?"

The Doctor smiled. "The foolish people of that world may have destroyed all visible life, but there is much that is invisible and not susceptible to bullets or bombs. Bacteria, germs, microscopic organisms—they all survive, and they will grow and evolve. One day that world will live again—it may even give rise to intelligent beings once more."

"Then I can only pray that they will be intelligent enough to realize the senselessness of war," Borel said.

The Doctor patted his arm. "Amen to that, my boy," he said.

Another iconic character I've always loved is Zorro. Ever since he first appeared in 1919 in The Curse Of Capistrano *by Johnston McCulley, he's also entertained a huge number of other people in every media. So when I had the opportunity to pen a tale with Don Diego in it, I leapt at it (not quite as gracefully as Douglas Fairbanks, though).*

The Wrath of Grapes

The mule train was barely an hour from the Mission when it was attacked. The journey from the port had been uneventful to this point, and neither Fray Quintero nor his Indian neophytes had any reason to suspect trouble. When the dozen masked riders rode down from the hills, their first reaction had been curiosity. Then the Indian at the head of the train gave a cry and pointed a wavering finger.

The riders had their swords drawn and raised as they raced down the slopes toward the train.

Fray Quintero did not know what to do. He was, after all, a man of peace, and no one in the train was armed with more than a machete. The approaching riders were clearly fighting men, unlike him. His Indian companions looked to the Father for guidance, and he shook his head. "Do nothing," he advised them. "Let us see what these men want." He strode forward, interposing himself between his followers and the new arrivals.

The riders encircled the mule train silently, gesturing the neophytes away with their swords. The lead rider bent from his saddle before Fray Quintero. "Tell your savages to abandon the mules," he ordered. "Or we shall kill them." His clothes were dark and simple, but clearly of rich material. His father was completely hidden by a cloth mask, save for two small holes for the eyes, and it muffled the man's voice.

"Do as they say," Fray Quintero ordered the Indians. "These are clearly brutal and unscrupulous men." Silently, the servants did as he commanded, withdrawing a short distance from the pack animals. The priest looked up at the leader of the raiders. "Why do you do this?" he asked. "These panniers do not contain money—merely clippings of vines."

"Treasure enough," the man growled. "And one destined never to reach your mission."

Fray Quintero did not understand. "You would rob the Holy Mother Church?"

"Why not?" he asked. "It would rob me. I merely return the favor. I offer you no violence, but you must be gone—and take those sorry wretches with you or I shall allow my men to slay them."

"You are a wretch!" Fray Quintero cried passionately. "To threaten unarmed men, to rob a priest of the church, to steal its property!"

"Enough!" the robber roared. "I have given you your lives—be grateful for that!"

"You must not do this thing!" Fray Quintero begged. "Those clippings are meant to improve the yield of the mission."

"I know what they are meant for, you whining cur," the man snapped. He returned his sword to its sheath. "And I have had my fill of your voice." He uncoiled the whip from his saddle. "Still your voice and be gone—or I shall drive you forth!"

Fray Quintero stood tall. He was six feet two inches of little more than skin and bones, and all of sixty years of age. But this man did not frighten him. "You are a miserable sinner!" he exclaimed. "Repent of your actions and God will forgive you."

"You weary my patience!" the robber cried. He struck out with the whip, still coiled, catching the priest a stinging blow across the face. Fray Quintero fell with a cry, his cheek burning and bloodied. "Leave now, or I promise you these swords will taste your blood!"

Two of his followers helped the priest to his feet. One of them dabbed at his cheek with a cloth, and the other offered his arm for support. The Franciscan realized that words would not help in this situation. "Come," he said, "we shall do as these men say." He turned to go, but looked back at the robbers. "You shall pay for your sins," he vowed. "Your actions will not go unpunished."

"Old man," the leader growled. "I would advise you to be silent—and be gone!"

Fray Quintero turned away again, and began walking, leaning gratefully on the arm of his companion. Silently, his small flock fell in behind him. As they headed on foot toward the Mission of San Gabriel Arcangel, he glanced back to see that the robbers had taken charge of the mules and were leading them into the hills. On the backs of the swaying beasts of burden were the panniers that held his precious clippings. Were they lost forever?

Don Diego de la Vega was seated on the veranda of his hacienda, skimming one of the books that had arrived the previous day on the latest merchant ship from Madrid. It was a fresh work on botany by the German naturalist Von Schtemper, and would certainly repay a more careful reading. But the day was hot, and Diego lacked the necessary interest at the moment to do the beautiful book justice. He was more than grateful when Bernardo appeared and indicated by gesture that Fray Felipe had arrived. He rose to his feet to greet his Franciscan friend warmly.

"And what brings you all the way out here on such a pleasant day?" he enquired, pouring the father a glass of fresh orange juice.

"A request for aid, I am afraid—as I am pressed to do all too frequently."

Diego grinned. "My aid—or that of... another?"

Filipe's lips twitched. "The other."

"Ah!" Diego nodded. "Perhaps you could tell me all about it." He gestured the Father to a seat, and took to his own once again.

Fray Felipe glanced at the book on the table. "I see you know that a shipment from Spain arrived yesterday—that is a new title. On the same vessel was a special cargo for the Mission—a hundred cuttings of vines, specially selected for Fray Quintero. You know he is the man who cultivates our vineyards?"

"Indeed," Diego said. "I purchase a number of bottles from him at every pressing. He is a skilled vintner, and his wines amongst the best in all of California."

"As you say. Fray Quintero enjoys his work and strives always to improve his crop. The money it brings in helps our mission to the Indians."

"And the product causes much pleasure amongst those who taste it," Diego said. "I take it the cuttings are intended to be grafted onto existing vines in an attempt to improve the yield?"

"That was the idea indeed, my son."

"I note the use of the word *was*," Diego observed. "I take it that there have been complications?"

"The mule train Fray Quintero was leading from the dock to the Mission was attacked last afternoon," Fray Filipe replied. "The robbers beat the good Father with a whip and stole all of the cuttings."

"I see." Diego's lips tightened in anger. "How is Fray Quintero?"

"He is recovering, thankfully, from his ordeal—but his cheek is likely to remain scarred from the blow."

"And you wish the robbers to be paid for the blow, and the vines recovered?"

Fray Felipe nodded. "The culprits offered an insult to the Mission by their actions, and this should not go unpunished."

"My thoughts precisely." Diego rose to his feet and started to pace as he thought about the matter. The Franciscans were gentle men, devoted to their work, and offered peace and

253

hospitality to all. There were few enough in California who would offer them violence. "And is there any clue as to who the robbers might have been?"

"Not directly," Fray Felipe admitted. "They were all masked. But they rode fine stallions, and their leader, at least, was dressed in expensive raiment, according to Fray Quintero. He felt that the man was no peon, but a person of wealth and breeding."

"Wealth and breeding, eh?" Diego muttered. "Insufficient breeding, it would seem, if he would steal from the Mission and strike a priest. It seems to me that the man must be taught a lesson in manners."

"We must first learn who the villain is," Fray Felipe reminded him.

"Come now, my friend," Diego replied. "I feel certain that it can only be the handiwork of one man—Don Jose Castiliano. Simple thieves would have no need for vines, and there is hardly a black market for them. Don Castiliano has large vineyards, and he produces the most successful wines in the county. He would have the most to lose if the Mission improved its production and competed more strongly with him. I have never met the Don myself, but I have heard two interesting pieces of information about him. The first is that he is a man of temper and avarice. That gives him motive."

"Perhaps so," Fray Felipe agreed. "But it falls far short of proving him the guilty party."

"Indeed it does," Diego admitted. "Which is where the second fact becomes of use. I hear that he has a very beautiful daughter—and my father is constantly urging me to marry and hastily produce him a whole tribe of heirs!"

"Maria?" Fray Felipe looked shocked. "She is the most spoiled and arrogant young lady on these shores!"

"Well, then—even better!"

"Better?" Fray Felipe was clearly confused. "Why is it better that a girl you wish to woo is spoiled and arrogant?"

"Because it gives me the perfect excuse not to go through with a betrothal," Diego replied. "One even my father can hardly object to!" He called for Bernardo. "I shall write to Don Jose immediately and suggest myself as a prospective son-in-law. I am certain it will at least pique his interest…"

Diego studied the ranchero as Bernardo drove the carriage up the road toward it. It was large and lavish, rather ostentatious. The gardens about the house were immaculate and well-kept, and the house itself large and slightly vulgar. It was no one thing by itself—the design and furnishings were quite stylish and pleasant—simply the accumulation of everything. It spoke of an owner who wished everyone to understand and acknowledge that he had wealth. It was the home of an egotist. Little wonder, then, that the daughter was spoiled. Don Jose was a man who denied himself little, so she had learned her manners at his knee.

An Indian servant opened the door for him, but a Spanish footman announced him to the owner. The interior of the house was like the exterior—every item was precise and expensive, and the total sum simply too much. Don Jose himself was more of the same—his trousers and tunic were crisp, clean and with overly busy decorative stitching. His bolero shirt flared out over his ample belly, and his boots were ornately-wrought rawhide. The kerchief about his throat was of fine China silk. The man was stout, tanned and with a trim dark beard tinged with the onset of gray. His hair was slick and gleaming, with a similar hint of gray at the temples.

"Don Diego," he said in greeting. "I know your father, of course. I trust he is well?"

"Indeed he is, Don Jose," Diego replied. "You yourself appear to be in excellent health. I trust the same is true of your daughter?"

"We both are fine. Maria will join us shortly—she is eager to meet you, of course."

"And I her," Diego replied. "I have heard glowing reports of her beauty, and am quite eager to verify their accuracy."

Don Jose smiled a trifle tightly. "As her father, I am naturally not unprejudiced, but she is indeed a lovely girl. She takes after her late mother. So, you are eager to wed?"

"Not especially," Diego replied. "But my father seems to view it as my duty, and as a dutiful son I strive to please him." As he had expected, this lukewarm response did not endear him to Don Jose.

"I had rather hoped that any suitor for my daughter's hand might be a trifle more... enthusiastic."

"But I have not yet met her!" Diego protested. "I can hardly be expected to enthuse over a girl I do not know. I am sure my passions will be aroused once your daughter has joined us."

"Of course," Don Jose agreed. "In the meantime, perhaps I can offer you a little wine? It is of my own produce—you know of my vineyard perhaps?"

"Indeed," Diego informed him. "I am in the habit of purchasing a good deal of it for my table and my pleasure. Not *too* much, of course! But it is excellent. I should appreciate a glimpse at the fields where the grapes grow, if that is not inconvenient?"

"Not in the slightest!" Don Jose assured him with pride. "I believe I can safely claim to produce the finest wines in California."

"I am strongly inclined to agree," Diego said. "Your only true rival is that produced by the Mission. Fray Quintero is a superb vintner himself."

Don Jose scowled slightly. "I would not compare their produce to mine—they manufacture theirs for the peasants, not for men with discriminating palates such as ourselves." The Indian servant had poured two glasses of rich red wine, and Don Jose handed one to Diego. "Taste this and tell me what you think."

Diego sipped it appreciatively. "A fine wine, senor," he said. "A full, rich taste, a hint of the oak... Most agreeable. Once it has aged a year or so I do believe there will be few wines this side of Madrid to match it."

"Ah." Don Jose was caught between enjoying the compliment and being pricked by the implied insult that he was serving it too soon. "You recognize it as this year's harvest, then," he finally compromised.

"Yes, indeed. It shows great hope for your future. And, speaking of which, I do believe this is your daughter now."

Don Jose bowed slightly. "It is indeed. Don Diego, may I have the honor of presenting to you my daughter Maria?"

Diego bowed. "A great pleasure, senorita," he said. "You are indeed as dazzlingly beautiful as I have heard." This was perfectly true, and Diego enjoyed the vision before him. Maria Castiliano was tall and slender, and her features delicate and excellent. Her dark hair hung in ringlets over her bare shoulders, framing her immaculate skin. Her eyes were dark and deep, with a hint of amusement. Her dress was—as he had expected—costly, overly ornate and very, very flattering to her splendid figure.

"I am glad I do not disappoint," she said demurely, half-hiding her smile behind her fan.

"I am certain you could never do that," Diego assured her.

At this moment the servant announced dinner. Diego offered his arm, which she accepted, and they followed the servant and Don Jose into the dining room. The meal that followed was superb, and carefully matched with truly excellent wines. It wasn't difficult to see why Don Jose was stout—his cook was a master or mistress. Conversation over the meal was light and pleasant, but Diego could detect the stirrings of Maria's selfishness even in the slightest of remarks. If she was not continually flattered or attended to, her voice became a trifle sharp, and the fire in her eyes became menacing. At the end of the meal, Don Jose offered sherry, and the three of them drank it together. This was a fair breech of etiquette, as Maria should have left the men alone. But she clearly wished to be privy to the conversation and studiously ignored her father's glare of annoyance, turning instead to Diego.

"And are you pleased with what you have found here to-night?" she asked him, pointedly.

He smiled gently back. "Do you speak of the wine or yourself?" he asked, lightly.

With the slightest of frowns, she said: "Why, both, of course."

"Then in order: the wine, as I told your father, is excellent. I am rather looking forward to a tour of the vineyard here. I am certain it will prove to be interesting. Yourself... You are as pleasing to the eye as everyone says, senorita—a rare delight. I am somewhat amazed that you have not yet been snatched up before now by some eager suitor. It is my great fortune to be the first, then."

Maria smiled, but did not blush as many young women would have done in her place. "You wish to press your suit for my hand, then?" she asked, pointedly—once again ignoring the dark glance her father gave her. It was not her place to inquire.

"I rather think I had better," Diego told her. "My father would never forgive me if I allowed a beauty like you to escape me. And he is most eager that I should start a family. I do trust I would not be too forward if I were to ask if you are prepared to bear him a large number of grandchildren? I am his only child, you see, and he has always dreamed of a home filled with many children."

The frown on her brow was definitely more pronounced now—as he had hoped. "I am still quite young to be thinking of children, senor," she said. There was a touch of ice in her voice also. "I am more interested at the moment in dances and enjoyment."

"Then I envy you," Diego said. "I am afraid I do not dance well myself—and I prefer to stay at home and read. The world is a fascinating place, and there is so much to learn—wouldn't you agree?"

"I should think you would learn more by going out than staying home," she said rather sharply.

"Ah, that is because you do not read much, I assume," he replied. "Books can be so transforming."

"Really?" The ice was chillingly thick in her voice now. The prospect of an end to amusement and the early onset of motherhood were clearly highly unappealing to Maria. "I prefer to enjoy life in its fullness."

"Perhaps, Don Diego, you would like that tour of the vineyards now?" Don Jose suggested, quickly.

Diego blinked as if caught by surprise, and then nodded. "I should enjoy it, certainly. I am most eager to see the source of such splendid wines. My servant, Bernardo, has my carriage waiting at your front door. Perhaps we can take that?"

"Of course." Don Jose turned to his daughter. "Please stay here and await our return." Diego caught the glower the father shot the daughter. She bowed her head demurely in acknowledgement.

Once he and Diego were seated in the carriage, Don Jose turned to him. "I must apologize for my daughter," he said. "Her mother died when she was quite young, and I have perhaps not been the best influence on her. She has a tendency to speak out of turn."

"I had noticed," Diego said—a remark that was just shy of insulting. "But, as you say, she is young, and it may be possible to cure her of that. But enough of her—tell me about your vineyards, Don Jose." Again, the change of subject so abruptly was *almost* insulting.

"Vineyards?" The other man scowled slightly. "Have your man drive around the house and you will see them—or, rather, the start of them. They extend for quite some distance."

Bernardo started the horses, and in a few moments the vines came into view. As Don Jose had said, they were quite extensive. Diego was impressed. Behind the house stood a secondary building.

"The press house," Don Jose explained. "We also store the casks for the wine in the cellar of that house. It is best to allow the wine to mature before I sell it."

"Of course." Diego frowned slightly. The sun would be setting shortly, but there were still several dozen workers weeding among the vines. They were all natives, most dressed only in trousers and sandals. As the carriage drew closer, Diego could see that most of the men had lash-marks across their backs. Many of these were fresh, but some were old enough to have scarred over. He could also now see that there were three overseers in the fields, keeping wary eyes on the Indians. The overseers all carried bullwhips, which clearly explained the scars.

"You allow your laborers to be beaten?" Diego asked Don Jose.

"It is the only way to encourage them to work," Don Jose snapped. "They are lazy, and would otherwise never finish their assigned chores. They will not listen to exhortations unless accompanied by the crack of a whip across their backs."

"I have never found brutality necessary," Diego said softly.

"It is not brutality, it is expediency," his host answered crossly. "You do not understand the Indians, it seems."

"I think I understand them far better than you," Diego replied. "They are human beings, not beasts to be whipped."

Don Jose glared at him in fury. "Don Diego, you are a guest at my house, otherwise I should have *you* whipped for criticizing me! I advise you to be very careful what you say to me, otherwise I shall be forced to issue a challenge to a duel." He thrust out his left arm and rolled the sleeve of his fancy shirt back. There was a scar across the forearm. "I received that when I was 17—and have never been touched by a blade in any fight since then. There is no man in this entire country who is my equal with a sword—unless you think yourself such an expert?"

"I use my mind, not my arms when I fight a man," Diego said calmly. "I assure you that if I wish to harm you, I am quite capable of it."

"Then you are more of a fool than I thought," Don Jose growled. "Even the Alcalde himself cannot touch me. I have powerful friends in Spain."

"Spain is a long way off, Don Jose," Diego reminded him. "And there is justice in this world that is not reliant on the Alcalde."

"Justice?" Don Jose gave a barked laugh. "My foolish friend, *justice* is what the weak bleat for when they are incapable of holding onto their own. I have no faith in justice—only in strength."

"Then there we differ," Diego said. "For I believe that justice will always triumph. You will surely be made to answer for your brutality—and for your thefts."

"Thefts?" Don Jose barely restrained himself from striking his companion. "You accuse *me* of theft?"

"I most certainly do," Diego replied. He gestured toward the vines. "I see fresh graftings on several of your growths. Since the only new vines that have arrived in this country in the past few months were those destined for the Mission, and since those were stolen before they arrived there, the conclusion is inescapable."

"Stop this carriage!" Don Jose roared. Startled, Bernardo did as he was ordered. The older man leaped down agilely. "Don Diego, you have insulted me and now accused me of theft. If we ever meet again, you had better be carrying a sword and be prepared to use it!" He turned to storm off back to his house.

"Then I take it that you look unfavorably on my courting your daughter?" Diego called after him, barely able to suppress a smile.

"To the Devil with you and your courting!"

"Father will be so disappointed," Diego murmured. "Well, Bernardo, my task here is done. I think it is time for Zorro to take a hand in matters…"

In the cave below the de la Vega hacienda, Diego gestured at a batch of small pots he had been filling. Each was the size of a soup bowl and filled with a thick, black, pungent material and a fuse. "Don Jose has about a dozen caballeros working for him," he explained. "Even Zorro might have trouble fighting all of them at once, so we need a way to remove them from the scene. These should do the trick." Bernardo raised an eyebrow in query. "These are filled with tar taken from *Los Bocanes de Brea*[3]," Diego said. "It will burn strongly and with smoke. You are to take them into the vineyards and start them going—but be careful not to get too close to the vines. I want them to *think* that the vineyards have been set ablaze but not to actually do so. Much fine wine would be lost if those vines are damaged." Bernardo nodded his comprehension. "Good. Then I think tonight Don Jose will discover that there is still justice in this world for all…"

The moon was close to full and low in the sky, casting a silvery pallor across the Castiliano Rancho. There were lights blazing in the main house, and also in the servants' quarters. The vineyards were deserted as Bernardo slipped off on his mission. Zorro watched as he set and lit the first pots, then saluted him briefly.

"On, Tornado," he urged his steed, patting his neck. The Andalusian gave a soft whicker, and then moved silently down the pathway to the hacienda. As soon as they were close to the house, Zorro slipped from the saddle, and led Tornado into the shadows beside the supply sheds. "Wait here," he murmured, and then faded into the shadows himself. He glanced back at the vineyard in time to see the first of his tar pots erupt into fire. It would be quite visible from the house if anyone were to glance in the right direction, but to be certain they would he cried: "Fire! Fire in the vineyards! Fire!'

There was a clatter at the rear door, and two of the servants looked out. Seeing a second pot burst into flames, they set up a wail of "Fire!" throughout the house. Zorro waited, pa-

---

[3] The then-current name for the Rancho la Brea, where the La Brea Tar Pits stand in the present day.

tiently, as the house exploded into noise and movement. Don Jose dashed out and stood, aghast, at what he believed he was seeing.

"The vines are aflame!" he exclaimed. He cuffed the closest servant. "Rouse my caballeros!" he ordered. "Get every man into the fields and make certain the fire does not spread." As he spoke, a third and then a forth gout of fire illuminated the night. "Hurry, you fools! I shall follow!"

The servant rushed to obey, turning the caballeros out of their separate sleeping quarters. Cries and confusion filled the night as men sought buckets to carry water to the fire. Others grabbed blankets to beat back the flames. Then began a stream of would-be firefighters heading toward the fields.

Don Jose reappeared in the doorway, with his daughter in a thick robe behind him. "Stay here," he growled at her. "I must lead those fools, or the fire will spread across the rancho!" Maria gave a bleat of fear and dived back into the house. Don Jose started toward the growing fires, and then gave an abrupt curse.

From the dark shadows had stepped a darker one—a man dressed all in black, and masked... Zorro gave a swift smile. "Good evening, Don Jose," he said softly. "I have been intending to visit you for a while."

"Who are you?" Don Jose roared. "No matter—out of my way! I have work to do!"

"You have sins to answer for," Zorro informed him. "Your men will be sufficient to tend to the fields—you have a more important and urgent meeting with your fate." He drew his sword from its sheath. "I hear that you consider yourself the finest swordsman in California. Permit me to dispute that."

Don Jose was struggling to make sense of all of this. "Who are you?" he demanded. "What are you talking about?"

"I am justice," the black-clad man informed him. "I am retribution. I am—Zorro."

"Zorro?" Don Jose blinked. "I have heard of you—the Alcalde says you are a bandit and a thief!"

"And I say the same about him," Zorro replied. "And his day will come. But, tonight, it is your turn to pay."

"You would attack an unarmed man?" Don Jose spread his hands to show he carried no sword.

"Why not?" Zorro asked him. "You do not hesitate to scourge the helpless, nor to strike and rob an elderly priest." He saw Don Jose pale, and then laughed. "But I am not like you—I give you a chance." He took a spare sword from his belt and tossed it to the landowner, who caught it nimbly enough.

"It is an insult to me to fight with a criminal," Don Jose spat.

"And for me to tackle a thief," Zorro replied. "But if I am willing to overlook this, then so should you. Prepare!" He raised his sword and moved forward. "*En garde!*" He thrust with his weapon, and Don Jose was forced to parry and step back. There was no further complaint from him that he was fighting beneath his station, for he had no breath to spare to talk.

His claim of being a fine swordsman was no idle boast. He was indeed skillful, and Zorro found himself giving ground more than once. The man was fighting for his honor, which meant a great deal to him—but Zorro was fighting for justice, which meant more. Blow by blow, thrust by thrust, attack by attack, Zorro beat the other man back. Swords clashed and sparked, muscles strained and the two men fought with every last drop of skill and courage. But Zorro was the more skilled—not by much, but sufficient.

"You would scar a holy man," he growled. His sword flickered out, and a thin, bloody line appeared down Don Jose's left cheek. "Receive a mark in return."

Don Jose snarled, and touched his cheek. "You dare!" he snarled.

"I dare more," Zorro assured him. "You would beat your servants to teach them their place? Then learn your own!" His blade flashed again, and a second mark appeared on the same cheek, parallel to the first.

"Swine!" Don Jose snarled. "You will pay for this."

"No," Zorro answered. "It is your turn to pay." For the third time his sword flickered out, and left the third line connecting the first two. "The mark of Zorro has branded you," he said. "All who see you now shall know you for what you are." His sword was a burning instrument in his hands, and in three further blows he had sent Don Jose's sword spinning into the night. His own blade dashed out, and the tip rested at his opponent's throat. "And now—an ending."

"No!" Don Jose whispered, his eyes bulging as they stared at his death. "Spare me."

"You do not deserve it," Zorro said coldly. "But you *shall* be spared, to be a lesson to others of your kind. However, there is a price to pay." He reached under his cloak and pulled out a parchment he had prepared. "We shall go inside and you will sign this letter to the Alcalde. It is a full confession of your guilt for stealing from the Mission and for scarring Fray Quintero. It says that in recompense for your sins you will donate your vineyard to the church."

"You would rob me of all I own?" Don Jose asked.

"No. Only the vineyard. Perhaps this deed will do your dark soul some good. But you are to leave California and return to Spain. The supply ship the vines came in on will commence its return journey in two days. You will be on it. The letter includes instructions to the Alcalde for him to sell your hacienda and the remaining lands and to forward payment to you in Madrid." Zorro smiled. "As you have powerful friends there, I am sure he will not cheat your too much over his...commission in this matter."

"You cannot force me to do this! I shall have justice!"

"Justice?" Zorro laughed. "Justice is the bleat of the weak when faced by those stronger." Don Jose blanched. "Yes, I heard you when you spoke to Don Diego—it is only appropriate that your own words rebound on you."

"I shall not go!" Don Jose insisted. "I have men and wealth, and you are just a bandit."

"A bandit who can slip into your home when he wishes, and hear what you say and what you plot," Zorro reminded him. "Where are your men to help you now?" He shook his head. "No, they will not be able to help you and your wealth will not save you. I come and go as I wish. I have granted you two days—if you are not on that ship, then you will be in your grave before the end of the week. This I promise you, and you have my mark on your cheek to remind you every day that I keep my promises." He whistled loudly, and Tornado hurtled from the shadows to his side, rearing and snorting. Don Jose fell back with a cry. Zorro vaulted into his saddle, and pointed his sword at the cowering man. "Two days!" He whirled and rode off. Only his laugh floated in the air behind him.

Don Diego sat by the wharf watching the workers loading Maria de Castiliano's voluminous luggage aboard the supply ship. Her father had vanished below deck as soon as he had arrived, his face heavily bandaged. He sipped at his wine and smiled across the table at Fray Felipe. "I hear that scoundrel Zorro had a hand in your latest land grant," he murmured.

"Indeed," the priest agreed. "He seemed to think it an appropriate penance."

Diego laughed gently. "Perhaps he is a padre at heart," he suggested.

"It is perhaps a good thing he never took holy orders," Fray Felipe replied. "I would think even the Holy Father in Rome might be dismayed by some of the penances he imposes."

"And you?" Diego asked more seriously. "Do you disapprove?"

"No, my son," his friend replied. "I think the payment... most appropriate."

"Then I suspect Zorro will sleep without regrets," Diego said. He raised his glass and smiled. "I can hardly wait to taste the new wines that Frey Quintero may now produce!"

Sources

Twenty Thousand Years Under The Sea
Tales of the Shadowmen #4: Lords of Terror, edited by Jean-Marc & Randy Lofficier, Black Coat Press, 2008.

More Imaginative Sins
Tales of the Shadowmen #8: Agents Provocateurs, Black Coat Press, 2011.

The Benevolent Burglar
Tales of the Shadowmen #9: La Vie en Noir, Black Coat Press, 2012.

Time To Kill
Tales of the Shadowmen #13: Sang Froid, Black Coat Press, 2016.

The Gutter God
Tales of the Shadowmen #15: Trompe l'Oeil, Black Coat Press, 2018.

The Eye Of The Hawk
Tales of the Shadowmen #16: Voir Dire, Black Coat Press, 2019.

Blood Calls To Blood
The Vampire Almanac #2, edited by Jean-Marc & Randy Lofficier, Black Coat Press, 2015.

Franklinstein
Dark Moon Digest #1, edited by Lori Michelle & Stan Swanson, 2013.

To Protect And Serve
Strife & Harmony, edited by Dixiane Hallaj & D.J. Stevenson, S&H Publishing, 2019.

Long Time Dead
Unearthed, edited by Kara Dennison, Altrix Books, 2019.

Now Departing
Dark Tales from Elder Regions: New York, edited by Anthony Burge & Jessica Burke, Myth Ink Books, 2014.

Pink Samurai
Midnight Rose, edited by Shannon Riley, Southern Rose Productions, 2002.

The Wrath Of Grapes
More Tales Of Zorro, edited by Richard Dean Starr, Moonstone, 2011.
Zorro tm Zorro Productions, Inc. All Rights Reserved.